Praise for

BELLA ANDRE

"Bella Andre hit this book right out of the park! An absolute home-run! I cannot get over how enjoyable and thrillingly sexy this book was. *Let Me Be The One* has shot straight to the top of my favorite books this year."
—*Under The Covers Book Reviews*

"Sensual, empowered stories enveloped in heady romance."
—*Publishers Weekly*

"The perfect combination of sexy heat and tender heart."
—#1 *New York Times* bestselling author Barbara Freethy

"Bella Andre writes warm, sexy contemporary romance that always gives me a much needed pick me up. Reading one of her books is truly a pleasure."
—*New York Times* bestselling author Maya Banks

"I can't wait for more Sullivans!"
—*New York Times* bestselling author Carly Phillips

"Loveable characters, sizzling chemistry, and poignant emotion."
—*USA TODAY* bestselling author Christie Ridgway

"I'm hooked on the Sullivans!"
—Marie Force, bestselling author of *Falling For Love*

"No one does sexy like Bella Andre."
—*New York Times* bestselling author Sarah MacLean

Also by Bella Andre

**THE LOOK OF LOVE
FROM THIS MOMENT ON
CAN'T HELP FALLING IN LOVE
I ONLY HAVE EYES FOR YOU
KISSING UNDER THE MISTLETOE
IF YOU WERE MINE**

Look for Bella Andre's next novel
COME A LITTLE BIT CLOSER
Available soon in print from Harlequin MIRA

BELLA ANDRE

Let Me Be the One

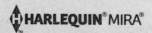
HARLEQUIN® MIRA®

If you purchased this book without a cover you should be aware
that this book is stolen property. It was reported as "unsold and
destroyed" to the publisher, and neither the author nor the
publisher has received any payment for this "stripped book."

Recycling programs
for this product may
not exist in your area.

ISBN-13: 978-0-7783-1600-8

LET ME BE THE ONE

Harlequin MIRA/January 2014

First published by Bella Andre

Copyright © 2012 by Oak Press, LLC.

All rights reserved. Except for use in any review, the reproduction or
utilization of this work in whole or in part in any form by any electronic,
mechanical or other means, now known or hereafter invented, including
xerography, photocopying and recording, or in any information storage or
retrieval system, is forbidden without the written permission of the publisher,
Harlequin MIRA, 225 Duncan Mill Road, Don Mills, Ontario M3B 3K9,
Canada.

This is a work of fiction. Names, characters, places and incidents are
either the product of the author's imagination or are used fictitiously, and
any resemblance to actual persons, living or dead, business establishments,
events or locales is entirely coincidental.

® and TM are trademarks of Harlequin Enterprises Limited or its corporate
affiliates. Trademarks indicated with ® are registered in the United States Patent
and Trademark Office, the Canadian Trade Marks Office and in other countries.

For questions and comments about the quality of this book, please contact us at
CustomerService@Harlequin.com.

Printed in U.S.A.

Dear Reader,

I've always wanted to write about a big, close-knit family full of brothers and sisters who laugh, love, tease and are there for one another no matter what. For the past year, I have been living, breathing—and writing!—Sullivans. I can't thank you enough for the thousands of emails, tweets, Facebook and Goodreads posts you have made about my Sullivans—and for launching Gabe's, Sophie's and Zach's books onto the *New York Times* and *USA TODAY* bestseller lists!

Ryan Sullivan has been in five previous books, so I thought I knew him. He's funny. Sexy. A great brother. And he can throw a baseball really, really fast. But until the moment Ryan and his old friend Vicki showed up on the page together, I didn't truly realize just how much love he had to give.

Right from page one, Ryan and Vicki care about each other. Deeply. And as I wrote this story, I quickly realized that it is somewhat different from the first five books in the series. Gentler in some ways—even as the sparks that ignite between them break the heat-o-meter—because there is no place in their story, or their friendship, for arguments, personality clashes or explosions. So while there is a bad guy, ultimately *Let Me Be The One* is a story about navigating the choppy waters between the pure sweet love of friendship and an even stronger and deeper (and much, much hotter!) love.

For the next few hours, I hope that you can find a quiet spot to curl up with Ryan and Vicki's love story…and that you love reading it as much as I loved writing it.

Happy reading,

Bella

One

Victoria Bennett couldn't take her eyes off Ryan Sullivan, who was standing in the high school parking lot laughing with some of the guys on his baseball team. As she continued on her way toward the art store on University Avenue, the image of Ryan kept playing on a continuous loop in her mind.

None of the other girls in her tenth-grade class could take their eyes off him, either. At least that was one thing that didn't make her stick out from the rest of her class. Her clay-stained fingers and clothes along with the "new girl" sign she felt like she was wearing during her first few weeks at every new school did that with no help whatsoever from Ryan...or his ridiculously good looks.

Normally, she would have gotten over his pretty face without much trouble. As an artist, she always worked to look beneath the surface of things, to try to find out what was really at the heart of a painting or sculpture or song. That went for people, too. Especially boys who, as far as she could tell, only ever told a girl what they wanted to hear for one reason.

No, what had her stuck on Ryan Sullivan was the fact that he was always laughing. Somehow, without being the class clown, he had a gift for putting people at ease and making them feel good.

Before she could catch herself, she put her fingers to her lips…and wondered what it would feel like if he kissed her.

She yanked her hand away from her mouth. Not just because dreaming of his kisses was borderline pathetic given the utter unlikelihood of that scenario, but because she needed to stay focused on her art.

She wasn't just another tenth grader mooning over the hottest boy in school.

She was studying her muse.

Vicki had never been much interested in sculpting formal busts before. Old, dead, overly serious guys in gray didn't really do it for her. But it had only taken a few minutes near Ryan at lunch her first day on campus to be inspired to capture his laughter in clay. She wished she could get closer to all that easy joy—if only to figure out how to translate it from her mind's eye to the clay beneath her fingers.

Yes, she thought with a small smile, she was perfectly willing to suffer for her art. Especially if it meant staring at Ryan Sullivan.

She was almost across the school parking lot when she noticed the traffic light turned from red to green. She could pick up her pace and make it across the street, but she slowed down instead. She'd been having such trouble getting the corners of the eyes and mouth just right on her *Laughing Boy* sculpture. Knowing there wasn't a chance that Ryan or his friends would notice her, rather than leaving the school grounds she closed the distance between them in as nonchalant a manner as she could. Surreptitiously, she observed Ryan from beneath the veil of the bangs that had grown too long over her eyes during the summer.

A few seconds later, his friends high-fived him and walked away. Ryan bent down to finish packing up a long, narrow black bag at his feet, which she guessed held his baseball stuff.

What, she wondered on an appreciative sigh at the way the muscles on his forearms and shoulders flexed as he picked up the bag, would happen if she talked to him? And what would he say if she asked him outright to pose for her?

She was on the verge of laughing out loud at her crazy thoughts when she heard a squeal of tires seemingly coming from out of nowhere in the parking lot. In a split second she realized an out-of-control car was fishtailing straight toward Ryan.

There wasn't time to plan, or to think. Without a

moment's hesitation, Vicki sprinted across the several feet between them and threw herself at him.

"Car!"

Fortunately, Ryan's natural athleticism kicked in right away. Even though she was the one trying to pull him out of the way, less than a heartbeat later he was lifting her and practically throwing her across the grass before leaping to cover her body with his.

She scrunched her eyes tightly shut as the car careened past, so close that she could feel the hairs on her arms lifting in its wake. Breathing hard, Vicki clung to Ryan. Wetness moved across her cheeks and she realized tears must have sprung up from landing so hard on the grass.

The seconds ticked by as if in slow motion, one hard, thudding heartbeat after another from Ryan's chest to hers and then back again from hers to his. He was so strong, so warm, so beautifully real. She wanted to lie like this with him forever, more intimately, closer than she'd ever been with another boy.

Only, as voices rose in pitch all around them, suddenly the reality of what had just happened hit her.

Oh, my God, they'd both almost died!

She was starting to feel faint when he lifted his head and smiled down at her.

"Hi, I'm Ryan."

The way he said it, as if she didn't already know

who he was, pierced through her shock. He acted as if it was normal to be sprawled all over a girl. Which, she suddenly realized, it probably was. For him.

Definitely *not* for her, though.

Her lips were dry and she had to lick them once, twice, before saying, "I'm Victoria." The words, "But my friends call me Vicki," slipped out before she could pull them back in.

His smile widened and her heart started beating even faster. Not from shock this time, but from pure, unfettered teenage hormones kicked into overdrive by his beautiful smile.

"Thank you for saving my life, Vicki." A moment later, his smile disappeared as he took in her tear-streaked cheeks. The eyes that she'd seen filled with laughter so many times during the first two weeks of school grew serious. "I hurt you."

She would have told him no, and that she was fine, but all breath and words were stolen from her the instant he brushed his fingertips over her cheeks to wipe away her tears.

Somehow, she managed to shake her head, and to get her lips to form the word *no,* even though no sound followed.

His laughing eyes were dark now, and more intense than she'd ever seen them. "Are you sure? I didn't mean to land so hard on you."

"I'm—"

How was she supposed to keep her brain working

when he'd begun the slow, shockingly sweet process of running his hands over the back of her skull, and then down to her shoulders and upper arms?

One more word. That was all she needed to be able to answer his question.

"—fine."

"Good." His voice was deeper, richer than any of the other fifteen-year-old boys she knew. "I'm glad."

But as he stared down at her, his expression continued to grow even more intense and she found herself holding her breath.

Was he going to kiss her now? Had her life just turned into the quintessential after-school-special fantasy, the one where the artsy girl caught the eye of the jock and the whole school was turned upside down by their unlikely but ultimately perfect and inevitable pairing?

"One day, when you need me most, I promise I'll be there for you, Vicki."

Oh. She swallowed hard. *Oh, my.*

He hadn't given her a kiss…but his promise felt more important than a mere kiss would have been.

Before she realized it, he was standing up again and holding out a hand to help her up, too. Instantly she missed feeling his heat and his hard muscles pressing into her softer ones. All the lies she'd been trying to tell herself about Ryan simply being a muse scattered out of reach.

"Can I walk you home?"

Surprised that he wanted to spend more time with her, she quickly shook her head.

He looked equally surprised by her response, likely because no girl on earth had ever turned him down.

"No, I can't walk you home?" he asked again.

She fumbled to explain. "I'm not going home. I was actually heading over to the art store to pick up some supplies for a new sculpt—"

She barely stopped herself from rambling on about her latest project. Why would Ryan Sullivan care? Besides, she reminded her racing heart with brutal honesty, he probably had some pretty cheerleaders waiting on him. And they wouldn't need an out-of-control car to get him to lie down on top of them.

No matter how tempting it was to believe that she had suddenly been cast in a happy-ever-after fairy-tale romance, the truth was that getting that close to Ryan had been nothing more than a fluke of fate.

And Vicki remained the star of her artsy, and often lonely, move-to-a-new-town-every-year-with-her-military-family teenage life.

Only, for some strange reason she couldn't understand, Ryan wasn't running in the opposite direction yet. *Probably because he felt like he owed her after she'd saved his life.* After all, hadn't he just told her that he would be there for her one day when she really needed him?

"What are you getting supplies for?" He asked

the question as though he were truly interested, not just acting like it because he felt he should.

"I'm making a—" Wait, she couldn't tell him what she was making. Because she was sculpting *him*. "I work with clay. Lately, I've been trying to capture specific facial expressions."

"Which ones?"

Never in a million years did she think she'd ever speak to him, let alone have this long a conversation. But what shocked her most of all was just how comfortable she felt with him. Even with all of her teenage hormones on high alert, Ryan was, simply, the easiest person she'd ever been around.

And she wanted more time with him than just five stolen minutes on the high school lawn.

Her nerves were starting to back off a bit by the time she told him, "I started with all the usual expressions every artist knows best." She played it up for him. "Tears. Pain. Suffering. Existential nothingness."

His laughter made her feel like she could float all the way to the art store and back.

"Sounds fun."

"Oh, yeah," she joked back, "it's a riot. Which is why I'm trying something different now." She took a breath before admitting, "I'm working on laughter."

"Laughter, huh?" He grinned at her. "I like it. How's it going?"

Being so close to the full wattage of his smile

made her breath catch in her throat. In an effort to cover her all-too-obvious reaction to him, she scrunched up her face. "Let me put it this way, I think I've started to resemble all those other expressions."

"Even the existential nothingness one?"

As if she were watching the two of them from a distance, Vicki knew she'd always look back to that moment as the one that mattered most. The one where she fell head over heels in love with Ryan Sullivan. And not because of his beautiful outside.

But because he'd listened.

And, even better, because he'd appreciated.

"Especially that one," she replied.

He picked up her bag from the grass. "Sounds awesome. Mind if I tag along?"

Okay, so maybe the two of them didn't add up on paper, but Vicki couldn't deny that they had clicked.

"Sure," she said, "if you don't have anywhere else you have to be."

He slung his equipment bag over his other shoulder and walked beside her. "Nothing more important than hanging out with a new friend."

This time, she was the one grinning at him. In the two weeks since she'd moved to Palo Alto with her family, she hadn't done a very good job of making friends at the high school. As an army brat who moved every year more often than not, she'd stopped making the effort. A long time ago, when she'd realized how hard it was to break into fully

formed cliques or maintain long-distance friend-
ships, she just stopped trying, knowing she would
inevitably have to move again.

But Ryan made everything seem so easy, as if
the only thing that wouldn't make sense would be
if they didn't hang out.

By the end of their trip to the art store she knew
all about his seven siblings, he knew she had two
annoying little brothers, he'd told her what he liked
about baseball, she'd told him what she loved about
sculpting and before she knew it she'd been invited
to dinner at the Sullivan house.

It was the beginning of a beautiful friendship.

The best one she'd ever had.

Present day, San Francisco

Ryan Sullivan threw his car keys to the valet as
he shot past him. The young man's eyes widened
as he realized that he was not only about to drive a
Ferrari into the underground parking lot, but that
it belonged to one of his sports idols.

"Mr. Sullivan, sir, don't you need your valet
tag?"

Ryan took his responsibilities to the fans seriously and made it a point never to let them down.
But tonight the only thing that mattered was Vicki,
so he waved off the valet's question as he hurried
toward the entrance.

Even though a half dozen missed connections

over the years after high school had kept them from meeting up again in person, he and Vicki had kept in touch through email and phone calls.

Vicki was his friend.

And he wouldn't let anyone hurt one of his friends.

Ryan pushed through the dark glass doors to the exclusive hotel foyer and made himself stop long enough to do a quick scan of the glittering room. The Pacific Union Club wasn't his kind of place—it was pretentious as all hell—and he hadn't thought it would be Vicki's usual stomping grounds, either.

So why was she here? And why hadn't she told him she was finally coming back to Northern California after so many years in Europe?

He'd been hanging at his brother Chase's new baby celebration when her texts had come in.

I need your help. Come quick.

Ryan had cursed every one of the thirty-five miles as he drove into the city from his mother's house on the peninsula. He'd called Vicki again and again to get more information, and to make sure that she was okay, but she hadn't replied.

He couldn't remember the last time he'd been so worried about anyone…or so ready to do battle. Vicki wasn't the kind of woman who cried wolf. She wouldn't have sent him those texts just to try to get his attention. She was the only woman he'd ever known, apart from his sisters and mother, who had ever been completely real with him, and who didn't want anything from him besides his friendship.

His large hands were tight fists as he surveyed the cocktail lounge, his jaw clenched tight.

Damn it, where was she?

If anyone had touched Vicki the wrong way, or hurt her even the slightest bit, Ryan would make them pay.

He was famous for being not only the winningest pitcher in the National Baseball League, but also one of the most laid-back. Very few people had a clue about Ryan's hidden edges, but it wouldn't take much more to set him off tonight.

He grabbed the first person in uniform, his grip hard enough on the young man's upper arm that he winced. "Is there a private meeting room?"

The young man stuttered, "Y-yes, sir."

"Where is it?"

His hand shook as he pointed. "On the back side of the bar, but it's already reserved toni—"

Ryan hightailed it through the lounge, and it shouldn't have been that hard to get through the crowd, but it seemed that every single person in the room had either got up to buy another drink or was trying to get his attention.

When he found a subtly hidden door just to the side of the bar, he nearly knocked it off its hinges in his hurry to open it.

Ryan saw the flash of Vicki's long blond hair first, her killer curves second.

Thank God. She was here, and in one piece.

But his relief was short-lived when he realized he'd interrupted her and her cocktail companion just as the man's hand was sliding onto her thigh.

Vicki jumped off her seat as Ryan strode into the room. The terror that had been on her face when the other man had touched her leg slowly morphed into relief at Ryan's arrival.

Her companion, on the other hand, was clearly surprised to see Ryan…and he wasn't happy about it, either. The man was probably in his fifties and was obviously loaded. Or at least he wanted people to think he was, holding meetings in a place like this, wearing a handmade suit.

Quickly conjuring up an expression of surprise, Vicki said, "What are you doing here so early, *honey?*"

Two

Ryan made sure not to give away his surprise at Vicki's greeting. Clearly, she needed to make it seem like they were an item, because the rich douche bag she was having a drink with in the private room had been hitting on her. And no wonder.

She was gorgeous.

She'd been a pretty teenager, but now Vicki was everything he loved in a woman, wrapped up in one gorgeous package. Long hair that brushed over the swell of her breasts, the sweet curve of her hips from her waist, killer legs in high-heeled sandals.

Oh, yes, the years had been good to his high school friend. So good, in fact, that it didn't take any acting ability whatsoever to reach for her hand and tug her into his arms.

"Sorry I'm early, *baby.* I could have sworn you said you'd be free by eight."

God, she felt good. Warm and soft in all the

right places. She smelled just as good, like flowers blooming in the sun mixed with the earthy hint of the clay she was always working with.

She was stiff for a moment in his arms before she seemed to remember that they were pretending to be an item. Her hands shifted around Ryan's back, before settling in just above his hips.

"Thank you," she whispered as she hugged him, before saying an even softer, "I'm sorry."

Didn't she know she didn't have a damn thing to apologize for? She'd saved his life when they were kids. He still owed her for that, would owe her for the rest of their lives.

Pretending to be her boyfriend for one night wasn't even close to paying her back.

Especially when it meant he finally got to live out his secret fantasy.

Six years after she'd moved away from Palo Alto, he'd headed out from California to New York City to surprise her at her college graduation. She hadn't mentioned having any guy in her life in the emails they frequently sent back and forth, so when he saw her walk into the graduation ceremony on the arm of an older man, who had clearly claimed her, looking so happy and glowing, the jealousy and frustration had almost flattened him.

He'd been too late again.

Ryan had left her graduation without ever letting her know he'd come and the next thing he knew there was a breathless voice mail from her saying that she'd eloped and was moving to France.

He couldn't help feeling that he'd just lost something vital…even though he'd never had her as anything but a friend in the first place. For the next ten years, Vicki had lived all over Europe with her husband and, after her fairly recent divorce, had settled in Prague. Ryan had been toying with taking a trip to see her at the end of the baseball season. Instead, she'd come to San Francisco. And he was damn glad about it.

As she pulled back from their hug, he threaded their fingers together. He'd seen several of his brothers and sisters fall in love this past year to know how two people in love were supposed to look.

Always touching.

Adoring glances.

Little kisses when they thought no one was looking…and even when they were.

"James, I'd like to you meet Ryan Sullivan. My b—" when she momentarily stumbled over the tag, he pulled her closer into him "—boyfriend. Ryan, this is James Sedgwick. I'm sure you remember me telling you that he's one of the foremost authorities on modern art?" She gave Ryan a blinding smile that didn't reach her eyes. "James and I have been discussing my latest project for the fellowship competition. He has some very constructive suggestions for me."

"What can I get you to drink, Mr. Sullivan?"

James gestured to the heavily laden glass table against the wall.

"Call me Ryan," he said in as easy a voice as he could manage, given the fact that he wanted to pound James's head into the marble tabletop. "A beer would go down great, thanks."

"Of course. If you will excuse me for a moment."

Ryan had counted on James needing to head out to the bar to get his drink. As soon as the creep left, he said, "What the hell is going on here, Vicki?"

She shook her head, looking too pale and worried for his peace of mind. "I'll tell you everything later. Just keep playing along. Please."

James returned seconds later and Vicki gulped from her wineglass as the man handed the beer bottle to Ryan, clear distaste upon his face. "The bartender assured me you wouldn't need a glass. I must congratulate you on your record season, Ryan." James turned his attention back to Vicki. "I'm surprised you didn't tell me who your boyfriend was before now. I'm very...impressed."

This time she didn't stumble as she smoothly replied, "I didn't realize you were a baseball fan, James." She turned to Ryan and smiled. "I should know by now that everyone is a fan of yours, shouldn't I?"

She said it with such affection that even Ryan found himself believing that they were a couple for a moment. It was pure instinct to gently smooth the pad of his thumb over the faint drop of wine left on the corner of her bottom lip.

Her eyes flashed with sudden heat at the unexpected touch, and he wanted to kiss her, needed to find out just how sweet she would taste. Telling himself it would help them look like an item in front of this guy, Ryan dipped his head and pressed his mouth to hers.

So many years he'd waited for this moment, and sweet Lord, if it wasn't even better than he thought it would be. The surface of her lips tasted like red wine and sugar and all Ryan wanted was to deepen the kiss and keep kissing her for hours. When he finally managed to pull back from the softest, sweetest mouth he'd ever tasted, Vicki's skin was flushed.

"James and I were just talking about how being able to take criticism is one of the most important elements of creating great art." Her voice seemed a little higher than usual and Ryan was pleased that one little kiss had had such an effect on her. "James, what was it you were saying when Ryan joined us?"

"Simply that anyone can mold clay into shapes," James informed Ryan with a nod. "But it takes a true artist to heed wise direction. I'm sure you experience the same thing with your pitching coach, don't you?"

Ryan shrugged, even as his hand fisted behind Vicki's back. "It's a give-and-take. The pitching coach trusts my experience on the mound." He paused a beat before adding, "And I trust him not to abuse his power by convincing me to do things I shouldn't be doing."

James's bland expression didn't waver the slightest bit at Ryan's not-so-subtle warning. Vicki, on the other hand, squeezed his hand hard enough for him to know she wasn't entirely pleased by the way he was playing the situation.

Ryan got it. She didn't want to piss the guy off. But she had to know when she texted him tonight, and then called him *honey* the second he walked into the room, that he would make damn sure to protect her.

No matter what.

"Sounds like I interrupted an important discussion," Ryan said with another easy smile that he didn't even come close to feeling. "I used to do the same thing when Vicki and I were kids. I'd swing by her house to hang out and she'd barely even look up from what she was working on. But I was totally mesmerized by her and her sculptures, even at fifteen."

Back in high school, everyone had expected him to stick with the other jocks and the cheerleaders but, especially after a night game, he was always glad to know he'd find Vicki in her garage at her potting wheel. Her hands would be covered in clay, with little splatters on her face and body. She'd look up and smile to let him know she saw him, but she wouldn't stop, wouldn't drop everything for him the way everyone else always did. He'd keep making jokes until she'd finally laugh and tell him he was bothering her, but then they'd talk. For hours, sometimes, as she created art right before his eyes. He didn't always understand what she was making with such intense purpose. But even though he wasn't an expert in modern art, he'd known without a doubt that she was special. Vicki was never afraid to reach, or head out of bounds, or screw up and start over a hundred times in a row.

"Vicki is pretty damn amazing, isn't she, James?"

James bared his teeth at Ryan in what he assumed was supposed to pass as a smile. "As I'm sure she's told you, everyone on the fellowship board is eager for her project to hit the mark. Which is why I was so pleased that we could meet tonight to address a few specific issues. Victoria wouldn't be a contender for the fellowship if I didn't think she had potential."

Potential? This a-hole thought Vicki had *potential?*

When she was a teenager she had potential. A decade and a half later, her sculptures were nothing short of masterful. Ryan should know, considering he owned a half dozen.

He had a choice to make. He could either grab James by the throat and slam him against the wall for minimizing Vicki's incredible talent...or he could get them both the hell out of there before he said or did something that would ruin her chances for the fellowship this guy was in charge of.

Turning to Vicki, he brushed a lock of hair back from her face. "I really feel like an idiot for getting the timing all wrong, *baby,* but Smith is holding the private screening of his new movie for us tonight, and you know how much he values your opinion." He worked like hell to feign regret at having to pull her away. "We'd better get you over to his house before he throws one of his movie-star tantrums."

James immediately stood up, clearly more than a little pissed off at the turn his evening with Vicki had taken. "I can see you have other plans, Victoria. And while I'm disappointed that we didn't make more progress together, I'm sure if you're as serious about this fellowship as you seemed to be at the outset, you will let me know when you have time to meet again privately. Good night to both of you."

"What were you doing in here alone with that asshole?"

Since the day she'd moved away at the end of their sophomore year in high school, whenever Vicki had thought of Ryan Sullivan, she'd always pictured him laughing.

He wasn't laughing now.

On the contrary, his gaze was so intense that a shiver ran up her spine.

Her breath had gone from the first moment Ryan had walked into the private cocktail lounge. It was no different from the way she'd felt around him at fifteen. No wonder, given that he'd only become better looking over the years. No longer a gorgeous boy, he was all man now.

And, oh, my, the way Ryan kissed, even when it was no more than just his lips against hers...

Working overtime to get her brain to click back into gear on the problem at hand, she was about to answer him when she looked down at their hands, still linked together.

The last thing she wanted was to let his hand go, but she knew better than to pretend that any of this was real, no matter how tempting it was to do just that. So even though she'd wanted to hold his hand like this since they were teenagers, Vicki forced herself to slide her fingers from his.

"James came by the fellowship building this morning and asked if he could stay to watch me work for a while. I assumed it was part of his critiquing style. You know, that he was just as interested in my technique as in the finished sculpture."

"How long did he watch you?"

"Twenty minutes, maybe." Twenty incredibly long and icky minutes in which she'd felt like James had been studying *her* more closely than her project. "The thing is, before he left, he really did have some brilliant suggestions for me."

So brilliant that she had let herself write off his slightly creepy behavior as purely artistic interest.

"And then later, at a welcome party the fellowship board threw for all of the applicants, he told me that the top candidates were going to be meeting here afterward."

"There were supposed to be other people here?"

"By the time I arrived, he said everyone else had already dropped in and that he was glad it was just the two of us tonight so that he could give me special attention."

Bile rose in her throat as she remembered the way he'd moved closer and closer during their conversation and started touching her arm and then her hands —even when he had to know how off-limits a sculptor's hands were. What he'd said to her hadn't been much better: *I've coached many other talented sculptors toward greatness. It's considered quite an honor to work under me. Especially as I know you're all alone in San Francisco, I feel that I could really help you make your way here by introducing you to everyone you should know. Doesn't that sound good to you, Victoria?*

It was one thing to trust the wrong man at twenty-two. But she'd been in the art world long enough by now to know better than to be so naively flattered by a powerful man's attention.

"Jesus, Vicki, why didn't you kick him in the nuts and get the hell out of here?"

"I wanted to," she said softly, "but the fact is that regardless of what you and I think of him, James Sedgwick is one of the leaders of the West Coast art world. The only thing I could think of doing that wouldn't jeopardize my chances at the fellowship was to pretend that I was seeing someone so that he wouldn't take my rejection of his advances personally and turn it against me. That was when I went into the bathroom to text you." She'd prayed that Ryan would not only get her messages, but come right away. Which he had, thank God.

But even after her explanation, Ryan still said, "You need to turn him in to the rest of the fellowship board."

She sighed. "I doubt it would do any good when everything he's done so far could so easily be argued as me mistaking friendly support for something more. He hasn't done or said anything blatantly threatening."

"I saw him put his hands on you," Ryan growled.

"He's an art critic and curator, with a specialty in sculpture, so everyone knows it's a very touchy-feely job in a lot of respects. I'm sure if I raised a stink and called him on it, he would just laugh and say he's like that with men and women and sculptures alike. And, in the end, it would only hurt my chances for the fellowship by deflecting attention away from my project."

Ryan stared at her for several long moments. "You really want this, don't you?"

In those final months leading up to her divorce, Vicki's ex-husband, Anthony, had told her again and again that the only reason she'd had any success at all was because he was one of the foremost sculptors in the world, and that she'd be nothing without him. Since then, she'd heard whispers from friends in the European art community that he'd been working to turn people against her. She wouldn't be at all surprised to find out that it was true. His once-awestruck wife leaving had been a blow that Anthony's ego had never seen coming.

Vicki had come to San Francisco to win the coveted fellowship and prove once and for all that she had what it took to make it as a sculptor. Not just to her ex, but to herself.

It was long past time to prove to herself that she hadn't wasted her life chasing a dream.

"I do want it, Ryan." She paused. "But even more than that, I *need* it. It's the next step for me and my career, the perfect way to start fresh and build my reputation as a sculptor in the United States. So if I win the fellowship—"

"*When* you win it," he cut in.

"—I want to know that I got it because of the quality of my work." Not because she'd agreed under pressure to sleep with one of the board members.

"I wanted to kill the creep for touching you." A muscle jumped in Ryan's jaw. "Hell, I still want to tear him apart for even looking at you the wrong way."

"All these years, when I thought about us seeing each other again, I never thought it would be like this. I'm really sorry for roping you into my mess."

"I like ropes," he teased her with the naughty grin he was so famous for.

How could she do anything but smile back at the most beautiful man she'd ever set eyes on? Vicki was amazed to find that nothing had changed since they were teenagers. Ryan was still just as able to send heat all through her body as he was to make her laugh.

She'd never met anyone like him before or since.

His hair was lighter than most of his siblings, shot through with highlights due to all of his time spent in the sun. His long-sleeved cotton shirt had an extra button open at the top, giving her a glimpse of just enough tanned skin to make her lose her train of thought all over again.

"Promise me you won't be alone with him again, Vicki."

"Don't worry, I won't make that mistake again. Thanks for being my ten-minute boyfriend."

"Ten minutes?" Ryan looked surprised to be let off the hook so easily. "When is the board going to decide on the fellowship?"

"Next week."

"In that case, sign me up to be your one-week boyfriend."

"What? No. You can't do that for me." When Ryan lifted an eyebrow at her quick refusal, she said, "Seriously, thank you so much for stepping in tonight. But you don't have to pretend to be dating me for a week. If James asks about the two of us,

I'll just explain that we had a fight and are taking a break. And I'll be beyond careful not to put myself in any more situations like this with him again."

Unfortunately, Ryan looked anything but convinced. "You asked me to come here tonight because you felt like you were all out of options, right?"

She blew out a breath. "Right."

"When we were kids, you were nearly killed pushing me out of the way of that car. You saved me, Vicki. Big-time. Now it's my turn to return the favor."

Everyone thought Ryan Sullivan was so easygoing. And it was true that he was quick with laughter, that he made everything look easy. But she knew how much focus went into his ease. When she'd be at her potting wheel in her parents' garage, he'd throw baseballs at a soft target he set up on her driveway over and over until her fingers were working in time to the constant thud of the ball into the target.

Now his focus was on protecting her from James's less-than-pure intentions. Ryan was too committed a friend not to back her up. And he wouldn't dream of walking away if he thought she needed him.

He reached into his wallet and tossed a couple twenties down on the table. "Let's get out of here. This place gives me the creeps."

She felt the same way, surrounded by all that leather and velvet. Everyone at the Pacific Union

Club looked like they had metal beams shoved up their you-know-whats.

Ryan stood up, then waited for her to scoot over to the edge of the couch. And even though she knew his sweetly seductive kiss had all been part of their big act, she was hyperaware of how her body was responding to him.

The fact that her dress was hiking higher and higher up her thighs as she slid along the couch. The knowledge that he must have a perfect view of her ample cleavage. The expensive, sky-high heels she'd put on to prove an army brat like her belonged in a place like this.

His hand was warm on her back as they headed for the exit. She tried to remind herself that it was no different than what any other gentleman would have done. But her body refused to listen.

How could it, when it felt so good to be touched by him?

She'd never been more glad for fresh air. Now all she needed to do was *stop thinking about that kiss* and everything would be fine. Which, unfortunately, meant she should probably call it a night. Because every second she spent with Ryan only made her want to do it again.

"Why didn't you call me to tell me you were back in town?"

"I know how busy you are with the team and your family and—" *your women* "—your social life."

"I'm never too busy for a friend."

It was exactly why she'd texted him. Because she knew that if anyone would come through for her in a pinch, it would be Ryan. He'd always been different from the other men she knew. Not just because he was worlds better looking than the rest of them, but because she'd never doubted how much he *liked* her.

After the starstruck valet asked for an autograph and then went to fetch Ryan's car, he asked, "Where's your hotel?"

Not wanting him to see the dump she was staying in for the time being, she said, "In the Mission. But I can take a cab." A bus, actually, because she didn't have the money to waste on a taxi.

His eyes narrowed. "The Mission? No way. We're going to get your things and you're moving in with me."

Shock rolled through her at his suggestion. "I can't move in with you, Ryan."

"Of course you can."

He was so sure. Was acting like it all made sense, like her moving in with him was no different than his giving her a ride home.

"You have a life, and I can't just barge in on it."

Honestly, just the thought of being in his house while he was making love to another woman under the same roof practically did her in. Plus, if she was being perfectly honest with herself, she wasn't at all sure she trusted herself to be that close to him without giving in to the urge to strip naked and beg him to take her.

"If I had known you were coming to the city," Ryan said as he pulled into traffic and headed toward the Mission District, "I would have asked you to stay with me. After not getting to see you for so long, I'm planning to keep you here for as long as I can this time."

It was impossible to hold back her smile. Over the years, whenever Ryan had texted or emailed, or if they'd managed to catch each other on the phone for a few minutes, he'd never failed to brighten her day.

It was lovely to know that he seemed to feel the same way.

How had the years come and gone between them so fast? She'd moved away from the Bay Area after sophomore year and slogged her way through to high school graduation in the Midwest before finally escaping to art school in New York City. She'd loved every minute of finally being with people she understood and who seemed to understand her. Still, she'd always missed Ryan and had even tried to attend a couple of his College World Series games on the East Coast, but the game dates and her test schedules had always conflicted.

Before she knew it, she'd met Anthony and graduated and was married and living in Europe. Her husband had been possessive and jealous of her platonic relationships with other men.

Especially her friendship with Ryan.

No wonder it had never worked for the two of them to actually meet up again. She'd been too worried about damaging her marriage, and Ryan had obviously been just as wary of getting in the middle of it. It wasn't until she'd finally left her husband that she felt she could reach out to Ryan again. But by then, according to the tabloids, he was dating an oil heiress. Of course she wasn't going to cry on his shoulder. It wouldn't have been fair to him—or to the heiress girlfriend. By the time the tabloids had declared his relationship to be over, she'd vowed to get her life back together on her own so she could laugh with him again instead of wasting any more time crying.

She'd thought this fellowship opportunity was going to be part of finally getting her life back on track rather than a reason to drag Ryan into her messy life.

He didn't say anything when they got to her motel, but he didn't need to. The disgusted look on his face said it all.

"You should probably stay with your car," she suggested. Wouldn't it be the icing on the cake if his fancy car was broken into or stolen, on top of everything else she'd already put him through tonight?

"Screw my car." He looked around at the very sketchy men and women loitering on the sidewalk. "I'm coming with you."

As they climbed the stairs, the sounds of yelling and crying and babies wailing felt like the perfect soundtrack to the fiasco of her life. She'd never wanted to be the woman in need of rescuing, had scoffed at girls like that.

And now here she was, with her very own knight in shining armor.

The only saving grace in the whole thing was that it was Ryan. But even though rationally she knew he wouldn't judge her, she was a little short on rational thought right now.

Mortification, on the other hand, was in healthy supply.

Especially when Ryan got to the bathroom before she could and walked face-first into the bra-and-pantie sets she'd hand washed in the sink. They were drying on the rusted shower rail, the towel holder and the doorknobs.

Was he shocked by the fact that her underthings were more suited to a high-class kinkster than a woman who had been a virgin until she was twenty-two and had only slept with one man in her whole life?

She watched as, almost in slow motion, Ryan reached for a pair of panties and the matching bra. Her breath caught in her throat as his fingers slid over the lace.

"Pretty."

She barely had enough breath left in her lungs to say, "Thanks." She moved into the very small bathroom with him. "I can grab the rest of them."

Only, to get to the colorful lace hanging from the curtain rod, she had to slide past the sink and the tub. Which was right where Ryan was standing, still holding her unmentionables. Every inch of her body that came in contact with his felt hot. Supersensitive. Flustered, she yanked so hard at a particularly naughty bright pink thong that it nearly shredded.

She forced herself to stop, to take a breath, to recenter.

Ryan was her friend. The two of them were never, ever going to be lovers.

Never.

Ever.

So getting all flustered and out of breath and nervous around him like this was ridiculous. They were friends, and friends would be laughing about this.

She turned around and looked pointedly at the lingerie he was still holding. "You planning on keeping those for yourself? Don't worry, I'm not going to judge you for whatever you're into," she teased.

He held the bra up to his chest. "Do you think it's my color?"

She laughed as she grabbed it from him and took the stack over to her bags. The dresser drawers had been too gross for her to take much else out, so she was ready to go as soon as she zipped her lingerie into one of her bags. Of course, Ryan took her bags, then held the door open for her, always the perfect gentleman.

Was it wrong that, instead of appreciating his manners, she momentarily found herself wishing he'd act like a caveman instead?

Three

Vicki tried not to act like a total doof when Ryan pulled into the Sea Cliff neighborhood consisting of oceanfront mansions.

All these years that they'd kept in touch over email and texts and the occasional phone call, in her head he'd still been the fifteen-year-old boy who liked to climb the big tree in his mother's backyard. Sure, she knew he'd been a top draft pick out of college and was one of the best pitchers in pro baseball. But she'd never actually put it all together into what his life must be like now, had never compared her transient life with her ex-husband as they traveled between artists' colonies in various countries with Ryan's top-flight life as a bona fide celebrity athlete.

Within blocks of leaving her seedy motel, the San Francisco neighborhoods had become progressively nicer. For all that she'd wanted to keep up with Ryan's life over the past years, she'd always been careful not to rub her friendship with Ryan into Anthony's face. So she truly had no idea how much Ryan's annual contract with the Hawks was worth even though at his level it was probably public knowledge.

"This is me." He clicked the remote that opened the front gate and drove into the driveway of a positively gorgeous two-story oceanfront home.

Trying to act cool about it despite the fact that her mouth was all but falling open, she joked, "Yup, I'd say your place is definitely at least a couple steps up from my motel."

He grinned at her. "I had a pushy Realtor, one of my Seattle cousins who was working in the city for a while. Mia knew I didn't have a prayer of saying no to her."

Vicki grinned at that, knowing exactly what kind of sucker Ryan was for his female relatives. It was so sweet, sweet enough that her heart did more of that melting thing it had already done way too much of tonight.

"When I told her the place was too big, she swore the value would double in under ten years. But she was wrong."

"How wrong?"

Another grin came. "It tripled."

"In that case, Chinese is on you tonight."

He grabbed all three of her heavy bags and she followed with her purse. She'd noticed the way he favored his nonpitching arm when they'd been leaving the motel earlier. Now she caught his slight wince as he adjusted one of the bags over his right shoulder.

Knowing he was too much of a guy to let her take it from him, she said, "Hey, Ryan, there's something I want to make sure I remembered to pack in that bag. Could you put it down for a sec?"

"I'm pretty sure there wasn't anything left in your room," he said as he set it on the floor of the garage.

"You know how disorganized I can be. It might take me half the night to root through everything I stuffed in here."

"I'll put these in the guest room and come back for that one."

As soon as she couldn't hear his footsteps anymore, she started dragging the bag across the floor, only bothering to lift it up when she stepped inside the house and hit hardwood. She'd planned on bringing it all the way into the guest room, but as soon as she saw the view from his windows, her feet stopped moving.

Water had always been her weakness. It was why she'd chosen to go to Prague after leaving her ex-husband. The river had soothed her as she walked for hours along it, out of the city and then back once her mind had been quiet enough to return.

As Ryan came down the stairs, she said, "Your view is incredible."

"It's better from over here."

He reached out a hand for her and she forgot all about her bag as she moved toward him. As she put her hand into his, warmth sizzled all the way up her arm.

He pointed with his free hand. "Farallon Islands to the left. Alcatraz to the right. Heaven's straight up."

She could feel his grin without needing to look at him. All those years she'd never forgotten the beauty of it.

"I'm so happy for you," she told him, "that all of this is yours."

Even better was that she could tell how much he appreciated it. Ryan wasn't one of those guys who bought something as a status symbol. Regardless of what he'd said about his Realtor cousin, Mia, pushing the place on him, if he hadn't also loved it, they wouldn't be standing here now.

"I'm glad you agreed to stay for a while, Vicki."

She'd been so worried about being alone with him, but now that she saw how huge the house was, she realized they could probably go several days without seeing each other if they wanted to.

Not, of course, that she *didn't* want to see Ryan. But if he needed some alone time—say, if he had a woman over—she could easily disappear. If nothing else, she could always happily head down to the beach to get out of his hair.

"I am, too."

He picked up her remaining bag. "Come on, I'll show you your digs."

Silly her. Even after the little pep talk she'd just given herself, her heart was still flipping around at the thought of being in a bedroom with Ryan next door. Silently reminding herself that she wasn't a teenager anymore, she started to follow him through the house when her mouth fell open in shock.

"You've been collecting my sculptures?"

He had several of them placed throughout the main level of his house. Not just that, but they were some of her favorites.

"I've always been a fan, Vicki."

His simple, heartfelt response warmed her inside and out. Still, she had to ask, "Why didn't you tell me you wanted them? I would have given them to you."

"That's exactly why I didn't. Your work is worth a hell of a lot more than what I paid for each of these. I can't tell you how many times over the years people have tried to buy them from me."

"They have?"

"All the time. For a huge profit." He looked around at her sculptures. "My answer has always been, and will always be, that they're not for sale. To me, they're priceless."

Feeling utterly dazed by what he'd just told her, Vicki followed him through the living room, past the open kitchen and up the stairs. Halfway down the hall, Ryan opened one of the doors to a room that had another great view of the San Francisco Bay and the Golden Gate Bridge.

Vicki did her best to focus on the view rather than on the big bed in the middle of the room.

"I'm just next door," he said in an easy voice, and she immediately looked at the wall he'd gestured to, her brain spinning off in entirely inappropriate visions. Ones where Ryan was stripping down for the night, pieces of clothing falling onto the floor one after the other—

"I hope you'll be comfortable here."

Her lips and tongue felt really, really dry as she came back to reality. "I'm sure I will."

Perfectly comfortable, and yet she already knew she wouldn't be able to sleep a wink with Ryan only a wall away.

She smiled over at him, but it froze on her face as she took in his expression. Just as it had been earlier tonight, the expression in his dark eyes was intense before it was replaced with his easy smile.

"How does the usual sound?"

It took her longer than it should have to realize that he was talking about dinner. So many nights when they were kids, he'd come over to her parents' garage with takeout. She'd learned not to eat much dinner with her family so that she could share those meals with him. He worked out half the day, so he usually ate about ninety percent of the food, but she loved that he always made sure to bring over her favorite things, anyway.

"Sounds great."

"Go ahead and unpack and I'll call for delivery."

It wasn't until he'd left the bedroom that she could finally take a full breath. She knew she was being ridiculous, that they were both adults now and could certainly handle being in close proximity again without things getting weird and complicated. But just because she knew that intellectually didn't mean her heart—or her body—was getting the message.

How many fantasies had she had about him over the years? Starting at fifteen and going on from there, when the nights grew dark and lonely and she'd get an email from him that made her laugh. The longing she'd felt for him on those nights had been nearly unbearable.

Were the weird vibes from James the only reason she'd texted Ryan tonight? Yes, she'd felt threatened and out of options…but hadn't she also wanted desperately to see Ryan? Had she grabbed on to James's creepiness as an excuse to reach out and see if she was still important to him after all these years?

Angry with herself, she tossed her clothes into the beautiful dresser. She'd never been a particularly neat person—only with her art supplies did she bother with organization—but she knew she was taking messy to a whole new level.

Stop.

She needed to stop. Chill out. And enjoy being

with the one person on earth she'd always completely adored.

Vicki made herself slowly take everything back out of the dresser and fold it neatly.

That was how she'd deal with everything from now on, she promised herself. Calmly, carefully, rationally, rather than following the impulses—and passions—that had always gotten her in so much trouble.

She took a deep breath and worked to center herself before going downstairs to have dinner with Ryan. Her entire body still tingled from the kiss he'd given her at the cocktail lounge, despite the fact that he'd simply been pretending to feel something for her as part of their act...not because he wanted her and needed her and couldn't live without her.

If and when they had to pretend again, she needed to remember that a second or third kiss wouldn't mean anything more than that first one.

Calm.

Careful.

Rational.

She could be all those things, if for no other reason than she *needed* to be all those things around Ryan.

She was just heading for the stairs when Ryan's deep voice rose up from below.

"Felicia?...Actually, that's why I'm calling. Sorry, I've got to cancel...No, I can't reschedule... It isn't because of that. You were always great."

Vicki hadn't meant to listen in on his phone call, but he wasn't exactly doing it in private. Obviously, he was breaking a future date with someone named Felicia, and just as obviously, Felicia thought he was dumping her because he'd found someone better to tangle up the sheets with.

Little did Felicia know that the woman who had just moved into his house wasn't ever going to get closer to Ryan's sheets than the ones in the guest bedroom.

When she thought he was done with his call, she started down the stairs. She was too far to turn back by the time she heard him say, "Janey? Sorry to call so late about this, but I've got to cancel for this week…No, next week won't work, either…No, you shouldn't think that. Of course we always had fun together."

Vicki winced as Ryan extricated himself from another future date…and from the nasty tug in her chest as she couldn't help but wonder just how "great" his previous dates with Janey and Felicia had been.

After so many months of feeling as if he was just going through the motions—and trying not to let anyone get wind of his growing discontent—the second Ryan had gotten Vicki's text, he'd been hit with the kind of adrenaline he used to get when he was pitching a shutout.

"Still a lady-killer, huh?" she teased.

He shrugged. "There were a couple events I needed to back out of this week." It wasn't Felicia's or Janey's fault that they'd never measure up to Vicki, so he'd tried to let them down easy.

She raised an eyebrow. "Events? This is me, Ryan. You were breaking dates with women who probably really like you. And you were only doing it because of the situation I dragged you into." She shook her head. "I know if we're supposed to be dating it doesn't make sense for you to be going out with anyone else, but I feel really bad about you having to break things off with them."

"Don't. It was nothing serious with either of them."

"Just hot sex, huh?" Her words made it sound as if she was joking, but her expression wasn't quite all the way there.

In any case, he couldn't answer her question when his brain was unable to even think about touching another woman when he was around her.

"Seriously, Vicki, I'd much rather spend time with you."

She blinked up at him a couple times before saying, "I always knew I could count on an old friend."

Ryan knew that was all he'd ever been to her. A friend. But after the kiss he'd given her had confirmed everything he'd ever wondered about how it would be if she let him be more than just a friend, it was damned frustrating.

The buzzer at the gate rang and he let the delivery person in. Ryan had never wanted to live behind a fence, but the past couple times they'd won the World Series, things had gotten out of hand to the point that he'd actually been glad he had an extra level of security.

The delivery boy looked as though one word from Ryan would make him faint. "Mr. Sullivan, I'm your biggest fan."

All Ryan wanted was to be alone with Vicki. Reminding himself that she'd be here for at least the next week, he took a few minutes to talk baseball and sign an autograph and let Vicki take a picture of the two of them.

When he'd closed the door and was heading over to the kitchen island to set out the boxes, she was smiling at him. "No wonder you're everyone's hero," she said softly. "You couldn't have been nicer to the valet when we left the hotel and then to that boy. I never realized just how much work it must be for you to be so good at what you do." Before he could respond, her eyes went wide at the white takeout boxes that were covering a good deal of his kitchen counter. "Do you think you got enough food?"

He slid onto a bar stool and passed her a fork. They always used to eat straight out of the cartons. "You say that now, but soon you'll be giving me a hard time about eating the last spring roll."

She pulled up a bar stool and speared some

lemon chicken. "Why don't you just hand over that carton before you scarf them all down?"

For a moment, as they mock-fought over the spring rolls, it felt as if nothing had changed.

Nothing except the fact that he could barely look at her without losing his breath.

Vicki had always been pretty, and he'd been attracted to her from day one, but the years had turned her from a cute teenager into a shockingly beautiful woman.

One he could barely keep his eyes—or hands—off.

Four

In an effort to keep his hands to himself, Ryan grabbed a couple bottles of beer from the fridge and handed her one. When both of them took a good long slug from their bottles, he got a couple more and put them near the boxes of food.

"Now that we're finally together again," she said, "I need you to fill me in on everything I've missed about your life."

Ryan had always been more comfortable coasting in the middle of a family full of loudmouths rather than talking about himself. "Life is good," he said, even as that faint sense of dissatisfaction tried to rear its ugly head.

He had everything. Maybe not as much as his brothers and sisters who were so in love and building new lives, but that didn't mean he had the right to sit around and complain.

"I'm still planning on playing baseball for as

many years as my arm will let me, hanging with my family, enjoying my new niece." He pulled out his cell phone and showed Vicki the pictures of the baby he'd taken at the party. "Chase and his wife, Chloe, had Emma a few weeks ago." He couldn't have been happier for his brother, who had already practically taken more pictures of his daughter than he had throughout his entire career as a photographer. "Emma is amazing."

"She's beautiful, Ryan. Everyone must be over the moon about her."

"We are. I was at my mother's house with all of them when you texted."

"Oh, no, I can't believe I pulled you away from your family."

"The party was winding down anyway." But he'd stayed because he didn't have anywhere else to be. He didn't have anyone to go home with or even a dog to feed. Used to be, he'd been glad for all that freedom. It was only recently that he'd started to feel as if he were waiting for something else. Something more. "And you know how glad I am that you asked me to come tonight."

"I'm not letting you off the hook that easily," she said to him, "but now that you've started, why don't you fill me in on the rest of your family? I thought I read about Marcus dating a pop star?"

"I never saw that one coming," he said about his oldest brother, who owned Sullivan winery, "but Marcus and Nicola are a surprisingly great match even though she's quite a bit younger than he is. Pretty sure we'll be seeing another engagement in the family soon. Maybe by Christmas."

"Another engagement? How many have there been?"

"Gabe is marrying Megan this winter up in Lake Tahoe. Summer is her seven-year-old daughter and she's a total spitfire. He saved Megan and Summer when their apartment went up in flames earlier this year and his station got called in to fight it." At Vicki's horrified look, he let her know, "Everyone was fine. Gabe ended up in the hospital for a couple days, but I'm pretty sure he wouldn't have wanted to miss that fire for anything. Actually, Summer's eighth birthday party is in a few days and I know they'd all love to see you if you want to come."

"Of course I would," she agreed with a smile, even as she marveled at the way Ryan was integrating her into his life without so much as blinking.

"Zach fell hard for his dog trainer and they're sickeningly happy now and heading to the altar at some point." He could still hardly believe how fast his brother, owner of Sullivan Autos, had fallen for Heather. "Only Naughty, Smith and I are still single. You'll never believe who Nice ended up with." Normally, he wouldn't have used Lori's and Sophie's nicknames, but Vicki knew his family well enough that she also used to call the twins Naughty and Nice when they were kids.

"Sophie's with Jake, isn't she?"

He stared at her in disbelief. Had she really thought his librarian sister and Irish-pub-owning friend were a good match? "How did you know that?"

She shrugged as if it were completely obvious. "Sophie had stars in her eyes every time she looked at him when we were kids. And Jake always went out of his way to steer clear of her. I'm glad he finally gave in and admitted his feelings for her."

Was Vicki trying to tell him something? Was this a sign that she wanted him to finally get up enough guts to make another move after that first pathetic attempt to kiss her had crashed and burned so hard back in high school?

Looking over at her, he could see she was busy picking up a container of mu shu pork and focusing on pulling out the slivers of cabbage with her fork. Not exactly looking at him with lust in her eyes.

Feeling like an ass for even thinking about hitting on her, especially when it had barely been three hours since they'd reconnected in person after so many years apart on separate continents, he said, "Only problem was, he got her pregnant with twins before he admitted a damn thing to anyone. Including her. She's due soon."

"Twins. That's amazing. I'm so happy for them." She picked up the second bottle of beer and took another drink.

"Your turn," he said, his words a little hoarse from wanting so badly to press his lips against the pulse point in her neck she'd inadvertently bared to him when she'd tilted her head back.

"Well, you already know about my marriage and divorce," she said, brushing off a good ten years in less than a dozen words. But he could hear the pain behind every single one of them. "After spending the past year in Prague, I heard about this fellowship opportunity in San Francisco and here I am."

Ryan could tell she didn't want to talk about herself any more than he did, but he'd spent so long wondering about the guy who had been lucky enough to marry her—and then was stupid enough to lose her—that he had to probe deeper.

"Was the fact that your ex is also a sculptor part of the problem?"

"Talk about stars in your eyes," she said in a hard voice. "I was fresh out of art school and he was a legend." She put air quotes around the word *legend*. She took another drink from her bottle as if she needed the liquid courage to talk about it at all. "I was so flattered that he was pursuing me, and life with him was such a crazy whirlwind that before I knew it I was married. Until one day I realized I would be way happier being single than I ever had been when I was married. Good thing I was smart enough, at least, not to take his last name. I could never stand the idea of trading on his success in any way, even if he thinks he taught me everything I know."

All of Ryan's protective instincts had already

been roused tonight, and hearing the hurt vibrating in her voice as she talked about her ex ripped even deeper into him. Thank God he'd been there to protect her from James, but she'd been all on her own with her ex-husband.

"Did he hurt you, Vicki?"

She shook her head, but wouldn't meet his eyes. "I made a big mistake with Anthony by focusing on him instead of moving my own career forward. I'm not going to be stupid enough to let a relationship sidetrack me again." She shrugged as though it was all just water under the bridge. "I'm fine, really. Chalk it up to being young and stupid."

"This is me you're talking to," he told her in an echo of what she'd said to him a few minutes earlier. "Just because we didn't see each other for too many years doesn't mean I didn't think about you all the time. I'm still your friend and you can still tell me anything."

"I know. It's just—" She licked her lips and took a breath. "I'm not trying to hide things from you, Ryan. Especially after what you did for me tonight. Ask me anything and I promise I'll answer. Better than I have so far."

Damn it, he didn't want to hurt her more by opening up old wounds. "Tell me about your sculptures. What are you working on right now?"

The relief on her face was palpable and even though he knew there was more to the story with her ex—way the hell more, and most of it likely to piss

him off and make him want to hunt the guy down—
Ryan was glad when the darkness left her eyes.

"I've been working on a piece called *Overflow*.
I don't know if you remember, but I was always so
inspired by water. How it feels. How it moves. The
way light and color play off it."

Some of his favorite memories as a teenager were
of the two of them going hiking out along the wetlands at night. No matter how cold it was outside,
Vicki always had to put her hands in the water.
He'd known just how much she'd love his view of
the ocean, and he'd always hoped he'd get a chance
to show it to her in person.

He scooted his chair back and reached for her
hand to pull her off the bar stool and out the French
doors in his living room. "Of course I remember.
Which is why I'm taking you outside to catch the
last of the sunset on the beach."

He grabbed a thick, oversize beach towel from
a storage container on the deck and headed down
the stairs after her. She'd kicked off her heels on
the deck, and her bare feet and legs were gorgeous
as she made her way down the staircase from his
house to the beach below. When she got to the bottom, she gave a happy sigh.

"I love the feel of sand between my toes."

It was the most natural thing in the world to wrap
his arms around her from behind. She was stiff for
a moment, before she finally relaxed into him and
leaned her head back against his chest.

"This is what I've been working on," she said softly. "I've been trying to sculpt water."

"Sounds amazing."

"More like crazy, but I can't stop wanting to do it anyway."

The wind blew the ends of her hair against his face and the sun was just falling behind the waterline. In that moment Ryan wanted her more than he ever had, with her soft curves in his arms, her passion for her art pulsing just as strong as her heart beating beneath his forearms.

"I can't wait to see it."

"It doesn't look like much yet. Just a bunch of blobs I'm hoping will actually come together at the end."

He could feel her being pulled toward the ocean and said, "Go do it already. I know you're dying to get your hands into the water."

She laughed as she pulled him toward the surf. The wind blew her dress against her figure and he was pretty sure he'd embarrass both of them when she finally noticed the effect she was having on him.

"You're the only one who doesn't think I'm weird for doing this."

She hissed as she walked into the cold water, but it didn't stop her from bending down to put her hands into it.

Ryan had already taken off his shoes in the house, but he didn't bother rolling up his jeans before moving beside her and doing the same thing.

"I guess that makes both of us weird, then. Because I've done it ever since."

It had been a way to remember her at first, but then he'd realized she was right: the water did feel different every single time.

She shot him a surprised look before looking down at his hands and saying, "Funny, I never really thought about the fact that both of us use our hands for our jobs."

Under the water, he reached for her and took her hand in his. Her eyes met his in surprise, but she didn't pull back. Instead, she closed her eyes and he knew she was taking in the way their connection changed how the water moved around both of them.

It was one of the best sunsets he'd ever seen, but Ryan couldn't tear his eyes away from Vicki. He stroked his thumb across her palm and she shivered.

Too soon, she slid her hand out of his.

"My hands and feet are numb already," was her excuse as she moved away from him to head for dry land.

He'd dropped the towel onto the sand when they'd arrived, and after she sat down on it, he sat behind her so that she could lean into his legs the way they had so many times before as teenagers, sitting out and watching the stars blink over the wetlands.

It had killed him to keep things platonic back then, but even though he was supposed to have more control as an adult than as a horny teenager, it was just the opposite.

"This is exactly what I needed." She turned her face to smile at him, and he was a breath away from kissing her when she said, "Thank you for still being the one friend I can totally relax with."

It didn't take a genius to hear what she was telling him, loud and clear: *I need you to be my friend, Ryan. Nothing else.*

So despite how badly he wanted her, Ryan knew he would never forgive himself for being like all the other guys who had wanted something from her... and had taken it from her without thinking about anything but their own needs and desires.

She yawned and leaned back into him. "You know, I've never been much of a sleeper, but the past few nights were really bad with all those cockroaches at the motel waiting for me to fall asleep so that they could come out to feast on me."

Her words had grown fuzzier and fuzzier as she spoke and he wasn't surprised when, a few minutes later, she fell asleep in his arms. It was hugely tempting to stay like that with her, to listen to her soft breathing, to memorize the feel of her beautiful curves against him...and to pretend that she was more than a friend.

Biting back a curse, Ryan easily lifted her up to carry her to the guest bedroom. Her legs were soft and smooth against his arm where her dress hiked up, and the feel of her breasts against his chest, her hips against his groin, made it difficult for him to think clearly.

Somehow he made it up the flight of stairs without giving in to the urge to kiss her gorgeous lips, but he barely bit back a needy groan when she turned her face into his neck and he felt her warm breath against him.

He was breathing hard by the time he made it to the guest bedroom. Not because of her weight—he had a good foot in height on her—but because of the fight to control his arousal.

At last, he laid her down on the bed, her beautiful hair falling across the pillows as she immediately moved to curl up on her side.

Knowing he was going to spend the rest of the night wishing he could be there wrapped around her, Ryan barely trusted himself to stay in the bedroom with her for another minute, let alone touch her again to get her under the sheets so she wouldn't wake up cold.

But even as he was pulling back the covers and getting ready to slide her beneath them, he knew she wouldn't be comfortable sleeping in her formfitting dress. It was going to have to come off…which meant he was going to have to stop being a jackass and remember how to be her friend.

One who just happened to want her like crazy.

Ryan was famous for his steady hands, and for the fact that nothing riled him. But tonight, just the thought of undressing Vicki had his hands shaking like a blade of grass in the breeze.

He thanked God that her zipper was on the side of the dress so he could reach it without having to touch her too much. As he slowly pulled it down, he was torn between wanting her to wake up and praying she'd stay asleep.

What would she think if she found him undressing her in the dark bedroom without her consent? Would she slap him and throw him out?

Or would she tell him to finish the job by taking off her underwear, too, and then invite him to press kisses to the skin he'd just uncovered?

By then the zipper was down, but he wasn't doing his control any favors by letting his mind wander into fantasyland when he still had the dress to slide off her incredible curves.

You can do this, Sullivan.

He'd learned early on, when the game stakes were high and it came down to him on the pitcher's mound, how to shut down everything but the one thing he needed to focus on: making enough good pitches to strike the batter out.

Tonight, that focus was entirely on getting out of the guest bedroom without kissing Vicki. Or stroking his hand over the curve of her breast. Or waking her up and begging her to let him make love to her.

Her dress was made of smooth fabric and it didn't take more than a couple slow tugs on the hem to get it to slide off. His jaw dropped at the sight of her in a strapless bra and lace panties, both of them red. The bold color looked like fire licking across her pale skin.

He knew it was wrong to stare at her like this, while she was asleep and he was all but drooling. Knowing he still needed to get her under the covers, Ryan tried to get a grip, and swore he almost had it when she stirred slightly, just enough that he was utterly mesmerized by the way her breasts moved beneath her bra.

Hard past the point of comfort—way past—he gave himself sixty seconds to get her under the covers and himself out of the room.

Steeling himself for the touch of her soft skin beneath his hands, he gently lifted her from the bed again before putting her back down on the sheet. And as long as he blocked out every ounce of sensation, if he didn't make the mistake of smelling her hair, or getting too close to her luscious mouth, he might be able to get out of the bedroom in one piece.

He had almost pulled his arms from her when she suddenly said his name in her sleep, pressed her lips to his neck and tightened her hold on him as if she didn't want him to leave.

Ryan went completely still everywhere—apart from his erection, which was throbbing painfully against the zipper of his jeans. His hands started moving with a mind of their own down her back, over her hips. When she moved closer to him instead of farther away, he almost gave in to the need that hadn't just been eating at him from that first moment he'd seen her with James at the Pacific Union Club.

It had been eating at him since he was fifteen years old.

Ryan didn't just want Vicki anymore. He *needed* her. With a desperation he'd never felt before for anything or anyone but her.

Black and white turned into a shade of gray as the urge grew bigger, stronger, and he teetered between right and wrong. And in the end, it took every ounce of self-control he possessed to gently lay Vicki back against the pillows and cover her with the sheets.

She trusted him enough that she'd actually fallen asleep in his arms down on the beach. He'd never forgive himself if he selfishly took advantage of her sleepy vulnerability.

Especially when she'd just made it perfectly clear to him at dinner, and then again on the beach, that she needed him to be her friend.

And *only* her friend.

After leaving her alone and soft and perfect on the bed, instead of going to his bedroom where he knew he wouldn't sleep worth a damn with Vicki only a wall away, he headed for his home office and picked up the phone.

"Hey, Rafe, it's Ryan."

His cousin worked as a private detective in Seattle. Ryan always made sure Rafe had killer tickets when they played in the northwest.

"Need some pointers for the game tomorrow?" his cousin joked.

"Not tonight," Ryan replied.

Realizing he wasn't calling to shoot the breeze, Rafe said, "What's wrong? Is everyone in SF okay? Your mom doing all right?"

"They're all good. Great, actually. I'm calling for a friend of mine. I need you to dig up the dirt on one of her colleagues."

"Sure thing. What's the name?"

Ryan spelled it for him.

"I'll hand over any info as soon I get it," Rafe promised him.

A female voice sounded in the background and Ryan said, "Thanks for your help. You can hang up and roll back on top of her now." The phone went dead immediately, his cousin obviously eager to do just that.

Ryan pulled out some new endorsement contracts that could have waited. A few hours later, when he couldn't put off going to bed any longer, the situation was just as he'd figured it would be. Every time he closed his eyes, he saw Vicki in her sexy red lace panties and strapless bra, reaching for him and pressing her lips against his.

At 5:00 a.m., he finally gave up and went to take a cold shower. One that wasn't even close to cold enough.

Five

Vicki would have happily remained under the softest sheets she'd ever slept in had it not been for the incredible smell of bacon and eggs coming from the kitchen.

How long had she been asleep? She couldn't remember heading to bed...or, she thought as she looked across the room and saw her dress draped carefully over the arm of a chair, taking off her dress for that matter.

Oh, God, she thought as she felt her face heat up, had Ryan undressed her last night? She had a vague memory of being in his arms, with her arms around his neck, and his skin warm beneath her lips.

She gasped aloud at the horrifying thought that she might have thrown herself at him, her gasp turning to a moan at the even more horrifying realization that if she had, the solo state of her bed and the intact state of her underwear meant he certainly hadn't taken her up on it.

Her heart was pounding hard as she stripped off her underwear and got into the shower. The water pressure from the multiple expensive showerheads running down the wall from her head to her calves was heavenly, but she could hardly enjoy it while worrying about what she had—or hadn't—done to Ryan last night.

She knew he'd be a total gentleman about her throwing herself at him…but that didn't mean she wouldn't forever be hugely mortified about it.

Not able to stand not knowing what had happened for another second, she quickly dried off, slicked her hair back into a ponytail that she'd pay for later when the top of her hair was flat and the bottom looked like a bunny's tail and threw on a pair of fatigue-print capris and an army-green tank top. Her heart thudded as she made her way down the hall to the stairs.

At the stove, Ryan's back was to her, but as soon as he heard her footsteps, he turned and said, "Perfect timing. Breakfast is almost up."

She carefully studied his expression for any awkwardness, but he looked just as easygoing as always. Relief flooded through her and she held on to the desperate hope that she hadn't made a complete idiot of herself last night.

Still, the near miss was a very good warning to remember to keep her guard up around Ryan. The last thing she wanted to do was make him uncomfortable in any way. Especially after he'd rushed to her rescue last night and was now letting her crash at his oceanfront mansion.

"Was the bed okay?"

He handed her a plate full of bacon and eggs and toast, and her stomach grumbled in appreciation. "Between the bed and the shower and now breakfast, I'm not sure you'll ever figure out a way to get me to leave."

She'd meant it as a joke, but he didn't so much as smile at her. "Sounds good to me."

Her skin tingled under the intensity of his gaze and she sternly told herself to snap out of constantly fantasizing that there was something more behind his words than there actually was. Still, she needed to make absolutely certain that she hadn't crossed the line last night.

"I feel really bad about falling asleep on you last night. You know what a lightweight I am, especially after a few sleepless nights at Roach Central Station."

He sat down at the breakfast bar beside her and poured them both coffee. It smelled like heaven, but she was still too churned up over being this close to him to do more than cup the mug in her hands.

"My ego will get over it eventually," he joked, but a moment later she was surprised to see her easygoing friend look a little bit nervous. "I didn't think you'd be comfortable sleeping in your dress, obviously."

Now it was her turn to joke. "Just as long as you kept your eyes closed."

The lacy undergarments had been her big post-divorce splurge, a last-ditch effort to try to feel the slightest bit sexy again. Now, even though they weren't exactly practical, she wore them as often as she could simply because they'd been so expensive and she was hell-bent on getting her money's worth out of them.

She couldn't help wondering if he'd liked what he'd seen, even though she knew tall, brunette, size-four supermodels were his type rather than small, blonde, curvy girls like her.

He held his hands up as if to admit that he had, in fact, taken a peek or two. "Sorry about that. Forgive me?"

If he had been anyone else and she hadn't been horribly, excruciatingly attracted to him—say, if he were gay—she would be rolling with this no problem.

Yes, that was what she'd do.

She'd pretend he was gay.

Or that she was.

Actually, it would probably be safer just to pretend both of them were completely, utterly into their own team.

Forcing herself to shrug, she teased, "Just so you know, the next time I fall asleep on you, I sleep best with nothing on at all."

Ryan choked on the bite of eggs he'd just taken

and she silently cursed herself for saying exactly the wrong thing to diffuse the situation.

"So," she said a little too brightly, "what's on your agenda today? Practice? Or a game?" She crammed a huge piece of bacon into her mouth to make herself shut up.

Ryan drank some coffee to wash down the rest of the eggs before saying, "There's an afternoon game."

"Are you pitching?"

"Tomorrow night. Any chance you can make it?"

"I can't today, but hopefully tomorrow." She'd never been a baseball fan until she'd seen him play in high school from her spot in the shadows of the big oak tree some distance back from the field and stands. "The board will be coming by this afternoon to check in on all of this year's fellowship contenders."

Ryan's expression tightened. "Is James going to be there?" When she nodded, he said, "Make sure you don't end up alone with him, Vicki."

"Don't worry," she said, "I'm not going to be that stupid ever again."

"He tricked you."

"Maybe, but I should have known better, enough to at least trust my instincts about him when he gave me the creeps at the studio. In any case, between his thinking you and I are an item and all the people who will be at the studio this afternoon, I can't imagine he'd try anything."

"He'd better not." Her friend's expression was fierce. "You mean too much to me. Why don't you give me the address of the studio, just in case."

He'd just typed it into his phone when it rang.

"It's my cousin. Sorry, I need to take this." Ryan put the phone to his ear. "Rafe, hold on a sec."

He rattled around in a kitchen drawer and pulled out a set of car keys. "I wish I could take you back and forth from the studio, but now that I've moved you way out to the edge of the city, why don't you use one of my cars so you're not stuck on my schedule?"

She knew he was right, that it didn't make sense for her to try to get from Sea Cliff to the Mission on the bus. But as she took the keys, she felt more and more as if she was taking advantage of him. Not only was he playing the role of her fake boyfriend, but he'd also given her an oceanfront mansion to live in and now she held the keys to one of the shiny cars in his garage.

Ryan gave her an absentminded kiss on her cheek before he walked away, but she could tell he'd all but forgotten her as he resumed his talk with his cousin.

Vicki took their plates over to the sink, then washed and dried them while trying to enjoy the view of the morning sun over the ocean despite feeling like a complete interloper.

As she watched the gold and green and blue water merge, then break against the shore, a buzzing began just beneath her skin.

It was that feeling she got when inspiration hit. *Big-time* inspiration. And she had to act on it immediately.

She rushed back up to the bedroom to put on some flip-flops and grab her bag, and then she practically ran downstairs, miming to Ryan that she was leaving, to get to the car. The luxurious interior of the Ryan's Porsche convertible barely registered as she raced against traffic toward the parking garage nearest to the studio.

She'd waited so long to feel this rush of inspiration again that she could literally feel the energy about to burst from her fingers.

After parking the car, Vicki quickly made her way over to the building the fellowship committee had made available to the candidates. Making a beeline for her small studio, she flicked on the light switch, dropped her bag to the ground and grabbed a new container of Plasticine modeling clay. Later, if she nailed a small-scale model, she'd render a full-size version in oil-based clay.

It was so easy to overthink this feeling, to stop and drill down to see where it had come from, to want to know not only where it had come from, but also where it was going. Fortunately, after years of experience, Vicki knew better than to make the mistake of wasting time thinking about any of those things.

All she needed to do today was to go with it, to

let the clay talk to her through her fingers…and pray that it all made sense when she was finished.

It was, she suddenly realized, a little like trusting the ocean tide to take her out before bringing her back in again, refreshed and renewed.

Slipping on her headphones and putting a recording of the ocean on repeat, she placed her hands on the clay and closed her eyes. Following her instincts, she let herself shape and carve, enjoying the sweet pleasure of the emotion flowing from the center of her chest, then down her arms and out through her fingers.

The rhythm of the soundtrack matched her heartbeat as she worked steadily, lost to time, unaware of thirst or hunger or anything but the pure, sweet joy of creation.

Ryan slipped his phone back into his pocket and stared out over the ocean as he thought about what Rafe had just told him.

The background check on James Sedgwick had come up clean. A little too clean, according to his cousin. Ryan was fully confident that if there was anything to find on the guy, Rafe would find it. Unfortunately, it looked as if it would take some time for his cousin to dig deeper.

While he'd been on the line with Rafe, Vicki had left, but not before doing a cute little mime that indicated she was off to do some sculpting. Unable to shake the feeling that he and Vicki had left things in a strange place at breakfast, Ryan decided to drop by her studio to see her and her project before going to the stadium for a pregame workout.

As he drove back into one of the seedier parts of San Francisco, just thinking about Vicki working in this part of town made it hard to keep his possessive, protective nature in check. He wanted so badly to make sure nothing ever hurt her again.

For all those years…if he'd known she hadn't been happy with her husband, he would have—

What?

What would he have done?

Chased her halfway around the world and begged her for what? To let him sleep with her like every asshole who wanted a piece of her?

Or, he suddenly found himself wondering, would he actually have been begging for something more?

Six

Ryan spent several minutes poking his head into one studio after another looking for Vicki, before a woman with blue-and-green hair finally took pity on him. "Who are you looking for?"

"Vicki Bennett."

"Lucky bitch. Talented as all hell and now you." She pointed down the long hallway. "She's on the first floor at the back of the building."

Ryan thanked her and his heartbeat immediately kicked up at the thought of seeing Vicki again as he made his way toward her workroom. Her door was open a few inches and he put his hand on the knob to walk through it, but when he caught sight of her, he stopped dead in his tracks.

If seeing Vicki last night in her bra and panties had rocked his world, getting to watch her with clay beneath her hands, her legs open around her worktable, her feet bare, her eyes closed as she worked…

was so far past world rocking he didn't think they'd invented a term for it yet.

Some of the best nights of his life had been shared with Vicki in her parents' garage. She'd gotten used to him hanging with her while she worked. Some nights, when she was really intensely working on something, he'd work on his aim with a bag of baseballs. And on the nights where she'd get frustrated and throw the clay against the wall, he'd take her stained hands in his and convince her it was time for a wetlands walk. They'd both wash their hands clean in the water and he'd want to kiss her so bad.

He could have sex with other girls. Plenty of it, if he wanted. But he couldn't get what he had with Vicki with anyone else.

Vicki was his friend, a real friend, who didn't care if he was a great baseball player. She didn't expect him to be the easygoing, athletic Sullivan brother. She didn't need him to be the guy who was supposed to have the world at his feet.

Vicki never put any pressure on him to be anything at all. Just himself.

He had always thought she was beautiful, but she was never more beautiful than when she was deeply, passionately creating.

Sun was streaming in through the windows along the back of her room, illuminating her beautiful skin, her long eyelashes fluttering over her cheekbones. She was biting her lower lip as she worked and then licking at the spot where her teeth had left a small mark. Now that he'd finally gotten a tiny taste of her, Ryan wanted so much more. He wanted to run his lips down past the pulse that beat on the side of her neck to the curve of her shoulder so that he could breathe in the clean, sweet scent of her skin.

She was small, but her fingers were long and strong as she worked the clay. But it wasn't just her hands that were moving. Every part of her was at least a little bit in motion, all the way down to her toes. She'd painted her nails with colorful stripes and it occurred to him that Vicki was just as beautiful and mysterious as a rainbow.

One he'd been chasing for years without ever coming close to reaching the pot of gold at the end.

Telling himself that if she didn't come to a good stopping point soon, he'd head out to the stadium, Ryan leaned against the open door and dragged his gaze from her to take a look at what she was working on. Even though he owned several of her major pieces, seeing so many of her sculptures in one place at one time proved yet again just how staggering her skill was.

She'd been a talented teenager, but she'd turned *talented* into *brilliant*.

Vicki was just pulling out her earbuds, her eyes still closed as she lifted her arms above her head to stretch, when she opened them and saw him standing in the doorway. A surprised little squeak came from her lips and she almost toppled off her seat.

"Ryan? How long have you been here?"

He finally walked inside her workroom. "Long enough to be reminded all over again how talented you are."

She stood up. Flushed, she reached to push a stray strand of hair back behind her ear, streaking her cheek with clay. "Did you need something?"

"Just to see your studio and to apologize for leaving you to finish breakfast alone." He moved closer to the sculpture she'd been working on. "Is this the one you were telling me about last night? *Overflow?*"

"No, it's something new I'm trying, but the inspiration came in such a rush this morning that I haven't even had a chance to look at it yet—"

Her words fell away as she turned to face the sculpture. She shook her head as if she couldn't believe what she was seeing.

She moved closer to it, her hand outstretched, then stopped as if she was afraid of getting too close.

Even though it was still rough around the edges, he could easily make out the shape of two hands entwined. It looked as if a surf was breaking over them, the water moving over, under and through the hands without breaking their hold on each other.

Ryan immediately flashed back to the previous night out on the beach, when he'd reached for her hand and she'd let him hold on to her for a little while.

"It's amazing, Vicki."

"It's just rough, raw clay," she said, but she sat back down on her seat as though her legs were on the verge of giving out. "Ryan?" She lifted her eyes to his and he couldn't tell if she was sad or happy. "I—"

He moved closer to her, instinctively placing his hands on her shoulders to try to soothe her, hoping that was what she needed.

He could feel the ragged breaths shaking her before she said, "I've been searching for this for so long." Without letting go of her shoulders, he shifted so he could see her face better and was rewarded with a gorgeous smile. "It isn't perfect. I'll have to take the time to sketch it, to make a much cleaner maquette to see where it isn't working and where it is. But for the first time since I got here— longer than that, actually, so much longer—I think I might have a chance at creating something good."

"Not just good, Vicki. Something amazing."

She jumped up out of her seat as quickly as she'd dropped into it and threw her arms around his neck. He pressed a kiss to the top of her head and enjoyed the sweetness of her curves pressed against him.

Her face was radiant as she tilted it up to look at him. "I'm glad you came by to share this moment with me."

How he managed to fight the urge to kiss her,

he'd never know. "Me, too." He looked around at the other pieces in the room. "Looks like you've been busy this week."

She barely glanced at anything. "Dozens of false starts is all they are. They can go in the trash now."

"You'd better be kidding." He ran his hand down her back to take her hand, then pulled her over to a shelf with several blue sculptures of waves that were so fine and translucent they almost looked like glass. "These are brilliant. How can you even transform the clay into this?"

"You know how. You saw me throw plenty of clay against the garage walls that year in high school when I was trying to get it to do what I wanted. I don't throw nearly as much at the walls anymore, thankfully."

"Remember that night you tried to teach me how to make a bowl?"

Vicki's laughter was the best sound in the world. "I'm afraid that even five-year-olds put your pottery-making skills to shame."

He'd been a horny fifteen-year-old boy so distracted by her nearness, her scent, her hands over his as she tried to guide him with the clay that, for the first time in his life, he'd been all thumbs. Plus, he hadn't liked not being good at something right off the bat. It had been easier to give up early than to consider the possibility of failing later.

"I need to take a little break to clear my head and hands before I get working again." She lifted his hand, then picked up the other one and studied them. Her eyes were sparkling as she said, "What do you say we give these legendary hands of yours another try?"

He had to work like hell to keep her from seeing just how much the idea of her trying anything at all with his "legendary hands" got him going. "I'm all yours."

At his response, her eyes met his again and he thought he heard her suck in a quick breath before she shook her head. "Go sit. I just need to dig out my wheel and some fresh clay. Put this on." She handed him a thick plastic apron. "We're going to get you all messy."

Holy hell, the way she said *messy* in that sassy way had him just about bursting behind his zipper. What he wouldn't give to get messy with her.

Glad that the thick brown plastic apron covered up his hard-on, he sat back and enjoyed watching Vicki gather everything and set it up in front of him. When she was concentrating, she'd always licked at the corner of her mouth where her upper and lower lips came together. Now, watching her little pink tongue wet her gorgeous mouth every few seconds had him losing control of himself for a split second and he groaned out loud.

"Is everything okay?"

Just taking in her beautifully flushed skin, her big green eyes, the hair falling out of her ponytail and brushing over her shoulders had him *this close* to saying, "No," and then grabbing her by her ponytail and dragging her mouth to his.

Instead, he forced, "Never better," from his lips.

"Okay, we're ready." She pulled over another stool beside him and sat close enough that her thigh pressed against his.

"Aren't you going to get dirty?"

She held out her arms. "Haven't you noticed? I already am."

He finally saw that she had clay splattered all over her, most of it over her perfect breasts. The air coming in through the window was cool enough to have them pebbling slightly beneath her bra.

Which one had she put on today? Was it the black one with the small blue bow in the center or the—

Ryan's hard-on spiked again beneath his jeans as he quickly fell deeper into the fantasy that was Vicki.

Why had he thought playing around with her like this was a good idea? But it was too late to get out of it now, even if he could have dragged himself away from her.

"Okay, first we need to center the clay. This is really important, so you're not fighting with it the whole time. Are you comfortable?"

No. He'd need a freezing-cold shower—or a few hours in bed with her—before he could even come close to getting comfortable.

When he nodded, she said, "Press your forearms

against your thighs like this," and unintentionally gave him a killer view down her tank top.

Pink lace. That was the bra she'd put on this morning. Worse still, it was cut low enough for her full breasts to almost spill out the top.

Just barely, he managed to do as she asked, repeating, "Forearms to thighs," like an idiot.

She handed him a wet gray blob. "Okay, now center the clay on the wheel with a nice firm toss, so it sticks."

His aim was dead-on and she hummed her approval. "Perfect. Now, with your foot, start the wheel spinning slowly and—"

The moment the wheel began to spin, the gray lump splooged against the rim of the wheel. He could see how hard Vicki was trying not to laugh.

"Go ahead," he told her, "let it out."

Her laughter immediately bubbled over. "I just had a major flashback to our old garage days. But don't worry, I'm not as easily daunted anymore. I think you just need to get a feel for the way it is when it's working. Then you'll be able to do it on your own."

His heart almost stopped in his chest when she moved behind him and put her arms around his. "Shoot, I can't reach the clay like this." She moved beside him again, frowning. "Probably the only thing that will work is if I face you on the other side or—" She stopped, shook her head.

"Or what?"

"I could try sitting between your legs." She gave him a crooked grin. "You know, in the classic *Ghost* position, but without the sex afterward."

He worked to keep his grin easy, his joke light. "And here I was sure that was your plan all along."

Her own grin faltered for a minute, her cheeks flushing before she shook her head and laughed. "You don't know how many *Ghost* jokes I've heard over the years. I can't believe I just made one." She was all business again as she moved her stool in front of his and pushed the wheel away slightly to make room for their arms and legs. "Okay, let's make magic happen, shall we?"

Heck, yeah, he was ready for magic. But since he wasn't ever going to get to the ultimate magic with her, he tried to be happy with what he did have.

With her small but strong hands over his, they threw the clay in the center and began to form it into a cone shape.

"That's it," she encouraged. "Can you feel how right that is?"

Sweet Lord, all he could think was that she could have been talking to him in bed while he was tasting her. He grunted a yes and let her keep manipulating his hands with hers.

She sped the wheel up with her foot, then wet both their hands one after the other so their fingers slipped and slid against each other until it was hard to tell where one started and the other ended. Just like in the sculpture she'd been working on that morning.

Keeping their left hands on the outside of the wheel, she had them press down with their right hands from the top of the clay. A few seconds later, she maneuvered their hands again so that they were pressing on either side of it to force the shape upward.

"We're ready to make the opening now. We're going to have to work together to keep our hands really still so that the hole doesn't get all wobbly."

Her voice sounded breathy and, pressed against her, he could feel her heart pounding through her back against his chest.

"Start with your thumb," she said as she moved his right thumb into the top center of the mound, then held it steady with their left hands. "When you feel like we're deep enough, you'll use both hands to widen the opening, like this."

Ryan couldn't make sense of a word she said after *deep enough,* not with all the blood rushing from his brain and pounding south. Fortunately, Vicki was moving his hands for him on the clay and all he had to do was let himself be led by her.

"How does that all feel so far?"

"Great."

She slowed the wheel and backed off the pressure of their hands on the clay as she looked at him over her shoulder. "Do you want to try pulling up on the sides?"

Thinking that he would barely have to move his head forward at all to kiss her, he blurted, "God, yes, I want to try it."

Her eyes widened. "If I'd known you would be this enthusiastic about it, I wouldn't have let you quit so soon when we were kids."

It took him several beats to figure out what she was talking about. Finally, he realized what he'd said…and what an idiot he must sound like. In any case, it was a good thing they hadn't done this as teenagers, because there was no way he would have had a prayer of controlling himself back then. Even as an adult, there wasn't much slack left on his self-control.

Before he could figure out how to backpedal from his earlier statement, she turned back to the wheel and said, "Oops, it's going to squash in on itself if we don't get moving. The quick and dirty fix is that you're going to reach in with your left hand and pull the walls up. On three. One. Two. Three."

He tried to let his hands go loose in hers again, but with the words—and visual of—*quick and dirty* playing over and over in his mind, he couldn't manage it. In under five seconds, the clay beneath their hands went from a well-formed almost-bowl to a haphazard blob.

She exclaimed in dismay at the exact moment he cursed.

And then they both started laughing, her back shaking against his chest.

"I was so sure you were going to get it this time."

"I guess this proves I'm not that good with my hands after all," he joked.

She laughed again at his wildly inaccurate statement and he was finally letting himself enjoy the feel of her hips against his thighs, her ponytail tickling his neck, when a figure appeared in the doorway.

Ryan felt Vicki's entire body tense...and his own hands fisted in the clay until it seeped out gray and viscous between his fingers.

"James." Her voice shook slightly as she said the man's name, but was perfectly steady again a moment later. "I didn't expect you to come by until later this afternoon with the rest of the board."

"Hello, Victoria. Ryan."

Vicki pushed the potting wheel away and stood up.

Ryan moved with her and nodded his greeting. "Hi." He made sure the single syllable came out as menacing as possible and was easily translated to read: *Hurt her and I'll find a way to hurt you back.*

James focused his attention on Vicki. "Has your solo work turned into a group project?"

He was smiling, but Ryan didn't buy it. He was about to advance on the man, but Vicki put her hand on his arm before he could get his fist any closer to the creep's face.

"Ryan and I were just taking a little break together." Despite how flustered he could tell she was, she sounded remarkably calm. "Is there anything you needed before this afternoon, James?"

"I wanted you to be the first to hear the good news about Anthony."

Hearing her ex-husband's name uttered from the douche bag's self-satisfied mouth had Ryan seeing red.

Bloodred.

Seven

Panic and—hot on its heels—fury skittered up Vicki's spine. She should have known her ex wouldn't be able to keep out of her business.

It didn't help, of course, that James and Anthony had been friends for so many years. In fact, she wouldn't be surprised to find out that James had been the one to recontact Anthony, simply to try to get under her skin.

"How is he?" she asked in an easy voice, remembering to play her part of happy girlfriend by wrapping her arms tightly around Ryan and leaning into his broad chest.

She thought she saw a flash of surprise cross James's face at her relaxed response and was pleased she'd pulled it off.

"Very well, actually. And quite generous to do us all the favor of joining the fellowship board at such a late date."

Vicki couldn't stop her eyes from widening this time. *Anthony had joined the fellowship board?*

Ryan beat her to the punch. "Are you saying that Anthony will be voting on Vicki's project?"

Despite the fact that James was wearing his best poker face, it was perfectly clear to Vicki just how pleased he was by this turn of events. He'd found the perfect way to punish her for turning down his advances.

"Yes, he will, along with the rest of the board, of course. He and I were just going over the fellowship contenders' portfolios, but naturally he's already quite familiar with yours." He gave Vicki an understanding look. "And while it's understood that he has a special familiarity with your skills, I have no doubt that he will be well able to judge your project on merit alone without favoring you unduly."

Favoring her? Nothing could be farther from the truth. Vicki was right at the bottom of his list of favorites…and had been since long before they'd divorced.

She could feel Ryan bristling with the need to defend and protect her. She appreciated the strong friendship that was behind that urge, but just having him here with her was enough.

She wouldn't rise to the bait, but she needed to know. "When will he be coming to San Francisco?"

"He will be judging via photos and video, but I have asked him to squeeze the awards ceremony into his very busy schedule." James smiled at both of them. "I believe he's making travel arrangements as we speak."

Vicki didn't bother smiling back. Why should she, when there was no point? Her refusal to sleep with James had lowered the lid on her coffin. Anthony's arrival—and vote against her fellowship sculpture—would nail it down.

Still, she refused to give James the satisfaction of thinking he and her ex had broken her. Not when it was so apparent what they were after. Between the two of them, they clearly wanted to destroy her career.

Pushing her rage down far enough to be civil, she said, "I know you have so many demands on your time, James," in a soft but steely voice. "I really appreciate your taking a few moments to stop in to see me."

It was the world's politest dismissal. One even he couldn't ignore.

"It was a pleasure seeing you again, Mr. Sullivan. Best of luck with your game this afternoon."

As soon as James left, Ryan said, "The fellowship organization can't do this, not when they know he was married to you. There's no way he can judge your work with any kind of impartiality."

"Of course they can do it. And I suspect they're thrilled about the drama of it all—that they all feel like they're choreographing a juicy reality show." She narrowed her eyes. "I won't give them that drama."

Ryan pulled her into him and held her there for several sweet moments. She wrapped her arms around him, too, and let the steady beat of his heart against her cheek soothe—and strengthen—her. She knew him well enough, and had a good enough sense of the power he must wield via fame and fortune, to guess just how hard her friend was working to push back his need to take care of the whole messy situation for her.

"I don't have to be at the stadium for another hour, if you want to get out of here for a while."

Vicki had never been a quitter, but she'd finally been pushed right to the edge of her bounce-back threshold. "I can't let them win," she said softly. "So that means I need to finish what I started here."

Ryan stroked a hand over her hair. "That isn't why you need to finish it, Vicki."

Surprised, she looked up at him. "Sure it is."

He pulled her over to the clay she'd been shaping with her hands when he'd walked in thirty minutes ago. "This is why you need to finish." He paused to give her time to study the sculpture she'd been so excited about before James had come to crush her like a bug. "Because your project is amazing."

Yet again, she wondered what she would have done without Ryan there.

"Are you going to be okay?"

She took a deep breath. "Yes, I think so." A quick shiver moved through her. "I still feel a little icky all over, but fine." She tried to smile at him. "I'm glad you were here, though. But not just because of him." She felt suddenly shy. "It was fun teaching you how to work the wheel again. Maybe we could try again sometime when we both have more time?"

"I had fun with it." He pulled off the apron she'd given him and gave her forehead a kiss as he handed it back to her. "And with you."

Vicki desperately wanted to read more into every word he said, into every brush of his skin against hers, even into the friendly kiss he'd brushed against her forehead. At the very least, James's visit had been a good reminder that anything with Ryan beyond friendship was just a game they were playing.

"I don't want you to be late to the stadium because of me."

"If he comes back again, without the rest of the board—"

This time she was the one pressing a kiss to his cheek. Just as friendly a kiss as his had been. "Stop worrying. After what he just saw, he can't possibly think we're fabricating our relationship."

She flushed as she realized, too late, what she'd just implied…that only two people who were dating would have been so close, so playful with each other at the potting wheel. She quickly moved to clean up the mess she and Ryan had made.

"How does a goulash dinner sound after you win the game? It's a Prague specialty."

"You don't have to cook tonight, Vicki."

"I want to. Cooking always settles me down when things go haywire."

He gave her a look that asked, without words, just how many times she'd had to deal with *haywire* before now. "It sounds so good that I'll keep my postgame meeting quick."

He was clearly reluctant to leave, so she put her hands on his back and pushed him toward the door. "Go be a superstar. I'll see you tonight."

When he finally left, closing the door behind him, she wanted to collapse against it. Both from the fury and frustration at what James and Anthony were pulling, and from just how hard she was working to keep her feelings for Ryan hidden.

She looked more closely at her new sculpture. She knew what she'd felt when she was making it… and she knew what she felt now as she looked at it. Ryan had felt it, too, she was certain of it. He might not be trained in art or sculpture, but she valued his opinion. And she'd believed him when he said he thought it was fantastic.

Of course, there were other things she'd felt during the past hour, in addition to the anger at her ex snooping in on her life and James trying to intimidate her.

Because when she'd looked up to find Ryan watching her from the doorway, she'd been hit with a level of silly-stupid giddy she'd never felt with anyone before. Not since she was a teenager, anyway, when she'd hear Ryan pulling his classic re-built car up to the curb outside her parents' garage.

It had been so easy to go down memory lane with him and to reenact that night when she'd tried to teach him to make a pot. Only, she'd never have been bold enough at fifteen to sit between his legs like that.

She'd known better today, hadn't she? Being that close to him, with her hands on his while his heart beat strong and steady against her back, his breath on her bared neck, was borderline stupid when she was trying to keep it together around him.

But how could she resist?

A knock came at the door and then her new friend, Anne, popped her head in. The clothing de-signer was in her mid-twenties, with bright green-and-blue hair and a shocking number of piercings. She also happened to be a brilliant artist with ex-tremely wise eyes.

"Did the best-looking guy I've ever seen find you?"

Vicki had to laugh at that far-too-accurate de-scription of Ryan. She was glad to feel the laughter rush through her, replacing some of the anger and frustration, if not the lingering desire.

"He did."

"And?" Anne held up her hand. "No, never mind. I don't want to have to hate you even more than I currently do, so it's probably better if you don't give me any details. So," she asked with a lightning-fast change of subjects, "are you ready for this afternoon?"

The board members—and James—would be here in less than four hours, along with someone to film the fellowship applicants' progress to send to her ex in Italy.

Forcefully pushing away the sense of impending defeat that wanted to ride her, she said, "Hopefully. You?"

Anne shrugged. "Who knows. They'll either love what I'm working on or hate it. But honestly, whether they do or don't, I don't much care."

"Wait a minute." Vicki was confused. "I thought you wanted the fellowship."

"Oh, I do. Badly. The money would be fabulous, not to mention the contacts." Anne shrugged. "None of that changes whether or not I like my project, though. So caring about their opinions is kind of beside the point, don't you think?"

Vicki had to nod. Because Anne was right. Beyond right, actually. "How'd you get to be so smart so young?"

"Battle scars, baby. Once I realized that I beat myself up more than they ever could, I decided to start with kindness at home." She made a funny face. "I've got to find a sexier way of saying that."

"No, you don't," Vicki said softly. "Kindness is incredibly sexy."

It was something Ryan had proved to her again and again.

"You want a coffee?" When Vicki shook her head, her friend grinned and said with uncanny precision, "In that case, I'll leave you to get back to your dirty thoughts about Mr. Gorgeous."

Oh, God, was she that transparent?

Eight

That night, when Ryan walked through the door, his smile made her tingly in the kinds of places friends shouldn't get tingly in when looking at each other. Still, she tried not to beat up on herself too much for being a normal woman with normal hormones. Of course she got tingly with him. Who wouldn't?

It was one thing to feel those zings of desire for the gorgeous man walking toward her. It was another thing entirely to be stupid enough to actually do something about them.

Of course, he sure didn't make it any easier for her to stuff down her perfectly normal and human female hormones when he drew her against him for a hug. Oh, what she wouldn't give just to melt here against him....

"It smells amazing. Did you find everything you needed in the kitchen?"

"Are you kidding?" She made herself step out of his arms. "Professional chefs don't have it this good. I didn't know you were into cooking."

He looked a little sheepish. "I'm not. One of the women I was dating for a while was taking cooking lessons, so..."

She turned back to the stove while trying to look as if it didn't bother her *at all* that some other woman had cooked for Ryan here, a woman who had probably been tall and slim, with perfect breasts and a small butt. Since Vicki couldn't change her lack of inches in height—or the extra ones around her hips—she silently told herself to stop acting like an idiot.

Of course, it didn't help having seen so many pictures of his beautiful companions in the international press over the past years. It was the downside of knowing someone so well for so long. There wasn't much that could stay hidden, even if you wished it would.

Wanting to push past the slightly awkward moment, she said brightly, "I caught the last few innings of your game. Congrats on the win." Ryan hadn't been pitching, but she'd enjoyed the glimpses of him in the dugout.

"It's a good group this year." He snagged a slice of bell pepper from her cutting board. "If everything keeps going well, I think we've got a pretty good chance of winning the World Series again."

When he uncorked a bottle of red wine, she shot

a glance at the bottle and then at him. "Can we agree in advance that if I fall asleep on you again tonight, we'll both pretend it never happened and that I can totally hold my liquor?"

"Agreed," he said with a grin. He handed her a glass before pouring his own, then lifting it in a toast. "Here's to finally making it past first base with the potting wheel today."

She laughed as she clinked her glass against his. "And to those ex-girlfriends of yours who went absolutely crazy at Williams-Sonoma." At his confused expression, she laughed again and said, "It's a cookware store."

She was about to take a sip when he leaned in as if he were sharing a secret. "She couldn't cook worth a damn."

Relief shouldn't have bubbled up in her hearing she had something on the supermodel who had previously graced his kitchen. But she forgot all about being petty as she got her first sip of wine.

A moan escaped her lips. "My God. What is this?" After one incredibly smooth taste, she wouldn't be surprised to find out it cost more than her monthly rent in Prague.

"One of Marcus's special vintages."

She took another sip and closed her eyes to really savor the taste. "Yet another reason why you have the best family ever. You don't know how many times I wished I was a Sullivan."

Her eyes flew open as she realized what she'd

just—stupidly—blurted out. Quickly putting her glass of wine down, she busied herself with turning down the burner, plating their salads and bringing them over to the small table by the windows rather than into the big dining room on the other side of the kitchen.

Ryan followed her with their glasses of wine. As soon as they sat down, he told her, "I always loved it when you came over to our house. We all did."

She jammed her fork into a cucumber and tried not to flush too brightly at his sweet words. It didn't help that he was pure female fantasy in his dress shirt, tie and dark slacks. Ryan in jeans and a T-shirt was yummy. In dress clothes he amped the yum *way* up. Especially when she thought about reaching over to help him off with his tie and then uncovering his tanned muscles one button at a time—

"How did your meeting with the fellowship board go? They must have loved your new idea."

She thought about it for a minute before saying, "You can never really tell what they're thinking when they put on their poker faces."

It occurred to her how nice it was to be able to share these feelings with a true friend who had known her since those early years when she'd been working so hard just to capture laughter with clay. With almost anyone else, she would have felt she needed to make her answer shiny and snappy.

It was even nicer when he said, "If they don't

love it—and if they let James or your ex sway them in any way—they're all idiots."

"Spoken like a true friend," she said as she smiled across the table at him. "Actually, Anne said something interesting to me this afternoon that I'm still processing."

"Is she the one with the blue-and-green hair?"

"It was orange a couple days ago," Vicki said with a laugh. "She was probably the only person there tonight who didn't care about people's opinions of her work and wasn't living and dying on every smile or frown."

"Isn't she up for a fellowship, too?"

"She is. And I know how much she wants it. But at the end of the day, the most important thing to her is that she's proud of her work. Not whether a random group of powerful people think she's talented enough to receive a grant."

"Aren't you proud of your work, Vicki?"

It was a good question. One she'd been trying to figure out the answer to for a very long time.

"I've had a few great moments," she said slowly, "but sometimes I wonder if the in-betweens are enough to make it all worth it."

Ryan put down his fork. "Do you know how many pitches I throw on average in a game?" When she shook her head, he said, "Almost a hundred and twenty. How many of those do you think are great pitches?" He didn't wait for her to answer. "Twenty. Maybe thirty. Some guys beat themselves up for that, but my first Little League coach made sure I knew that baseball wasn't about being perfect. It was about having fun first, winning second."

"It sounds like you had a really great coach."

"One day I hope I'm as good with my kids as my dad was with all of us."

Vicki's heart turned to mush. "I wish I could have met your father." She looked at him and mused, "Although, I suppose in a way I have, just by knowing you and your siblings. He was obviously an extraordinary man to have created such a wonderful family."

Ryan's answering gaze was so intense she wondered for a moment if she'd said something wrong. Finally, he said, "As long as you love what you're doing, Vicki, it's all worth it."

That flutter in her belly at the way he was looking at her had her feeling light-headed as she took away their salads and brought one large plates of goulash and a basket of crusty bread.

"How was your meeting after the game?" He hadn't told her what it was for, but she assumed it had something to do with the Hawks.

"It went all right. I thought it would be easier to get people excited about bringing sports back to schools, but it's taken three months to pick up our first serious donor. Fortunately, I think this couple is pretty close."

She couldn't get over how different Ryan was from her ex-husband. If Anthony ever did anything nice for anyone, he broadcast it from the rooftops. Would Ryan even have mentioned his charitable work if she hadn't asked about his meeting?

"You're raising money to bring sports back to schools?"

"Sports are my first target, and then the arts programs if I can pull in enough for both."

She knew she was grinning at him like a fool, but he was *that* great. "I think that's so fantastic, Ryan. Because, honestly, I don't know if I would be a sculptor if it hadn't been for the class I took in eighth grade. Mr. Barnsworth told me the ashtray I made in his class belonged in a museum. Becoming an art teacher was always my backup plan. At least until the school districts got rid of those positions."

"P.E. teacher was my backup plan."

"You were thinking about being a high school teacher?"

"Until the scouts came calling, yeah, I was."

How could she not have known this about him? And why did it have to make him even cuter? She could just imagine what it would have been like in the halls of their old high school if he had become a teacher instead of a pro baseball player. Every time Mr. Sullivan walked down the hall, the giggling from crushed-out girls would have been deafening.

"I substituted for a while," she told him, "right after college." Until she'd married Anthony and he'd supported them both with his sculptures. She'd been grateful, but not nearly as grateful as he'd expected her to be.

"Oh, man, I'll bet those lucky punks in your classes didn't hear a word you said."

She had never thought about herself as the object of teenage crushes. Was Ryan right? Had she been?

"That could explain why they all seemed so spaced out all the time."

"They probably didn't want to come up to the front of the class, either."

She almost spit out her sip of wine. "Just eat already. It's not nearly as good cold."

Finally, Ryan took a bite of the goulash. And then another. And then one more before saying, with his mouth full, "I can't believe you made this." He shoved another bite in. "It's the best thing I've ever tasted."

"Thanks, but we both know your mother's straight-from-Italy spaghetti sauce is better. Just barely," she joked, "but still better."

It had been years since she'd sat down at the boisterous, crowded Sullivan dinner table, but she'd never forgotten how good the food had always been. Or how much fun it had been to be surrounded by all the laughter.

"By the way," she said after they'd both eaten in companionable silence for a few minutes, "I was thinking more about the latest turn of events with Anthony joining the board. I really don't think James is going to try anything again, not knowing my ex-husband will be coming in from Italy." She put down her fork and pushed the rest of her goulash away. "You're amazing for stepping in and pretending to be my boyfriend, but I can't let you keep putting your real life on hold for me."

He was frowning at her as he said, "I'm not putting anything on hold."

"I heard you cancel those dates," she reminded him.

"If I'd known you were back in town, I would have canceled them anyway." He grabbed their plates and headed over to the sink. When she got up to help clean the pots and pans she'd used, he poured her another glass of wine. "You cooked. I'll clean."

There shouldn't have been anything sexual about what he'd just said. They were talking about dirty dishes, for God's sake. And yet the subtle command to relax sent a flutter of heat down deep in her belly. But even as she reached out to pull up a stool at his kitchen island, Vicki couldn't stop herself from enjoying the picture he made—a big, strong man elbow-deep in suds, even though he could easily have employed a full-time staff to cater to his every need.

Which was why, instead of sitting down, she grabbed a clean dish towel and started drying off the plates he'd just washed. She needed to fill her hands with cotton and porcelain and keep them too busy to accidentally fill them with Ryan's hard muscles instead.

"Hey," he said with a raised eyebrow as he watched her put the dry plate away, "I thought you were relaxing with a glass of wine?"

"I was, and now I'm helping you clean up."

She pretended she didn't see the look in his eyes that told her he wasn't used to being ignored when he wanted a woman to do something. Would he be like that in bed, too? Would he tell her how he wanted her and how he—

She caught his dark gaze on her and almost dropped the wineglass in her hand as she realized she'd just been caught fantasizing about him. Moving to put the plate away, she prayed he couldn't figure out what was making her so fumble fingered. God, she hoped he couldn't tell how aroused she was from nothing more than drying dishes next to him at the sink.

"I don't want you dropping your guard around him, Vicki. Not yet. Let's wait a few more days before we drop the high-school-sweethearts act."

How could she blame Ryan for being concerned about her when she was the one who'd dragged him into the situation by panicking twenty-four hours ago?

And why did it hurt so bad when he called their act exactly what it was?

"If it will make you feel better, I guess we could do that."

"It *will* make me feel better. A lot better."

Working well together, they soon had the dishes cleaned and put away and he was taking their glasses of wine into the living room. He put them side by side on the coffee table and clicked on the TV.

"What do you want to see?"

Two hours on the couch next to Ryan. How on earth was she going to survive that?

"A horror movie."

He shot her a surprised look. "Seriously? You want to watch a horror movie?"

"Love them." Not really, but maybe if she was scared enough, she could forget about how much she wanted him.

"I thought you were into indie comedies in high school?"

Warmth spread through her at his remembering something so small about her. He was right. She'd loved movies like *Clerks* and *Muriel's Wedding* but, even more, the fact that the scrappy filmmakers had followed their visions and found their success. She'd hoped for even a fraction of success like that for herself one day. She still did.

"Don't worry," she teased, "I won't tell anyone if you need to cover your eyes during the scary scenes."

"Nothing like knowing my friend has my back," he teased as he started scrolling through the available movies. "How about this?" *Halloween* was up on the flat screen. "It's a classic." He grinned and added, "This first one was practically indie."

"Sounds great." She curled her feet up under her and pulled a blanket draped over the arm of the couch onto her lap, even though sitting so close to Ryan already had her feeling way too hot and bothered to need it.

In reality she had only ever seen a handful of horror movies and even then it was mostly through her closed eyelids, daring to sneak a peek every few minutes. But she knew enough about horror movies to expect blood and gore shortly after the opening credits. Instead, *Halloween* opened with a teenage couple getting hot and heavy on a couch.

Vicki clutched the blanket tightly in her fists as she tried to keep her breathing slow and even while the kiss grew hotter and hotter. Her heart felt as if it was going to pound out of her chest by the time the teenagers pulled apart and headed upstairs to the girl's bedroom.

Thank God, she thought as she let herself relax back into the cushions. Maybe, if she was really lucky, someone would be slashed in the next scene.

Normally, she would have been dreading seeing the crazy little brother wield the large kitchen knife, but anything was better than continuing to watch the two young actors, who were her and Ryan's age when they first met, making out and grinding against each other. Yes, she was totally prepared for—

"Oh, my God!"

The little boy on the screen plunged the knife into his sister and Vicki couldn't stop herself from leaping into Ryan's arms and burying her head on his chest.

Nine

Ryan immediately clicked off the TV. His hands stroked down her back and even though somewhere in the back of her mind she knew what a bad idea it was to get this close to him, she couldn't even think of moving from his lap while her heart was still pounding so hard and she couldn't get the picture of spurting blood out of her head.

"It's okay, Vicki," he said in a gentle voice. "It's just a dumb movie. It isn't real."

"I know," she said, but her voice was shaking as she confessed, "I've only ever watched the *Chucky* movies, with the doll that comes alive." Those movies had been scary, but nothing like the slashing they'd just witnessed.

"We could have watched something else. Just because I'm a guy doesn't mean I can't hack a chick flick every once in a while."

By then, her fear had receded enough for her

to feel a little idiotic. "I don't know what I was think—"

She should have known better than to lift her head and look at him instead of moving off his lap first, but between her fading horror and rising arousal, her brain wasn't functioning quite right. Unfortunately, with his mouth so close that she could practically taste the red wine on his lips, it was too late to get that thinking done.

Ryan's hands stilled on her back and his arms tightened around her. She couldn't look away from his eyes, which were growing darker by the second. All she needed to do was lean forward the barest amount and her lips would be on his and she could kiss him the way she'd been dying to kiss him for half her life…and not just because they were putting on a show for someone else.

Only, just as Vicki was about to close the gap between them, her brain finally clicked into overdrive with all the reasons why this would not be a good idea, most of which started and ended with a crystal-clear vision of Ryan trying to be kind while helping her off his lap…and away from his mouth. He'd have to search for the right words to tell her that while he was flattered by her attention, he valued their friendship too much to do anything to jeopardize it, and then she'd be left feeling like a fool for actually trying to convince herself it had been okay to give in to temptation.

Moving as quickly as her suddenly clumsy

limbs could manage, she shifted off Ryan's lap. "You know what? I've got a big day tomorrow and you've got to pitch, so we should probably just head to bed." She stood up, then concentrated on folding the blanket into a perfect rectangle.

She was laying the blanket over the arm of the couch when Ryan also stood and said, "You're right, we should probably skip the movie tonight."

Vicki forced back her disappointment that he wasn't even going to try to convince her otherwise.

It was for the best. She wouldn't risk their friendship. Especially not now, when they were finally together again after years of living on different sides of the world.

She was halfway up the stairs to the guest bedroom with Ryan a step behind her, when he asked, "Any chance you'll be able to make the game tomorrow?"

If it had been anyone else she was lusting after inappropriately she would have said no out of self-preservation. However, not only did she not want to let Ryan down, but she also really wanted to see him play again.

She smiled at him as she put her hand on her doorknob. "I wouldn't miss it."

He smiled back, but it didn't erase that dark intensity in his eyes. "Great." He paused, and she could have sworn he was fighting with himself over something before he finally said, "Good night, Vicki."

After she stepped into her room and closed the door behind her, she sagged against it and put her head in her hands. She'd called Ryan to help her out of a sticky situation with James. Only, she was starting to feel as if she'd walked into an even stickier one with Ryan.

One where her nearly unstoppable fantasies of being more than a friend ran the risk of breaking apart the friendship she'd always held so dear.

Ryan felt like hell the next morning. Two nights of virtually no sleep combined with a hard-on that wouldn't quit had him out on the beach at first light, trying to run off what felt like a hangover. He was pitching today and knew better than to push himself too hard, but after his run, he went straight to his home gym anyway.

He could still feel Vicki's warm breath on his lips from last night when she'd leaped into his arms, and the way her soft curves had pressed against his groin and chest as she let him soothe away her fears. Despite how much the movie had frightened her, he couldn't find it in himself to regret the fact that he'd been able to hold her for a few incredible moments because of it.

Sweet Lord, he'd never wanted to kiss anyone the way he wanted to kiss her. And he'd almost convinced himself that it would be okay to give in to the powerful urge when she'd scrambled off his lap and practically run up the stairs to her bedroom to get away from him.

He'd offered her his guest room because she needed a friend to help her out.

He'd never forgive himself if she thought he expected any kind of sexual payment for the favor, but the way he was acting with her, he wouldn't blame her for thinking that.

Added to that were his worries about how quickly she seemed to want to chuck in their "relationship." As soon as he finished his workout, he was going to call Rafe to push for more information on James.

Hard-rock music pounded as he worked with the machines before moving to the free weights. But even though he was frustrated as hell by an arousal that had absolutely no outlet, he wasn't stupid enough to push himself past the twinge in his right shoulder. He grabbed a clean towel from the shelf on the wall and wiped off his face as he headed down into the kitchen.

Vicki looked up just as she turned off the blender. "Want to share my fruit smoothie?"

"Sounds great. Thanks." He absentmindedly rubbed his shoulder as he grabbed an ice pack from the freezer to put on it. "You sleep okay?"

"How could I not in that bed?"

Her smile seemed just a little too bright but, then again, how would he know? He was a grumpy—and horny—bastard today.

"Is your arm hurting?" She slid a full glass over to him and he drank from it gratefully.

He shrugged. "I always ice down after a work-out."

"I had a friend who was working with marble. By the end of her project, she started to hurt pretty bad." She gave him a tentative smile. "She claims my massages are the reason she was able to see it through to the end." She flexed her fingers in front of him. "You're looking at really strong sculptor's hands."

Oh, hell. There was nothing he wanted more in the world than one of her massages, but he wasn't sure he had the strength of will this morning to actually keep himself in check if she touched him.

"I appreciate the offer—"

Her face fell, but she quickly pasted that too-bright smile over it. "I'm sure you've got amazing masseuses among the team trainers who actually know what they're doing."

Damn it. He'd just hurt her feelings. It was the last thing he wanted to do.

"Actually, a massage would be great." When she hesitated, he said, "Where do you want me?"

"One of the kitchen chairs is probably best, so you're the right height."

He willed down his erection as he sat on the chair. He could smell her fresh, clean scent as she moved behind him and had to brace himself for the moment her hands touched him. By the time she laid them down on his shoulders, his muscles had never been tighter.

"Let me know if you need it harder. Or softer."

His erection immediately told him his ideas of what was right and wrong in a friendship could take a hike.

Vicki started rubbing him and heaven and hell rolled into one as pleasure and torture came at him in crashing waves. Fortunately, she didn't speak, so he didn't have to, either. She'd opened the French doors out to his deck and he worked to focus on the surf hitting the shore rather than how good she smelled…or the fact that she seemed to know exactly how he liked to be touched. Because if she knew how to rub his shoulders, did that mean she'd also know exactly how to rub his—

He cursed aloud.

Vicki jumped back. "Did I just hurt you?"

"No." How the hell was he going to stand up without her seeing what her innocent touches had done to him? *Down, boy!* "It was great. I just remembered something I should have taken care of last night." Namely, beating his desire for her into the ground.

By the time he had his erection under control enough to turn around, she was picking up her keys and bag from the counter.

"I should get going now anyway. I'll see you at the stadium this afternoon."

She was gone before he could apologize for being a jerk.

His phone rang just as he was about to get into a very cold shower. When he saw it was Rafe, Ryan turned off the water and picked up. "You found something."

"Maybe. James Sedgwick is into some pretty creepy things. Heavy-duty S and M mostly, although that isn't that much out of the ordinary considering some of the things I see."

"But you're still not convinced he's clear."

"This friend of yours he was hassling is a sculptor, right?"

A muscle jumped in Ryan's jaw as he unclenched his teeth long enough to say, "She is."

"I'm guessing she's pretty, huh?"

Ryan thought about the way Vicki had looked the night before on the couch, her big green eyes slightly dilated from the darkened room, her mouth plump and begging to be kissed. "You can't even imagine how pretty."

"As far as I can tell, every year he picks a girl just like your friend to be his. And then at the end of the year, after sending the girl on her way with some career prize, he gets a replacement. I'm guessing he wants your friend to fill his current vacancy."

Ryan nearly crushed his cell phone in his fist as he stared blindly out at the ocean. "That. Is. Never. Going. To. Happen."

Just the thought of letting the pervert look at

Vicki while fantasizing about tying her up and hurting her to get his sexual kicks had Ryan's fists tightening.

Vicki thought they could "break up" and everything would still be fine. She'd thought she'd overreacted to the creep's advances.

If anything happened to her, Ryan would not only never forgive himself, he'd end up in jail—because he'd kill James without even blinking an eye.

That was when the truth hit Ryan hard enough to jolt him with the force of an earthquake rolling beneath his feet.

Of course Vicki's friendship meant a great deal to him. But it was also a given that he'd always wanted her, right from that first moment he'd landed on top of her in the high school parking lot. That was why, these past few days, it had been easy to focus on first their friendship and then the wanting—the bottomless pit of desire he felt for her—as his reasons for wanting to protect her and keep her close.

But the real reason went so much further, so much deeper, than friendship.

Ryan didn't just want Vicki, didn't just crave her laughter, her curves, her mouth beneath his.

He loved her.

And every other woman he'd been with since that day she'd come into his life had only been a placeholder for the real thing.

Ten

Ryan timed his arrival at the Hawks' parking lot perfectly in order to intercept Judy, a reporter for ESPN.com. Some of the reporters were all business, but since he had pretty much been responsible for introducing her to her husband a few years back, they'd always had a friendly rapport.

Still, just because they were friendly didn't mean she wouldn't release any and all dirt that she could dig up on him.

Today in particular, he was counting on Judy to do her job.

"How's John?"

She smiled, looking just as happy about her marriage now as she had a couple years ago when he'd attended their wedding. "Great, thanks, although we've recently adopted a puppy who is running us in circles. And pooping pretty much everywhere."

"Let me know if you need a dog trainer. I know one of the best."

"Honestly, I'll take any help I can get at this point."

After he gave her Heather's name and the number for Top Dog, she got down to their standard order of business. "It's been another great year for you so far. One more game to go before the play-offs. How are you feeling about tonight's game?"

"Never felt better."

Her eyebrow rose at his emphatic response. "Really? Any particular reason why?"

Ryan grinned and leaned in closer. "Actually, there is."

Despite all the nonsense with James and Anthony, Vicki couldn't remember the last time she'd had such a good day in the studio. It was probably all the repressed sexual desire she was channeling into her work that had her kicking it up a notch.

Lord knew she had to put all that tamped-down lust somewhere.

She stopped to stretch her back and neck and enjoy the way the sun was filtering into the windows in her small room, when she jumped up out of her chair with a curse, her iPod and headphones clattering to the floor.

Crap, it was already 6:00 p.m.!

She'd been planning to go back to Ryan's house to take a shower and blow-dry her hair into submission, maybe even put on some makeup before heading out to his game. Instead, she barely had time to wash her hands and change out of her clay-stained leggings and tank top to put on the old, faded flowery sundress and flip-flops she'd worn into the studio. Vicki groaned as she realized her breasts were half falling out of the dress. She hadn't been planning to wear it in public, but consoled herself with the fact that no one would be looking at her. Especially not if any of Ryan's brothers or sisters came to the game and sat near her.

Since there was no time to make a difference with styling products and mascara, she didn't bother to look at her reflection in the window as she grabbed her bag, sunglasses and Ryan's car keys from the tiled counter. She didn't even want to know how bad her frizzed-out hair was.

Fifteen minutes later, when she'd arrived at the private parking lot behind the stadium that Ryan had directed her to, she had to scramble around in her bag to find the special key card that would let her past the security gate. By the time she'd dealt with the guard's rigorous round of twenty questions and ID checking, a loud roar of applause from the stadium told her that the game had begun. A bead of sweat trickled down between her breasts as she parked between two shockingly expensive imported cars. No wonder it was like Fort Knox getting in here.

She was making a dash for the stadium entrance

when she felt a buzzing against her hip. She rooted around in her bag again for her phone and was surprised to see several text messages and missed calls from Ryan.

Call me as soon as you get this.

Ryan's first text had come in several hours ago, but she'd had her headphones on all day while she'd been working and she hadn't thought to check her phone. He knew she listened to music while she worked, but he probably didn't remember she always had to wear headphones at the studio so as not to disturb the other artists. After fifteen minutes he'd texted again.

No cell reception for a while. If I don't pick up, come by the stadium early and ask for me.

And then, five minutes ago, he'd sent one more.

Game's about to start. Where are you?

Picking up the pace, she showed her ticket at the door. The bowels of the stadium were a maze of dark hallways and it took forever to find the right door and emerge into the light.

She was still hunting for her row and seat when she felt strong arms wind around her neck.

"Vicki!" She instantly recognized Ryan's sister,

Lori. Aka Naughty. "I can't believe how long it's been since I've seen you. I was so psyched when Ryan told me you were coming today. He asked me to keep an eye out for you."

As Lori grabbed her hand and pulled her down the steps to their seats, she quickly filled her in on everything in the same rapid-fire way she'd had as a girl.

"Sophie wasn't feeling up to the game today. I swear she's been pregnant forever. You know she's having twins, right? Good thing she's having two, because I'm totally out on the whole baby thing after watching her and Chase's wife get so huge." Lori stopped a step before their row. "You remember Zach, right? This is his fiancée, Heather. I won a bet that he'd fall in love with her."

Vicki couldn't hold back her laughter at Lori's runaway-train-of-thought soliloquy as she said hello to Zach and Heather.

She was just getting settled in her seat when a low, instantly recognizable voice said, "Sorry I'm late."

Oh, God. Vicki couldn't believe Ryan had neglected to tell her that Smith Sullivan was coming to the game. He was going to pay for that little surprise.

But before she could turn around to say hello to one of the biggest movie stars in the world, the inning turned over and Ryan walked out to the pitcher's mound.

He stopped halfway out to look up into the stands, and she could see the relief on his beautiful face as he caught sight of her.

She waved before she thought better of drawing attention to herself like that. He winked at her before heading out to do his job.

As dozens of eyes turned to her—not only because Ryan had just winked at her, but also because Smith Sullivan was sitting right next to her—Vicki realized how surreal her life had become.

A short time ago, she'd been renting a studio apartment in Prague while making a daily decision to spend her precious cash on either food or clay.

Now not only was she living in an oceanfront mansion and driving a sports car around San Francisco, she was also hanging out with the coolest kids on the block.

On the surface it looked as if she'd come a *really* long way from being the freaky-geeky art girl in high school.

Funny how deceiving appearances could be.

Of course, once she and Ryan would no longer need to pretend to be dating, all of this strange fun with fancy cars and famous friends would soon be over.

Truly, she wouldn't miss any of the luxury.

It was Ryan she'd miss.

"I can't remember," Lori said. "Did you ever meet Smith when we were kids? Or was he already in college?"

When all Vicki could manage was to shake her head like an idiot, Smith smoothly said, "It's great to meet you, Vicki. So how do you know this unruly lot?"

Smith was even bigger, even better looking in person than he was on the screen. But strangely, although his fame made her feel more than a little nervous, she was stunned to realize she wasn't getting all hot and bothered for him. Only one Sullivan made her girlie parts tingly.

Too bad *that* Sullivan was too important a friend to even think of screwing things up by adding any benefits to it.

"Ryan and I were friends in high school. I just moved back to San Francisco."

Smith grinned at her and she lost her breath a little. Okay, so maybe she didn't want to jump him, but she was only human. And billions of happily attached women around the world would have just gone breathless if they'd been in her flip-flops right then.

"Moved from where?"

"Prague was the last place I lived."

"She's a sculptor." Lori shoved a handful of Jelly Belly beans into her mouth. "An awesome one. Want some?"

Vicki took a few of the colorful candies, but didn't dare put any in her mouth just in case she did something embarrassing like choke on them.

"What does Ryan think of your sculptures?" Smith asked.

Vicki felt caught in Smith's gaze, was sure he could see exactly how she felt about his younger brother. She flushed as she finally replied, "He's always been really encouraging."

Lori leaned over to say, "Ryan owns a bunch of them and he thinks her sculptures are the freaking bomb, Smith. And so do I. We all do." She turned back to Vicki. "After Ryan mentioned you were back in town and working on the fellowship, Heather and I went by the gallery last night and bought a couple of those gorgeous river sculptures. One day when I'm loaded, I want one of the big ones. I had to pull out all my tricks to buy them out from under Heather, didn't I?"

Heather smiled at Lori with what Vicki could only describe as affectionate irritation. "I saw them first and then she bought them when my back was turned."

"Sorry my sister's such a brat," Zach said to his girlfriend, and Vicki couldn't miss the way he looked at Heather like she was the most beautiful woman in the entire world.

"Don't pretend you didn't teach her everything she knows about being sneaky," Heather murmured, which made Zach laugh before he kissed her long and deep as if they weren't sitting in the middle of a sold-out baseball stadium.

"They do that *all* the time," Lori said with an eye roll that had Vicki laughing again.

Zach's girlfriend was very pretty in an unflashy way, and she was utterly down to earth. Who would have thought lady-killer Zach, who had been a year ahead of Vicki and Ryan in school, would settle down with such a lovely, unpretentious woman? One who seemed to give it back to him as good as he dished it out.

Lori interrupted her musings by telling Smith, "Vicki's art is beautiful and smart and incredibly sexy."

"I'm not surprised to hear that," Smith said in his deep, billion-dollar voice.

Vicki felt herself flush all the way down to her chest at the implication that he thought she was sexy, and Lori threw a Jelly Belly at him.

"Take some time off the clock, Smith." She made a face at Vicki. "Just ignore him. He can't stand it when a woman doesn't throw herself at him. Zach used to be like that," she said with a jerk of her thumb over her shoulder, "until he found *true love*."

Lori said the words a little sarcastically, even though it was clear that Zach and Heather were wildly, and truly, in love with each other.

"You were married for a while, right, Vicki?"

"I was."

"Do you miss it?"

She was surprised by Lori's question. "Being married or being with my ex?"

"I'm assuming you divorced your ex because he was an ass," Lori replied.

A laugh bubbled out of Vicki's mouth. "I didn't realize you knew him," she joked.

Lori grinned back before clarifying, "I mean the living-with-a-person part. Knowing you'll wake up and see the same person every morning. Having someone who's always the first person you call with good and bad news. Knowing that when you fall asleep in front of the TV with him at the end of the day, not having hot monkey sex that night doesn't mean you don't love him."

"My ex was also a sculptor and he—" Vicki paused "—he embraced the artist lifestyle, if that makes any sense. There wasn't a lot of rhyme or reason to our hours, or our life."

Or any kind of accountability. It was all so exciting at first. The only thing he'd done traditionally was marry her. But he'd had his reasons for that, most of them having to do with who held the power in the relationship. It was that way from the very first day she'd met him as a starry-eyed young sculptor.

Just then the inning started and she could let the conversation drop away to train her gaze on the field where Ryan was throwing his first pitch of the game. He was magnificent. All that raw talent from when he was a kid had matured into athletic stardom.

In a matter of minutes, he'd struck out each of the

batters. The crowd chanted his name and she was surprised when he grinned up at her again.

And then, suddenly, the chants turned into cheers.

"Oh, my God. I can't believe neither of you said anything." Lori gave a happy little sound and threw her arms around Vicki. "Congratulations!"

Over Lori's shoulder, Vicki finally learned the reason for everyone's cheers.

Congratulations Ryan Sullivan and Vicki Bennett on Your Engagement!

Below the huge message was a photo of Ryan on one half of the huge screen and, right beside it, a still shot of Vicki laughing at something Lori had said just a few minutes ago. A dozen red and pink hearts were layered between their images.

This stunt had James written all over it. Couldn't he be satisfied knowing he had pulled Anthony back into her life? Did he have to go to the press about her relationship with Ryan, and then make it even worse by upping the ante and telling the entire world they were engaged, rather than just dating?

When she looked back toward the field, Ryan was still standing on the mound looking up at her. She knew she needed to pull herself together, but how could she when her big fat lie had spiraled off in ways she'd never planned?

She felt like everything was happening in slow

motion as Ryan put his hand to his lips and blew her a kiss.

The crowd cheered again, so loud this time that her ears actually started ringing. Smith put his arm around her, leaned over and said, "Smile if you can, Vicki." His voice was calm. Soothing. "Look at Ryan and pretend it's just the two of you here. One smile. That's all you need to give him, and then you'll be off the hook for now."

Somehow, Vicki managed to follow Smith's step-by-step instruction, all the while trying to convince herself that they'd probably look back and die laughing about this one day. Somehow, she managed not only to smile back at Ryan, but she also sent him a kiss.

A total showman after all his years as a star athlete, Ryan reached into the air with his glove and caught her "kiss" as it blew by.

"Well done," Smith murmured, and she was beyond glad the big movie star had been there to coach her through the most horrific moment of her life.

"As soon as the game is over, I need to know everything," Lori said. "Absolutely everything."

The temporary glow that had moved through Vicki when she and Ryan had been smiling at each other immediately drained away. Vicki absolutely, positively hated lying to Ryan's family. But she needed to talk to him first to figure out their plan together before she confessed everything to his siblings.

Eleven

It was the longest baseball game of Ryan's life.

He'd never missed a pro game, barring being injured or sick enough for the team doctors to bench him, but tonight he'd been on the verge of bailing on it to go out and hunt for Vicki. After he'd called the number at the art studio nonstop for thirty minutes, someone had finally picked up and told him she wasn't there. But they had been pretty sure she'd been working at the studio all afternoon.

Then, when she hadn't been sitting with his siblings at the start of the game, the elemental panic had come back. For fifteen years he'd barely seen her and now he was flipping out because he hadn't heard from her in a matter of minutes. He knew he was acting crazy, but he couldn't help it. He was worried about the possibility of James getting hold of her *and* what a massive screwup it would be if she found out what he'd planned tonight before he had a chance to explain it to her himself.

Ryan had been in the fame game long enough to know the surprise story of his engagement would hit the internet pretty darn fast. But he'd figured some stranger at the stadium might say something to Vicki about it, maybe congratulate her, not that Hawks management would blindside her with the big-screen congratulations. He'd told the journalist they were engaged to protect Vicki, but he would have never embarrassed her so publicly the way his team just had.

He knew he shouldn't be pissed at management. When one of their players was happy, they were happy. If he and Vicki had really been engaged it wouldn't have been a big deal—apart from the fact that she was clearly uncomfortable being in the spotlight.

But when it was all one big fabrication—a lie he'd orchestrated because he couldn't stand the thought of allowing her to walk out of his life before he had a chance to convince her that they could be more than friends. It all added up to one huge failure.

As he walked off the field, the reporters were lined up to talk to him. One after another they all said the same thing: "Another shutout, Ryan. Looks like love agrees with you."

He knew part of his job was giving them the sound bites they needed for their papers and TV shows and blogs, but after only a handful of minutes, he couldn't do it anymore. Especially when he looked up into the stands and saw that Vicki was finally there, completely surrounded by his brothers and sister. But he was the one who really needed to be there. Protecting her. Explaining it all to her.

And praying that he could make their fake engagement sound like it made some sense.

The group of reporters immediately parted for him, but as he rushed to get to the stands, the team owner suddenly appeared, stopping him. "Congratulations, Ryan. Both on the spectacular win and your upcoming nuptials."

This was the guy who signed Ryan's massive paychecks. He had to slow down, find a smile and get out a "Thanks."

"I'm looking forward to personally toasting both of you at the team celebration tomorrow night."

"Thanks so much," Ryan replied. "I appreciate it." Nodding toward the stands he added, "If you'll excuse me, I'm just going to head up there."

Ryan wanted nothing more than to show Vicki off, to claim her as his in front of his teammates and bosses. Even though she wasn't his.

And he hadn't even come close to claiming her.

Ten rows down from his family's section of the stadium, he could hear everyone talking to Vicki at once.

"Congratulations!"

"We're so happy for you!"

"What's it like to be engaged to the best pitcher in baseball?"

"Have you set a date yet?"

"Where's your ring?"

Ryan tried to hold on to his cool as he forced his way into the crowd of well-wishers. He wished he'd done a better job of thinking this whole thing through, now that he fully appreciated just how much it would put Vicki into the public eye. Even though he was well used to being a public figure, even by his standards, this engagement hysteria was pretty brutal.

Smith wasn't anywhere to be seen, but judging by the half dozen large men attired in black, Ryan suspected his brother had called in his security staff to watch over Vicki. Lori had her arm around her, and his little sister was doing most of the talking to the crowd. Zach and Heather were flanking Vicki's other side, his brothers and sister doing all they could to watch over the woman who meant everything to him.

For this alone, Ryan owed them so much more than he could ever repay.

Finally, he was close enough to reach for her, to pull her into him and press a kiss to the top of her head. She smelled so good, like clay and woman all mixed together. He closed his eyes for a moment as the pleasure of holding her rocked through him.

When he finally looked around at the crowd, he could see they were all waiting for him to say something. Slipping his hand through Vicki's, he smiled and said, "Thanks so much for your support and excitement. You've got my personal promise that we're going to do our best to win the play-offs and take the World Series again this year." He made sure to widen his grin as he said, "But for the next few days, I'm sure you can understand that all I want is to be alone with my fiancée."

With that, he left Lori, Zach and Heather to deal with the crowd while he escorted Vicki out of the stands. They managed to get to one of the back doors to the clubhouse, not stopping until they'd reached one of the private batting cages.

"I was so sure that everything was fine, that James was going to leave us alone," Vicki said as soon as the door clicked behind them. "And I can't believe he said we were engaged instead of just dating! It's like he knew exactly what to do to try to force your hand and make you admit that we're not actually together." Her voice was shaking and Ryan felt as if he'd swallowed cement that had now hardened in the center of his gut as she added, "I'm so sorry I dragged you into this, Ryan. If I could do it all again, I wouldn't have told that first lie. I should have known it would spiral off into something bigger. Lies always do."

The final eight innings of the game should have given him time to figure out how to tell her the truth without sounding like a complete a-hole.

But they hadn't.

"Don't come down on yourself for trusting your instincts about James," he told her, and even though he meant every word, Ryan knew he was stalling. He just needed to man up and say it already. "You're right about him being a nasty scumbag, but he wasn't the one who leaked news of our engagement to the press."

"What do you mean it wasn't him?"

She was frowning so hard that Ryan had to reach out to smooth his thumb between her eyebrows. He wanted to press a kiss there, and he wanted all this crap to go away so that he could start all over again.

"It had to be him. You and I and James are the only ones who know that we're supposed to be dating."

"I was trying to reach you all afternoon to explain."

"Explain what, Ryan?"

"Why I had to do it."

She stared at him in shock. "*You* did this?"

"My cousin Rafe is an investigator. He did some looking into James. That guy is a class-A creep. And I don't want him coming anywhere near you. I was worried that a guy like that wouldn't even blink at playing a boyfriend for a fool. But if he thought we were getting married—" The look in her eyes, horror mixed with anger, stopped him. Ryan attempted to continue, adding, "After talking to Rafe, all I could think about was keeping you safe."

"You should have asked me first." Each word vibrated with emotion as she took a step back from him. "Why didn't you ask me first?"

Because I don't want you to leave me.

Ryan ran his hand over his face. "I'm sorry, Vicki."

"Did you know they were going to do that congratulations thing up on the big screen...and with me wearing this awful dress?"

"No. I swear I didn't." He reached for her and took her hand, even though it was perfectly clear just how upset she was with him. But he couldn't stand the idea of losing even more of her, not after finally getting a chance to be close to her these past few days. "And you look gorgeous in that dress."

"I look like I just finished washing the floor."

"In that case, every guy who sees a mop from now on is going to get a hard-on." She just stared at him for several long moments, long enough for him to worry that he'd lost her for good. "I know I screwed up, Vicki, but I can't stand the thought of anything happening to you."

Finally, her eyes softened. "I still wish you had talked to me first—I would have tried to convince you not to do it. But I know you had the best intentions."

Ryan had been working to convince himself of that very fact all afternoon but, the truth was, he'd had just as many selfish motives for doing what he'd done as he'd had selfless ones.

"At the very least we need to tell your family the truth and try to explain things," Vicki said.

"No." The one word came out sharply. And hard enough that Vicki's eyebrows went up.

"I hated lying to them today."

"They'd understand if they knew the reason."

Telling his family the truth felt like the beginning of a slippery slope—one where Vicki would end up sliding out of his reach. But he'd had his way one too many times already today.

"I won't lie to your family anymore. I trust them and I know you do, too." She pulled her hand from his and crossed her arms beneath her breasts. "If you won't tell them, I will."

He knew she was waiting for his answer, but he could barely think about anything but kissing her gorgeous mouth, slightly pursed from her irritation with him. The urge was strong enough that he didn't stand a chance of doing anything but following his instincts. He pressed his lips softly on hers.

A surprised gasp sounded against his mouth as her arms uncrossed so that she could steady herself against him.

"You're right," he told her. "We'll tell them. How does breakfast tomorrow morning sound? We'll tell my mother, too. I know how thrilled she'll be to see you back in town again and to know we're spending time together. You were the only girl I ever brought home."

"I was?"

"Yes, you were."

He was *this close* to kissing her again when she

abruptly took a step away from him and out of his arms. "I just hope they don't hate me for using you."

"No one could ever hate you." Her phone rang in her bag and he said, "Have you checked your phone since the billboard went up during the game?"

She shook her head and pulled it out. "Oh, my God. I have forty-five missed calls."

She dropped the phone like a hot potato and he caught it just before it hit the ground. Quickly scrolling through the callers, he saw the messages were all from the usual suspects: journalists, bloggers and gossip columnists who had easily ferreted out her private cell number.

Damn it, he should have thought this out well in advance of the impromptu ESPN interview this afternoon. He'd wanted to help Vicki…not hurt her even more with all of this media attention that she wanted none of.

On the other hand, he found himself thinking, maybe they could use the media interest to bring more attention to her sculptures. Then all this would not be for nothing.

"One more thing," he told her before they left the batting cage.

"There's more?"

Hell, yes, there was more.

For one thing, there was the fact that he was in love with her.

But even though he'd proved himself to be a total ass hat tonight by broadcasting the news of their fake engagement without running it by her first, he wasn't quite far gone enough to also blurt out the four-letter word he was longing to say.

Friends-to-lovers was going to need a hell of a lot better transition than that. He needed the rest of this week with her if he was going to figure out how to pull it off. At least a week.

So, for tonight, he would drop just one more bomb on her.

"The owners are throwing a party tomorrow night to celebrate the end of the regular season and to send us off in a blaze of glory to the play-offs. I'm pretty sure you and I are the guests of honor."

She took a deep breath that elevated her breasts up to the top of her dress in a shockingly sexy way. "Smith told me all I needed to do was smile. Maybe I can just keep doing that."

Ryan made a mental note to give his movie-star brother yet another round of thank-yous for giving Vicki such great advice.

"Well, you do happen to have a pretty damn gorgeous smile." He pulled her hand up to his mouth and pressed a kiss to it. "What do you say we hit my beach with enough booze and pizza to forget all about this for a little while?"

The smile Vicki gave him then almost had Ryan forgetting to keep that one little four-letter word to himself.

Twelve

The next morning, they had a date with Ryan's family. As they walked from his parked car toward the diner on the corner, Ryan rubbed a soothing circle on her back. "Relax. They're your friends, not a firing squad. You didn't sleep well, did you?"

Did he have any idea what it did to her when he looked at her like that? As though she was the only person in the world who mattered?

Vicki couldn't bring herself to pretend again that she had, in fact, slept well in his awesome guest bed. "I'm not a big sleeper."

Sleep had often eluded her, even when she was a kid. Back then it had been as if she always had to be ready to throw her things in a bag and head off to the next town at any given moment. Still, last night had been a particularly bad night. More than ever before, she'd wanted to go into his bedroom and climb into his bed, just so that he could hold her in his arms.

But that wasn't what now had her blinking once, twice and then just plain gasping.

Her face was plastered on the front page of the newspapers lined up in the rack outside the front door of the diner.

Vicki read the headline out loud. "'Who Is the Mystery Woman Engaged to San Francisco's Most Eligible Bachelor?'" Each word created a hollow feeling in her stomach. To top it off, the paper had paired the article with an old, and very unflattering, picture of her.

Ryan's jaw was tight as he pulled her away from the curb. "Ignore it. We'll be yesterday's news soon."

His siblings were already at the table by the time they walked inside. Vicki was surprised by the low-key restaurant the Sullivans had chosen to meet in. Then again, she supposed they'd have to know good places off the beaten path if they had any hope of being left alone with Smith and Ryan in a public place.

Lori jumped up to give the two of them a simultaneous hug, and her energy was so infectious that Vicki smiled despite her dark mood.

Sophie pushed out of the faded brown booth before Vicki could tell her to stay where she was.

"Oh, my, you're gorgeous, Sophie! Congratulations on the babies," Vicki exclaimed.

Sophie hugged her, or tried to, anyway, with her

belly big and round between them. "It's so great to see you again, Vicki. It's been way too long."

"When are you due?"

Sophie laughed. "Not soon enough." She put her hand on her stomach. "I think they're starting to get a little too happy in there."

Gabe was the next one to pull her in for a hug. He looked every inch the rugged fireman. "Look at you," Vicki teased, "all grown up."

"Same goes for you," he said, pulling back just far enough to give her an appreciative glance that made her blush.

Chase had attended high school at the same time she and Ryan had attended and, even though she'd never gotten to know him very well, she'd been following his photography for a long time.

He held out his hand and shook hers. "It's great to see you again, Vicki."

"You, too. And I have to tell you what a fan I am of your photography."

"Right back at you," Chase said with a grin. "Your sculptures are fantastic."

Ryan slid into the large booth and pulled her in beside him, holding her hand in his on top of the table as everyone else settled back into their places.

"You met Smith at the game yesterday," Ryan said, "so I think we're all good here. We're heading to Palo Alto to talk to Mom about everything after breakfast."

The gray-haired waitress came by to take their

orders and Vicki didn't see even the barest flicker of excitement or recognition in her eyes when she looked at Smith and Ryan. It was clear she couldn't care less who was eating at the diner that morning.

Even though Vicki doubted she could swallow a thing, she ordered a fruit salad.

"She'll also have a side of bacon and a short stack," Ryan told the waitress before he launched into his own order.

Part of her wanted to rebel, to tell the waitress she *didn't* want those things, but she knew Ryan was only trying to look out for her. He was the kind of man who couldn't stand to see her want for anything. And hadn't that been why she'd texted him? Because she knew he'd drop everything and come to help her?

And yet she continued to wonder how much of what he'd done for her this past week had been because he still felt he owed her for saving his life when they were kids. After all, hadn't that been one of the first things out of his mouth that night she'd apologized for dragging him into her mess?

As soon as the waitress went into the back, Ryan shot her a smile and she knew he was about to tell his siblings the truth. But Vicki had already decided she needed to be the one to explain it.

"We're not really engaged," she said in a voice that couldn't possibly be overheard by anyone but Ryan's family.

Everyone's eyes automatically moved to their

linked hands on the table, but even though her fingers immediately stiffened, he only held on tighter.

"I hated lying to you yesterday," she said to Lori and Smith. "In all the places I moved to as a kid, your family was the only one that ever took me in and made me feel like I belonged." Her voice dropped to a whisper. "I'm so sorry."

Ryan pressed a kiss to her forehead. "You have nothing to apologize for."

Lori spoke up first. "I'm totally bummed to hear you're not actually going to be marrying my brother, because you'd be such a *great* addition to our family. But I have to admit, I thought you seemed a little too surprised by the public congratulations at the game yesterday. Something seemed off. So what *is* going on with you guys? And what's with the whole engagement story?"

"Well, we're not dating, either," she clarified for them, even though Ryan was still holding on to her and she was praying he wouldn't let go anytime soon. She made herself meet his siblings' eyes. "The long and short of it is that I ended up in an unwanted and unfortunate situation with one of the board members who will be voting on my fellowship. Ryan stepped in when it seemed to make sense to pretend that I was already involved with someone."

Sophie's eyes were wide with shock and concern. "Are you okay?"

"I'm fine," she said. "Thanks to Ryan, who came when I panicked."

"So you told the guy you were getting married to Ryan—" Gabe began.

"No, that's all me," Ryan interjected. All eyes turned to Ryan. "When I found out what a sadistic bastard the guy was, I couldn't stand the thought of him even coming near Vicki again. It seemed like an engagement might do an even better job of keeping him away than just allowing him to think we were dating. This seemed like the sensible thing to do—at least until she wins the fellowship in a few weeks. I'm the one who told the reporter about us yesterday. Unfortunately, I wasn't able to reach Vicki to let her in on the new twist before the team decided public congratulations were in order."

"How much influence does this guy have over the fellowship choice?" Chase asked.

Vicki unclenched her teeth enough to say, "A lot."

"And to make matters worse, her ex-husband has just been appointed to the board," Ryan added, a grim expression of annoyance on his face.

Smith gave Ryan a hard look before turning to her. "Things like this happen all the time in my business. But never on my movies if I can help it. Who is this guy? I'd like to make a few calls."

Oh, God, the last thing she needed was for Smith Sullivan to get involved. Talk about juicy drama. Not to mention the fact that people would be afraid to have anything to do with her and her sculptures, just in case they looked at her wrong and she sicced the Sullivans on them.

"I appreciate that, Smith," she said, "but it's bad enough that I roped Ryan into this mess. I don't want you to get involved, too."

The waitress came over with a huge tray laden down with their breakfasts and they stopped the conversation. While the waitress refilled coffee cups, Vicki thought again how great this family was.

What, she suddenly wondered, would it be like to *actually* marry into the Sullivan family?

But she already knew. It would be fantastic.

Apart from Ryan, they were what she'd missed most when they'd left California at the end of her sophomore year. Spending time with Ryan's mother and siblings in their kitchen, hanging around in the backyard, feeling like she was part of a family, had been the happiest part of her high school years. She'd been in love with Ryan from the start, but it hadn't taken her long to fall for his family, too.

Now, as she looked around at all of them, it struck her again just how much they were *there* for one another. And even though she knew they had their arguments and irritations like any family, it was clear just how much they all loved one another, too, and that there wasn't anything they wouldn't do for one another. No matter what.

Hence this morning's meeting.

Yet, somehow, she'd managed to spoil it all by coming here today to ask each of them to lie for her.

"I can't do this," she said suddenly, and everyone stopped with their forks halfway to their mouths. "I can't ask all of you to lie for me." She looked at Ryan. "We need to tell the rest of the world that our engagement isn't real."

"No."

Ryan's voice was hard. Unyielding. Even his siblings looked surprised by it. But she'd seen him like this several times in the past week, each time when he was angry or worried on her behalf.

She knew he thought he owed her a debt, but she would have saved him a hundred times over and never once asked for anything back other than the chance to be his friend.

"I don't want the fellowship this badly, not if it comes at the expense of my friends. And not if it means even more lies are spiraling out one after the other."

Ryan's hand cupped her cheek, stilling her from saying anything else. His touch was gentle, but enough to make her look into his eyes.

"The two of us pretending to be engaged isn't hurting anyone, Vicki. All that matters to me is your safety, and that you and your art aren't unfairly penalized because you're a beautiful woman."

She felt herself flush, both at the intimate way he was touching her in front of everyone, and the fact that he'd just called her beautiful in front of his family.

"I think Ryan's right, Vicki," Sophie said softly. "Beauty can, unfortunately, be a liability around men sometimes. Especially powerful ones who think they have a right to everything they see."

Vicki was suddenly hit with a memory of the first time she'd met her ex-husband. She'd been with a group of nearly graduated art-school students out touring a few studios. Anthony had taken one look at her and claimed her. First, by insisting she work out of his studio. Second, and far worse, by slowly but surely convincing her she was far better at making statues of people and animals rather than the more nature-inspired sculptures she'd been interested in creating up until then.

At the time, it hadn't occurred to her that he'd been abusing his power. But hadn't he? Especially since she'd been so young and so inexperienced and he'd seemed like an all-knowing god of a world she longed to be part of?

"I agree," Chase said. "Chloe had some trouble with her ex-husband and I would have done anything to protect her. She ended up spearing him with a pair of scissors, which took him down pretty damn well, but I'd hate for your situation to come to that."

Gabe nodded. "In my job, Dispatch calls in with too many incidents that start out the way you're describing. You trusted your instincts and were smart enough to call Ryan before anything could escalate."

"Besides, we love having family secrets like this," Lori said with a small grin. "And who knows, maybe you two will be inspired to actually get together for real by the time you get the fellowship."

Not knowing what to say to that absolutely mortifying bit of pressure Lori had just put on Ryan to throw her a dating bone, Vicki said, "Excuse me," and bolted for the bathroom.

"Jesus, Lori, could you have made her feel any more uncomfortable?"

"Sorry," Lori said, even though it was clear she felt anything but. "I just really, really like Vicki and think you two would be perfect together."

Ryan wasn't actually angry with Lori. He was pissed at himself. Swearing, he said, "You guys probably remember how hung up I was on her in high school."

Gabe looked confused. "The way I remember it, you two were just friends in high school."

"We were."

"And you were always going out with other girls, weren't you?" Lori asked in a far-too-innocent voice.

He knew Lori's question was meant to grate on him. "I was an idiot. But it didn't matter because she wasn't interested. She still isn't."

"Why don't you just tell her how you feel and that you wish it all was real?"

He'd asked himself that question a thousand times by now, but every time it came down to the same important reason. "I can't risk losing her as a friend by coming on to her."

He'd meant it when he said she shouldn't have to pay a price for being beautiful. Not just with some creep who had power over her career, but with her friend who could barely remember to keep his hands off her.

Ryan ran a hand over his face. "Plus, her ex was such a dick that she isn't exactly looking for a replacement right now." He looked up and realized his brothers and sisters were staring at him like he was speaking Greek. "What?"

Sophie looked around the table before saying, "I think we're all a little bit stunned. Not about what you and Vicki are doing with the whole fake engagement thing. That seems to make sense, strangely. But because—" she paused to weigh her words "—everything has always seemed so easy for you."

"Well, it isn't," he snapped.

"Tell us what you need and we'll do it," Smith said.

Ryan was pretty sure the subtext behind his brother's question had just as much to do with helping him to get Vicki to fall for him as it did with making sure some creep on her fellowship board didn't hurt her.

Knowing there was nothing anyone could do to get her to change her feelings, that she was too strong to be manipulated by anyone, he said, "If anybody asks about us, just back up our story of two old high school friends who reconnected and realized we weren't going to let our second chance pass by without taking it. We're going to go talk to Mom after breakfast to clue her in."

Vicki returned to the table just in time to hear Lori say, "Your story really does sound romantic. Like every fantasy of how things could go with the one who got away. Unrequited love made right is the ultimate, isn't it? No wonder the press is all over you guys."

Vicki's face was perfectly blank as she slid back into her space beside him. Before Ryan could smooth over Lori's ridiculously on-point statements, their waitress came to the edge of their booth.

"Something wrong with your food?" She glared at the table of untouched plates.

It was the perfect opportunity to change the subject, especially because he hadn't missed the way Vicki had tensed up at the word *romantic*.

"Everything's great, thanks." Ryan picked up his fork and shoved a bite of egg into his mouth before saying to Smith, "So how's preproduction going on the film?" It was his cue to all of them that they were done talking about the fake engagement.

And he was definitely done with everyone in

his family feeling sorry for him because he was in love with a woman who had only ever looked at him as a friend.

After Ryan and Vicki left the diner to head down to Palo Alto to meet with Mary Sullivan, Sophie said, "Ryan's never been like this before. So frustrated...almost angry. I'm worried about him."

"Vicki sure looks like she's crazy about him to me." Lori made a face. "Maybe he's wrong about her not returning his feelings."

"She was terrified when they put her picture up on the big screen," Smith reminded her. "Even if she does feel something for him beyond friendship, she might not want to deal with everything that comes with being with Ryan. Marcus has had to make a lot of sacrifices for Nicola's music career over the past year."

"And if Marcus were here, he would tell you every one of them has been worth it," Lori shot back stubbornly.

"Maybe," Chase said, "but since Ryan is probably going to be a pro coach one day, the pressures on whomever he's with are only going to get bigger. And even more public. I'm guessing Vicki's happiest when it's just her and her art."

"She's also happy when she's with Ryan," Lori argued. "I remember how much fun they used to have together. I haven't ever forgotten the look on her face the day she came over to say goodbye when we were kids, when she'd found out she was moving away again. She looked like her heart had just broken into a million pieces. So did his."

Gabe nodded. "If you ask me, he's just using the friend thing as an excuse. He should stop making excuses and make his move. I wanted Megan and I went after her."

Sophie rolled her eyes. "Sure you did, Gabe, after Summer and I totally schemed to throw you guys together."

Everyone grinned at Gabe and he had to laugh. "Okay, so maybe I needed a little help getting my head straight. Thanks, Soph."

As they all threw cash down on the table, Smith said, "We did our part by convincing her to keep the fake engagement on. Now it's up to Ryan to make the most of that extra time with her."

Smith scooted out of the booth and held out his hands to Sophie to help her up as she said, "Mom always did like Vicki." Sophie grinned at her siblings. "I wouldn't be surprised if she has some ideas about how to make sure everything works out the way we all know it should."

Thirteen

"**I** really do love your mother," Vicki said to Ryan a couple hours later as they headed back into San Francisco from the suburbs where Mary Sullivan had raised her family.

Ryan's mother had made them coffee and listened patiently as they explained their strange situation. Stranger still, she'd almost seemed pleased by their fake engagement, laughing with honest humor when Vicki had recounted her horror at the big public congratulations on the huge screen at the baseball game.

Although all of Ryan's siblings had been in support of keeping up the ruse, it wasn't until Mary Sullivan had laughed over it with such easy humor that Vicki finally decided maybe they were right... and she should stop feeling so guilty about it all.

"Mom was so happy to see you," Ryan informed her, "that she doesn't care about the reason behind it."

After they'd dispensed with the fake engagement news, Mary had coaxed Vicki into telling her all about her travels through Europe over the past decade. Vicki had loved hearing Mary share her own stories about when she'd traveled the world as a young, in-demand model before she'd married Jack Sullivan and had eight kids keeping her busy at home. Chatting with Mary and Ryan in the comfortable living room with the big oak tree out in the backyard, Vicki had felt just as at home with her as she had when she was a teenager.

She planned to hold on to that deep, comforting warmth—that beautiful feeling of unconditional love and support from Mary Sullivan and her children—no matter what else happened.

Ryan hit the brakes at a red light and glanced over at her. "Feel better now?"

Finally, she was able to give him a real smile. "So much so you wouldn't believe it. How about you?"

He covered her hand with his. "As long as you're smiling, I'm good."

From any other man's lips, those words would have been nothing more than just that: empty words. But when Ryan said it, she knew he meant it.

A few minutes later, they pulled up in front of the studio building and Ryan said, "Call me if you need anything today. Anything at all."

According to Anne's texts, reporters and bloggers had been calling the studio all morning to try to find Vicki. It didn't sound as if any of them had come by yet, but she suspected it might not exactly be a safe haven for her—especially now, in the aftermath of her engagement news to the hottest bachelor in the city. She and Ryan had called her parents from his car to explain, but when no one was home she'd left a quick message just saying hi. She wasn't crazy about them believing she and Ryan were actually engaged, but then, they hadn't ever much followed sports or the tabloids, so maybe they didn't know.

"Thanks. I'll keep my phone in my pocket just in case you need to reach me again today." She'd already programmed a special ring for him so that she could tell when he was calling. That way she could ignore all the other calls from strangers who had managed to find her cell number and were calling to try to get a sound bite out of her.

The day had already been so full that it was only at the last second that she remembered. "What time do we need to leave for the team party tonight?"

"The limo will come for us at eight."

Vicki worked to push away the new flutter of nerves at having to publicly pull off the ruse that she was the woman Ryan Sullivan had decided to spend the rest of his life with.

He lifted her hand to his lips and pressed a kiss to the back of it. "See you tonight."

Rather than heading straight for her workspace, Vicki detoured to Anne's sewing room and walked in without knocking.

"Do you have anything I could wear to a swanky cocktail reception tonight?"

"Hey!" Anne jumped up from her sewing machine. "You're going to be Mrs. Gorgeous!" She threw her arms around Vicki. "How's it feel to be famous?"

"Weird," Vicki said, smiling at her friend through the guilt that burned in her gut over lying straight to her face about the validity of the engagement.

Plus, unlike her ex, fame had never been what she'd gone after. She just wanted to be able to make a living with her art and know that she'd created a sculpture that made people *feel* something they might not otherwise have felt.

"I think it's awesome that you snagged the best-looking man this side of anywhere. Of course, a little heads-up on the engagement would have been nice."

"Sorry." And Vicki really was sorry that she didn't know Anne well enough yet to let her in on the real situation. Still, she felt it was safe to tell her, "Does it make it any better if I tell you it was as much of a surprise to me as it was to you?"

Anne raised an eyebrow at that. "You didn't see his proposal coming?"

"No. Not at all." But since that was just about as honest as she could be at present, and before her friend could ask for any more details, she said, "You wouldn't have anything cut and sewn for a nonsupermodel, would you?"

Anne grinned at her, a little wickedly. "Actually, I'm glad you asked. I've been wanting to see a couple of my dresses on someone with curves instead of prepubescent girls who look like they should be sucking on lollipops."

Anne walked to one of her hanging racks and pulled out a dark red dress. From the back Vicki could see that it was sleeveless and knee-length. It looked simple and comfortable and she'd always felt good in that color. The cut of Anne's dress was spectacular, and the fabric looked stretchy enough that Vicki was hopeful it would look all right on her. It was certainly better than anything she had in her closet anyway.

It wasn't until Anne handed her the dress that Vicki saw the zippers crisscrossing the front.

Before she could protest, Anne waved to the small curtained area in the corner. "Go try it on with these shoes. They look like they're probably the right size."

There was no way Vicki could keep her underwear on under the dress so, after folding her bra and panties into a pile with her hip-length sweater, long tank and leggings, she walked out from behind the curtain to take a look in the full-length mirror. Vicki had never known a dress could be both elegant and sexy at the same time. The beautiful dress looked like it had been made to fit her measurements exactly.

Anne started clapping. "I knew it. You look great in my awesome dress."

Vicki flushed as she took in her reflection.

Anne moved behind her and lifted her hair from her neck to pile it on top of her head. "Perfect. Absolutely perfect. Now all you have to do is tell everyone who asks tonight that the fabulous dress you're wearing is courtesy of a hot new designer." She grinned into Vicki's eyes in the mirror as she added, "Make sure they spell my name right when they take all those pictures of you and Mr. Gorgeous."

Ryan's heart had been pounding hard all afternoon...ever since he'd put the ring box in his pocket. Sure, he knew it wasn't a real engagement ring, that she would just wear it to perpetuate their fake engagement story. But since he'd never given any woman a ring, it felt like a big deal.

And, real or not, he wanted Vicki to like what he'd picked out for her.

When he finally heard the front door open, he immediately left his bedroom, where he'd been doing up the final buttons on his dress shirt, to meet Vicki. It had only been a handful of hours since he'd dropped her off at the studio, but he still had to pause for a few seconds to drink her in. He wanted to pull her into his arms, but reined himself in with a kiss on the top of her head instead.

"I'm all sticky and covered in clay," she said as

she stepped away from him and clutched a garment bag to her chest. "I need a shower. You look so great, I'd hate to get you dirty."

He loved the smell of her skin after she'd been working all day. Especially when one of the things he wanted most of all in the world was to get dirty with her.

She put down her bags and looked up at him. "I ignored all of the calls and emails and luckily no one came by the studio. Or if they did, Anne scared them away before they could get to me," she added with a smile. "You never called, so I'm hoping that means everything was okay for you today?"

Ryan had been hounded with interview requests for both him and Vicki, but he didn't think she needed to know that. They'd get through tonight's event first and then they'd figure out the next steps to take.

"I spent some time watching game tapes with my pitching coach and getting in a workout."

Mostly, though, he'd sweated it out over the ring. For all his legendary cool on the pitcher's mound, he was going to lose it if he didn't give it to her already.

He reached into his pocket. "I got you a ring."

"A ring?" She looked at him with no small measure of alarm. "You got me a ring?" He watched her work at pulling herself together before she said, "I guess that would help things between us look more real tonight, wouldn't it?"

He went to flip open the box and couldn't believe

his hand was shaking. Jesus, he needed to get a grip before he completely freaked her out.

"I hope you like it." His voice was gruffer than usual.

"Oh, Ryan." Her eyes widened as she stared at the ring. "It's beautiful."

But instead of reaching for the platinum band set with a scattering of dark red rubies and brilliant diamonds across a large, flat base, she simply continued to stare at it.

"Can I put it on you?" His voice was raw, his words rough.

She licked her lips, never taking her eyes from the ring. "Okay."

He took the ring from its velvet case and dropped the box onto the entry table before reaching for her hand. Vicki's fingers were shaking slightly as he slowly slid it onto the ring finger of her left hand.

"I—" She finally looked up at him and the emotion in her eyes had him wishing he could pull her into him and never let go. "I haven't had a ring on my hand since I left—"

Silently cursing himself for not realizing how conflicted she would feel about wearing an engagement ring again, he said, "I know you won't be able to wear it when you're working, so I got you this necklace to put it on during the day."

She took the necklace from him. "You thought of everything. Even the fact that a sculptor can't wear a big ring to work. No one else would have thought of that." She paused, shook her head. "Even Anthony forgot about that when we got engaged."

"You should probably wear it tonight to solidify our story, but if it brings up too many bad memories after that, you don't have t—"

"The ring is beautiful, Ryan," she said, giving him a small smile. The metal cage that had closed in around his chest loosened as she looked down at it again. "It's just perfect. How did you know?"

Because I know you, sweetheart. Everything you are, inside and out. And I don't ever want you to give the ring back to me.

"Lucky guess."

She went up onto her toes and pressed a kiss to his cheek. "Thank you for giving me the most beautiful ring in the world. Even if it's just on loan for a little while, I still love it. But, really, I'd better go get ready. I won't be long."

The next thirty minutes were hell for Ryan. He couldn't stop thinking about Vicki in the shower with water sluicing over her curves, soap bubbles sliding over her beautiful skin.

His hard-on throbbed beneath his dark slacks and he worked to will it down before Vicki came out of the guest bedroom. By the time he heard the click of her heels coming down the hall toward him, he felt fairly confident that he wasn't going to embarrass himself.

Until he saw what she was wearing.

Holy hell.

Vicki was wearing a dark red dress that made the most of her lush curves and sweet softness. All those zippers made him want to yank them open with his hands and teeth. It didn't matter how he did it, just as long as she ended up naked...and he was allowed to touch her.

"You're gorgeous, Vicki."

A friend could say that to another friend, so he wasn't worried that she'd take it the wrong way.

It would be ripping the dress off her and taking her against the wall that would screw everything up.

Her cheeks were beautifully flushed as she said, "Thank you."

The limo pulled up outside his house a few minutes earlier and he held out his hand to her. Her skin was extra soft from the shower and she smelled incredible, like soap and beautiful, perfect woman.

"Thank God everyone thinks we're engaged, or I'd be fighting the guys off you tonight."

Her smile was wide and oh-so-pretty. "No wonder the girls always went crazy for you in school. You always know what to say."

He hated that she was acting like he was only saying it to keep her nerves in check. Frustrated enough by the whole damn situation, he didn't control the urge to run his knuckles down the side of her cheek.

When she shivered beneath the stroke of his hand, Ryan knew if he didn't pull away from her soon, they wouldn't be going anywhere tonight...

and then she'd hate him in the morning. But he couldn't stop touching her entirely, so he picked up her hand and slipped his fingers through hers. Just like the close friend he was.

"Ready for tonight?"

"No." She followed up her totally honest answer with a crooked little smile. "But I'm bound and determined to pull this off, so I've decided it doesn't matter if I'm ready or not."

Fourteen

Vicki tried not to grip the stem of her champagne glass too hard, even though she was tense enough to snap it in two. She felt like such a fraud on so many levels and keeping up a false pretense this evening was going to be tough. She and Ryan had just stepped inside the Bently Reserve building in the heart of downtown San Francisco and all eyes had immediately turned to them as glasses of bubbly were thrust into their hands. Ryan's arm was warm and steady around her as they moved deeper into the large group of his teammates and their wives and girlfriends. The toasts and congratulations came from one and all. She hadn't been able to eat much all day, and now her head was spinning from the seemingly unending supply of delicious bubbly.

"So," one of the women asked, "how did you two meet? Wasn't it in high school?"

Ryan gave her waist a little squeeze as he said, "Vicki moved into town when I was fifteen. I noticed her right away, even though she never seemed to look my way."

The men all rumbled with laughter at the image of a hard-up fifteen-year-old Ryan, while Vicki worked to mask her surprise that Ryan had even noticed her back then.

"Of course I noticed you," she said softly. "How could I not?"

This was all supposed to be for show but, in that moment, as he turned to look at her, his own surprise evident in his eyes, everything became completely real.

"As I remember it," he replied, "I had to step in front of a car for you to pay any attention to me."

"Whoa, hold up a sec," one of his teammates said. "What's this about getting hit by a car?"

Despite the way her head was spinning over Ryan's version of the story, Vicki quickly clarified, "There was an out-of-control driver in the school parking lot and he was headed straight toward Ryan. I helped get him out of the way."

"Thanks again for that," Ryan said quietly as he brushed her hair back from her face with his hand, gently stroking her jaw.

Ryan was so good at this, at both playing the crowd and making everyone believe that his feelings for her were real. How on earth was she supposed to hide what she really felt for him in front of all these people, many of whom were looking at her so carefully?

"So if you guys were teenagers when you met, what took you so long to make it happen?" one of his teammates asked. "I thought you were known for speed, Sullivan."

Ryan didn't take his eyes off Vicki as he said, "She moved away, and the next thing I knew, she was marrying some other guy."

She swallowed hard as his hand moved down to gently caress her neck and then her shoulders, before settling in again at the small of her back.

"I should have gone and fought him for you." He wasn't telling the story to the group now. Instead, he was speaking every word directly to her. "I regret every single day that I didn't chase after you. Now that you're mine, I'm never going to let you go."

All of the players' wives and girlfriends, along with the women who worked in the back office, sighed as Ryan put words to every one of their fantasies.

Sadly, Vicki found herself doing the exact same thing. How many times over the years had she wondered what Ryan was doing, who he was with, whether he missed her?

Stop it, Vicki! Ryan was playing his part so beautifully he could have given Smith a run for his money on the big screen.

Cool.

She needed to keep playing it cool.

"So," one of the prettiest women Vicki had ever set eyes on said, "how does it feel to have tamed the ultimate bad boy?"

The cool she'd been struggling for was quickly replaced with a hot rush through her veins. Vicki bristled not so much at the question, but at that hint of knowledge in the woman's eyes and voice.

Clearly, Ryan had slept with her.

It shouldn't matter. Vicki knew that on a rational level. After all, she and Ryan were just friends and he could do whatever he wanted, both before and after their fake engagement. But right here, right now, and for as long as they were pretending to be engaged, he was off-limits.

Vicki was aware of the smoky laughter coming from her own throat. It was almost as if she were across the room watching another woman in a sexy zippered dress standing with Ryan's arm around her.

"Are you kidding?" She looked straight at the beautiful woman Ryan had slept with. "He's nowhere close to being tame." She put her hand on Ryan's chest and felt the heat of him through her palm before she added her final zinger. "Thank God."

When the other woman could barely fake a laugh, Vicki let herself relish the flush of victory.

Unfortunately, she didn't get to enjoy it for very long. Because mere seconds after the words had left her lips, everyone in the room started chanting for a kiss to seal the deal.

Oh, no, she thought as she looked up into Ryan's dark eyes, *what have I just done?*

Did Vicki have any idea how gorgeous she was when she blushed like that, the perfect combination of sexy and shy? It was exactly the kind of expression that had a guy ready to do anything he could to amp up the sexy—to make her forget everything except calling out his name from under him in his bed.

Ryan knew what everyone was picturing after what she'd just said about not being able to tame him—her naked curves beneath his muscles, the two of them in a rough and sweaty tangle in his bed.

He knew every guy in the room thought he was the luckiest bastard alive for getting to make love to Vicki. They all assumed he would be unzipping her soon and putting his hands and his mouth on her. No doubt it was Vicki they'd be imagining later tonight, regardless of who they were actually in bed with.

He put his drink down and then hers before turning to her and cupping her face in his hands. "Should we give them what they want?"

She waited to answer him for long enough that he thought she might say no, regardless of the show they'd come to give tonight. He didn't realize he'd been holding his breath until the moment she nodded.

All his teammates wanted was to see a kiss, but Ryan couldn't resist brushing the pad of his thumb over her full lower lip first. Her eyes held his as she shivered in his arms and her breath sped up.

When he lowered his mouth to hers, he intended to give her a soft and simple kiss, similar to the one he'd given her at the cocktail lounge. Hot enough to appease the watching crowd, but still just barely on the right side of the friendship line. He'd done it that first night in front of James, hadn't he? Lips, but no tongue. No one expected anything more in public, so he knew he couldn't use that excuse.

But when his lips touched hers, she was so sweet, so pliant in his arms, that all of Ryan's plans for the kiss immediately crashed through the window and flew out over the bay.

He had to tilt her face to get a better angle on her mouth, and as she opened her lips on a gasp of pleasure, his tongue stole into her mouth in a desperate search for hers. When he stroked over it, Vicki's tongue immediately licked his back. He slid one hand down from her face to pull her closer against him and her hands tangled in his hair as they deepened the kiss together.

It wasn't until the sound of catcalls and hooting and hollering broke through the blood pounding in his ears that he remembered where they were… and what he was doing to Vicki in front of a roomful of spectators.

She must have realized it at the same time, because she looked shocked, then horrified, as she pulled back from him at the exact moment he forced himself to stop plundering her mouth.

Half-afraid she would run after what he'd just done to her, he forced himself to whisper, "That was perfect," as if he'd just been acting, rather than feeling the kiss all the way down to his soul.

He kept her close enough to his side to cover his hard-on, but not close enough that she'd feel it digging into her hip. "Show's over now, folks. Go get your jollies somewhere else," he joked, before turning away with Vicki and heading out onto the balcony for a private moment.

"You okay?"

Her cheeks were deeply flushed as she replied, "Sure."

Well, that made one of them, then, because he wasn't even close to okay after that kiss. He wanted another and another and another. But even that one had been pushing things.

Way over the friendship line.

Which was why he tried to joke, "I think we really convinced them with that kiss."

Her eyes went translucent for a moment and he thought he saw a surge of emotion rush through her before she tamped it down. "Great. I'm glad we're pulling this off." Her mouth moved up into a smile that didn't reach her eyes. "We should probably go back inside, don't you think?"

Damn it, she wasn't afraid to be alone with him now after the way he'd mauled her inside, was she?

He put his hand back under her chin and turned her face up to his. "Are you sure you're okay? You can tell me if you're not, Vicki. You can tell me anything."

"I'm just not used to so much attention. I don't know how you live like this all the time."

"We'll get out of here soon, I promise."

"No," she said with a small shake of her head, "this is your big party before the play-offs. We need to stay."

That, right there, was one of the reasons he loved her. Where everyone else just thought about themselves, Vicki was never selfish. Whereas, even knowing how wrong it was to steal that hot kiss from her, he'd taken it anyway.

Because he'd *had* to take it.

Hating himself for crossing the line he'd sworn not to cross, he said, "I'm sorry I kissed you like that, Vicki. I'm sorry I took advantage of the situation. And of you."

She went completely still, her expression freezing on her face. "There's nothing to forgive. They wanted to see you kiss your new fiancée, so you did." She looked colder, harder, than he'd ever seen her before as she said, "And since I kissed you back, I hope you can forgive me, too."

A moment later, she was walking into the room and he was feeling like more of an ass than ever as he followed her inside. He didn't know what he'd said wrong...just that he had definitely screwed things up even worse.

And he didn't have the first clue how to fix it.

Fifteen

It was too much.

Ryan was too much.

They'd left the party ten minutes ago, but after the night she'd just had—and a kiss she didn't think she'd ever be able to forget—Vicki simply couldn't be this close to Ryan anymore.

She reached blindly for the silver handle inside the limo, but the door wouldn't budge when she tried to push it open.

"Vicki?"

Her breath caught in her throat at nothing more than the sound of her name on Ryan's lips, nearly choking her. So many times over the course of the night he'd said her name while reaching for her. And every single time, she'd tried to forcibly remind herself that it was all pretend, that none of it was real, that she wasn't really his…and wouldn't ever be.

Maybe, just maybe, she might have been able

to succeed at heeding those constant reminders, if only he hadn't added in the brush of his fingers over her shoulder, the stroke of his knuckles over her cheek, the press of his hand at her lower back as they moved through the room to talk with his teammates.

With every caress, every inch of his hard body against hers, she lost hold of her own body—and her heart—a little bit more. Until, at the end of the party, she'd been a quivering mess of nerves and lust and overwhelming *need*.

"I need to get out." The desperation in her voice was painfully clear. But she was long past the point of being able to hide anything from anyone. Especially herself.

Which was precisely why she needed to get away.

Away from Ryan.

And away from her own desires.

"Stop the car, please!" Her voice was shrill as she teetered on the edge of shattering, right at the cusp of her breaking point.

A moment later, the limo smoothly pulled over to the side of the road and the lock clicked open. She nearly fell into the gutter in her hurry to escape its confines.

She didn't have a plan, hadn't thought ahead as to where she would go. When she looked up and saw the door to a bar, it seemed like divine providence.

A drink. Or maybe a dozen.

She'd do anything right now to dull the pulsing

need, the potent memories on her skin of Ryan's hands and mouth on her, his arms around her.

Vicki pushed in through the black-and-red door. Her fingertips brushed over paint that had been scratched off and repainted likely a hundred times since the bar had first started serving, and she tried to focus on the stickiness of the wood, the small and large divots in the grain where pieces had been knocked out by fists. Somehow, some way, she needed to fill up her well of tactile sensation with something other than Ryan.

All night long he'd been under her hands. For a sculptor, there was nothing more sensual than touch. All those touches had tipped her over the edge into near madness.

The soft cotton of his dress shirt beneath her fingertips.

His incredibly honed muscles just beneath the fabric.

The lines of his ribs.

The tendons that held everything together.

Her hands had shaken as she tried not to do what the artist in her demanded she do—trace the rises and falls of his body.

At the same time, tonight's party had brought everything into such sharp relief that there was no way she could even try to deny just how wrong they were for each other.

Everything was easy for Ryan. His career, his relationships, his family. She, on the other hand, had struggled her whole life with her art, with making friends while always heading to a new town, with fitting in as an artist in a military family. Where Ryan was so utterly comfortable in his own skin, she'd never known quite how to feel about her abundance of curves on a body that wasn't nearly tall enough to carry them.

And yet, strangely, she never used to worry about those things when she was with Ryan. Because she'd always been so sure that he didn't look at her as a woman. As much as she'd often wished that he had over the years, it had also been tremendously freeing not to have to worry about any of that nonsense.

She'd always been herself with him. Regardless of what she wore, or whether or not she had makeup on, or whether she ate all her food and then grabbed the last bite of his, she'd always known that he would still be her friend.

Vicki absolutely, positively couldn't lose that just because she was letting ridiculous fantasies take her over, minute by minute, day by day.

Once and for all, she needed to kiss all those "what if this turned real and my dreams came true?" fantasies goodbye.

Ryan needed to be with someone who could carry the pressure of being the partner of a famous athlete. It was laughable to think she could ever be that woman, not when it gave her hives even to think about it, especially now that she knew exactly how hot the spotlight was on his life.

Fact was, she didn't fit into his world as anything but a friend and, one day, when he found the woman who would be his wife, no doubt their friendship would be relegated to the background.

And she'd deal with it.

Probably in the same totally unhinged way she was dealing with it now, she thought with more than a little inner sarcasm as she pushed into a group of men and women, young and flirting and already drunk, and put her hands flat on the bar.

"I need a scotch. Make it a double."

The sea of youth and blatant sexuality parted for her, likely because they didn't want her obviously impending mental and emotional breakdown to kill their buzz.

And yet it wasn't until the bartender slid the drink over that she realized what she'd ordered.

Scotch was the first drink she'd ever had when Ryan had smuggled a bottle of Johnnie Walker into her garage late one Saturday night. The perfect Ryan Sullivan had actually taken booze from one of his friends' houses, then left the fun to come hang out with her instead.

They'd gotten drunk together that night. Well, at least she had, and it had been so fun. She'd felt so loose, and warm, and even when she'd started to slur her words and had knocked over one of her brother's bikes, she'd felt so safe.

There wasn't another soul in the world with whom she could have let her guard down like that. And the fact that Ryan had chosen her that night over his other friends, at least for those few hours, warmed her as much as the alcohol had.

It was also the night he'd almost kissed her and she'd freaked out and pushed him away.

Vicki sighed at the memory. Even at fifteen, she'd known that if he couldn't bring himself to kiss her unless he was drunk and horny because his usual cheerleaders hadn't been available earlier, she wasn't going to have a prayer of respecting herself in the morning. So she'd pretended it was all a joke and pushed him away.

He'd never tried to kiss her again. Not until the night she'd called him in on his white steed and he'd arrived at the cocktail lounge ready to protect her at any cost. Even if it meant pretending that he loved her as much as she had always loved him.

Vicki took a shaky breath as past and present overlapped in her head, her heart. She wrapped her fingers around the cool glass, and the rubies and diamonds on her pretend engagement ring glinted in the light from above her head as she lifted the glass to her lips.

"The same for me."

The sound of Ryan's low voice had the glass nearly slipping from her fingers as he slid onto the bar stool beside her. But she couldn't drop the drink, not when she needed it so badly. The scotch burned like fire as she gulped it down.

She put her empty glass on the bar with a clack and kept her eyes trained on the bartender. "Another, please."

Ryan put his hand on her arm, but she was so sensitive from a full night of touches that she flinched. It was either that or throw herself into his arms, right then and there.

She couldn't.

She wouldn't.

But, oh, how she wanted to.

She hated feeling him stiffen beside her as her flinch registered, hated the way he so carefully removed his hand when he'd been so free with his affection earlier, hated it even more when he said, "I'm sorry, Vicki. I should have realized how tired you were. I should have gotten us out of there earlier."

She was long practiced in control, had made an art form out of it the past few days by channeling all that lust, all that need, into her art.

All night long she'd held on to her self-control for dear life, had kept it tightly grasped in her strong hands. But as she reached for it one more time, she felt it fluttering just out of reach.

Her hand shook as she lifted the glass to her lips.

"You don't have anything to be sorry for." She could see bits and pieces of her reflection in the rusting mirrors behind the bar, enough to know she looked just as tired, just as weary, just as beaten as she felt.

"I'm the one who told the reporter we were engaged," he reminded her. "I've seen the way the team celebrates news like that. I knew what was coming. You didn't."

She still wished he had run the plan by her first, but his intentions had been for the best. Just like they always were where she was concerned.

Even that made her angry now, the knowledge that even a man known to be the baddest of bad boys remained utterly and completely full of good intentions around her. And, in the end, it was so much easier to give weight to that frustration than it was to accept her forbidden feelings for the shockingly gorgeous man sitting beside her.

"You only did it to help me," she said in a voice that dared him to contradict her, "so how could any of this be your fault?" Especially the part where she was head over heels in love with him.

God, if he weren't here, she'd have a couple more drinks and then lay her head down on the bar top and pretend it was all just a bad dream.

But there wasn't time for her next breath before Ryan's hand was on the back of her neck and he was moving over her, his strong thighs trapping hers between his, his dark eyes flashing with heat as he stared down at her.

His mouth was a breath from hers before she had time to react, before she could get a single synapse to fire, or send out another silent reminder to herself about control and self-restraint and impossible futures.

"Here's how."

His words were a breath on her lips, and then he was covering her mouth with his and kissing her like she'd never been kissed before in her life—not even by him.

This kiss was a full-on slick of his tongue against hers, as if he was trying to learn all the shades of her taste. As his kiss spiraled deeper, darker, hotter, he pulled her closer and savagely took everything she could give. How could she do anything but give in—at least for a split second of heaven—to the need to taste him for herself?

She wanted him so bad—years of need culminating in this moment in a bar. He kissed her with all the passion of a dying man who needed the very breath from her lungs to breathe.

The two drinks she'd just gulped down, plus the champagne that had been refilled constantly for her at the Hawks' team party, were making her reactions slower, fuzzier, looser.

She could use being drunk as an excuse.

Only, even when she was a teenager, hadn't she known better? Hadn't she been smart enough to realize that being the drunk lay was so much worse than not being laid at all?

And if Ryan didn't want her when he was sober, it meant he didn't actually want her.

She forced herself to pull back from his mouth. She retreated from the heat that poured from him, from the pull that drew her hands to his strong arms, his broad chest, his tight, muscular hips.

"No one's watching us now," she made herself say, the words escaping her mouth between her panting breaths. Even back when she'd thought herself to be in love with her ex, his kisses had never left her this out of breath. Or anywhere close to the edge of giving over every last part of herself. "No one in this bar cares about baseball or whether we're engaged or not."

With those reminders in place between them, meant to douse the fire jumping and flickering so wildly, she would have scooted away from him.

But he didn't let her move.

And, oh, if she didn't end up even more lost to desire, to pleasure, at the way Ryan used his muscles, his strength, to keep her right where she was. Still, she had to try, at least one final time, to try to save herself before she went all the way under.

"The show's over now. You don't have to do this, Ryan."

"Yes," he growled, "I do."

And then his mouth was back on hers and he was pulling her from her bar stool to fit tighter between his legs, his hands hard on her hips, his tongue forcing hers to dance with his again in a kiss that was as close to making love as she'd ever come with all her clothes on.

The groan she'd been trying so hard not to let go of sounded wanton and breathless into his mouth as Vicki gave in to what she'd wanted for so long…to be in Ryan Sullivan's arms.

At least for one beautiful night.

It had been a hell of a night.

As one second had ticked through to the next, Ryan had wanted Vicki more and more. He'd been hyperaware of every sensual shift of her body, her mouth, her hands, her eyes. Her laughter had repeatedly lit up the party, and her innate sensuality had inflamed every guy—and many of the women, he suspected—at the party.

He'd worked to hold on to his self-control, but being so close to her tonight while pretending to be more than they actually were had kicked him right over the edge.

It didn't help any that he was jealous as hell of anyone else who made her laugh, who looked at her with appreciation, who couldn't take their eyes off her luscious curves. If one more guy at the team party had asked to see her sculptures, he would have pounded his skull into the nearest tabletop.

Only, when they'd gotten in the limo to head back to his place, the madness had gotten worse. She smelled so good and, as the party had worn on, he'd gotten used to the pleasure of reaching for her, stroking her soft skin.

He hadn't wanted to stop, didn't see any reason

why he couldn't pull her into him so that she could lay her head on his shoulder. Two friends who had made it through a rough evening together.

But when he'd reached for her, she'd slid just out of reach and then started shaking the door handle like she couldn't wait to get away from him.

Finally, he'd seen how shattered she was. How tired.

He had been putting on the pro-ballplayer show for more than a decade. But she didn't have his years of practice. Ryan felt terrible about the situation he'd put her in. And that was why he'd followed her out of the limo into the seedy bar.

To apologize.

At least, that was the reason he gave himself, the only reason he could allow.

He'd silently sworn up and down that he wasn't going to touch her again, that he wasn't going to give in to the urge to take her mouth...or to his desperate need to know if she would respond to him the way he'd always dreamed she would.

Only, now that he had her lips under his and her body wrapped tightly against him, despite all those years of wanting, regardless of the few kisses and caresses they'd already shared while playing girlfriend and boyfriend this past week, it was a goddamned revelation how good she smelled, how soft her lips were, how sweet her curves felt...and how much he wanted to be able to give in to the need to drag her against him like this whenever he wanted.

She was tired. Maybe even a little drunk.

Ryan knew he was taking advantage of both those things.

But, suddenly, he didn't care anymore.

Not when everything he'd ever wanted, everything he'd ever dreamed of, was finally on the verge of being his.

The chance to make love to Vicki was fifteen years in coming.

And Ryan Sullivan wasn't going to waste another second of it.

Sixteen

Ryan pulled his mouth from hers, but he didn't remove his hand from her neck. She felt branded by his touch as he reached into his pocket for his cell phone and called them a cab to replace the limo he'd sent home. His eyes never once left hers as he spoke, and the second he hung up, his mouth was right back there on hers.

Taking.

Demanding.

He wasn't asking permission to kiss her.

He wasn't trying to convince her with coaxing, persuasive words that they should sleep together.

Instead, he was simply showing her in the most elemental of ways that what they'd been building up to all night long was definitely going to happen.

Amazingly, it was exactly that which drew her passion all the way out of her. Regardless of her previous reluctance, there was no denying that this one moment—pulled tight into Ryan's arms, her lips and tongue tangling with his in a dark room that smelled like beer and grease—was perfect.

He was a man. She was a woman. And they would share with each other what men and women had been made to share from the beginning of time.

He barely pulled his mouth from hers as he led them through the room and out the front door to the sidewalk, and it occurred to Vicki that if anyone saw them now and recognized Ryan, there would be absolutely no doubt in anyone's mind that they really were a couple.

How crazy this was, this one night of passion they were about to have in a world where what looked real wasn't…and what was false could become mind-blowingly, momentarily true in a sweet moment of desire.

Back in the bar she hadn't let herself reach for him, hadn't touched him for fear that if she held on to him, she would never be able to let him go. But she'd had no choice but to wrap her arms around him when they'd been moving through the crowded bar. Now, even as he opened the back door of the waiting taxi for her, he kept his other hand over hers, holding her against him as if he feared she'd go running if he let go for even a second.

Vicki had never been the kind of woman who made out in the back of a cab. Her ex-husband had told her many times that she was too uptight to be a "real" artist, that if she could ever figure out how to loosen up, she might have a chance of tapping into her true artistic self.

She'd hated him every time he said it, hated him even more once they'd split up because she'd felt he was right. But now, for the very first time, she realized it hadn't been all her fault after all.

Because when Ryan was kissing her, when his hands were on her and he was stroking the bare skin just above her kneecap, she couldn't do anything but be in the moment.

She had no choice but to *be* that woman.

It took being with Ryan for her to realize that her ex simply hadn't been man enough to draw that passionate a response out of her, no matter how wondrous everyone thought him to be, no matter how sought after he was by both women and men in their insular art world.

Ryan lifted his mouth from hers again for the briefest of seconds to give his address to the taxi driver, and then he was all hers again. He sat back against the leather seat and effortlessly lifted her onto his lap so that she was straddling him.

She gasped at how thick and hard and throbbing he was, pressed up tight against the vee between her legs. His fingers on her upper thighs and then the curve at the bottom of her hips drew the next gasp from her.

She'd laughed with Ryan a thousand times. They'd talked late so many nights about family and travels and their dreams. But in all that time, she'd never known this side of him, had never guessed that the easygoing boy she'd had such a crush on could ever be such a possessive man.

No one had ever claimed her so completely in any moment, not even the man she'd married.

With nothing more than Ryan's eyes and hands on her, she felt irrevocably his. It thrilled—and scared—her in equal measure.

Confused by the riot of emotions moving through her, pulled at by arousal and desires she'd never thought would see the light of day, she did the only thing she could: she put her sculptor's hand on his beautiful face and closed her eyes.

She needed to see him. Really see him in the only way she truly knew how to see anything.

Vicki let her hands rest on Ryan's cheekbones for a long moment, settling into the feel of his skin and bones just as she had a thousand times before with clay.

It should have settled her. Only, clay didn't have a heartbeat.

Clay wasn't warm.

Clay didn't breathe raggedly in and out.

And clay didn't say her name in a breath that was as much a plea as it was an expression of pure gratitude.

His hands tightened on her hips as he drew her even closer to him and she couldn't stop herself from rocking once, twice, three times into the pleasure his thick heat gave her just at her core. A low groan came from his throat, and as she arched into him just one more time, he pressed his mouth to the hollow of her neck and licked against her skin.

Oh, God, that one slow stroke of his tongue was almost enough to pitch her over the edge. Just a few more brushes on her overheated, oversensitive skin, just a handful of thrusts against him, and she'd not only be the kind of woman who made out in the back of a cab...she'd also be the kind that climaxed in one.

But, amazingly, it wasn't her sense of propriety, it wasn't even a last grasp at self-control, that had her shifting back on his thighs just enough to keep from imploding. It was the fact that her hands were even more insistent, simply craved the chance to finally touch the man she'd only been able to admire visually for so long, that had her refocusing on the planes and hollows of his face.

She could have explored Ryan's face for hours—the slightly irregular bone over the bridge of his nose where he'd once been hit with a baseball, the peaks and valleys of his upper lip, the bristling stubble across his chin and cheeks that scratched at her fingers and palms, the perfect curve of his earlobe, the strong beat of his heart at his pulse point.

How different, she had to wonder, would all of this feel against the insides of her thighs rather than her hands?

And would she find out tonight?

The decadent questions had Vicki shifting closer

to him again, and her eyes fluttered open. Until now, Ryan had always been the one to kiss her. Right from that first night in the cocktail lounge when their game of pretend had begun, Ryan had been the one to claim her mouth in the gentle kiss.

They both knew he could take anything he wanted from her right now, even in the back of a cab. He was bigger. Stronger. And she wanted him. Badly. And yet he remained perfectly still beneath her.

Watching her with those dark eyes.

Waiting, as if to see whether she was brave enough to demand from him what he'd demanded from her in the bar.

Vicki told herself her heart shouldn't be thudding so hard in her chest over yet another kiss. But it was.

Because she knew this was so much more than a kiss.

It was the difference between allowing herself to be seduced by Ryan…and being an equal partner in seduction.

Ryan hadn't said a word, but she could hear his voice just the same. *Come on, Vicki. Just one little kiss. Give it to me. You know you want to.*

As if he'd said the words aloud, his dark eyes lit with the humor that was never far from the surface, the perfect combination of wicked and daring, safe and sweet.

That was when Vicki knew she was a goner.

Not just for one kiss.

Not just for one night.

But forever.

They'd make love tonight. It would be beautiful and thrilling and, likely, the culmination of every sexual fantasy she'd ever had.

But Vicki didn't need to sleep with Ryan to know that he'd already conquered all the corners of her heart.

And that making love would likely cause irreparable damage between them come morning.

She kissed him anyway.

Seventeen

Vicki's mouth was a soft press of sweetness against Ryan's lips as she finally kissed him.

God, she tasted good. He loved the way her tongue found his before pulling back slightly to stroke against his lips and teeth.

Even more, though, he loved the fact that she'd finally reached for him.

Not just with her mouth on his, but the way she'd put her hands on his face and closed her eyes as if she were sculpting him. Sitting in the cab with all of his clothes on and her hands on him, he'd felt naked. And completely transparent. As if Vicki had a direct line to his heart…and soul.

He'd wanted her to know it all, everything he didn't know how to say but couldn't stop feeling.

When the taxi driver hit the brakes hard, Ryan was glad for the excuse—for any excuse—to hold her even tighter. He'd never felt anything as good as having her in his arms, and when she'd been rocking into him a few minutes ago, he'd been close to losing it fully clothed.

She tried to slip off his lap as he reached for his wallet, but he wouldn't let her go until the last possible second. Still, he held fast to her hand so that she couldn't leave the cab until he did, too.

The taxi sped away from them, and in the light of the streetlamp outside his front gate, Vicki's beautiful face was flushed. Her eyelashes were covering her eyes from him and he wanted to tip her chin up to his, make her look at him and really see who was claiming her before he took her right then and there on the street.

Somehow, a faint glimmer of common sense got through. Once he had her inside his house, however, all bets were off.

There wasn't going to be any embarrassment tonight.

Or any holding back.

He'd waited too long for her. Had she waited just as long for him? Or was she simply swept up in the moment?

Even though he told himself it didn't matter, that they'd work it all out in the morning, he wasn't quite able to push away the twinge in his chest that seemed to say it did, in fact, matter very much whether this was just an impulse for Vicki.

Damn it, he'd never wanted anyone as much as he

wanted her. But if she was at all hesitant, he knew what he'd have to—

"Let's go inside, Ryan." He was surprised to see Vicki's eyes darkened with the kind of passion he'd only ever seen her give to her sculptures. "I want to feel more of you beneath my fingertips." She licked her lips before whispering, "All of you."

Ryan throbbed hard behind his zipper and he quickly punched in the security code and led them up the steps to his front door, then inside the house they'd shared for the past few days as friends.

Together, they went to the couch where they'd been watching the movie together just the night before. Even for the five minutes they'd seen of the movie, it had been torture not to reach for her, not to lay her down on the leather and strip her naked so that he could taste every inch of her body.

What a difference forty-eight hours had made.

Thank God.

It was the most natural thing in the world to put his arms around her and pull her right where he wanted her. Her green eyes were big and so damned beautiful as she blinked up at him when he came over her. She was so much smaller than he was that he wanted to be careful, didn't want to put too much of his weight over her, even though it killed him not to get even closer.

She took advantage of the small distance he'd put between them to push his jacket from his shoulders. He helped her get it off and then she was using those incredibly gifted and clever hands of hers to undo the buttons of his dress shirt.

Ryan's breath was coming faster and faster, his control slipping more and more with each brush of Vicki's fingertips over his chest as she worked her way down the front of his shirt.

He needed to rein himself in, enough at least that he wouldn't scare her with all that he wanted from her.

Everything.

She lifted her eyes to his again just as the word resounded inside his brain.

"You're so beautiful, Ryan," she said, and then she laid her hands on the chest she'd bared, palms flat, fingers splayed.

He wanted to see her, too, needed to strip the sexy dress from her gorgeous curves and find out if all of his fantasies about her naked body were, in fact, real. But then her eyes were closing again and she began to move her fingers over his skin.

Her fingernails scraped slowly through the dark hairs that curled over his pecs, and he was powerless to control a rumbling groan at the sweetness of her touch. Another smile tipped her lips as she played with him some more.

"I love the way you're vibrating through my hands," she whispered as she moved her hands higher, up toward his shoulders.

He'd thought he wanted her hands lower, but the way she traced each line of muscle and sinew over his shoulders, then up onto his neck, was hands down the sexiest thing any woman had ever done to him.

If she wanted to just keep touching him like this, he would happily let her for as long as she wanted.

But then she moved her hands down from his neck, over his shoulders, to his upper arms. Shoving the fabric of his shirt down so that she could touch his skin, she wrapped her hands over his biceps and triceps, which were bulging from holding himself up over her, and gave a happy sigh.

Her eyes fluttered open, stunning him all over again with their beauty as she said, "You're so perfect. I love touching you."

He couldn't resist dropping his mouth to hers then, and taking her lips in a kiss that told her he thought she was absolutely perfect, too. She gripped his arms as he deepened the kiss, her hips arching up into his. Her legs were pinned between his, and he took advantage of the position by pressing himself hard into her. This time she was the one groaning as pleasure took them both over.

Ryan hadn't lain on a couch fully clothed, grinding against a girl, since high school. It occurred to him through the fog of lust in his brain that it was fitting they should be here like this, almost as if they were revisiting all those lost opportunities when they were teenagers.

If he had ever gotten her like this in high school, he would have lost his freaking mind, he'd wanted her so bad. All the years between then and now had only amped up that want, and he had to fight not to just rip her clothes off and take her.

Hell, who was he kidding? That was exactly what he needed to do. A second later, he was shrugging off his shirt and reaching for one of the zippers on the front of her dress.

"I've wanted to do this all night long."

He finally unzipped her a couple inches, baring perfect soft skin. He would have kept going all the way if surprise hadn't lit her eyes.

"You did?"

He'd thought she'd known exactly what she was doing with the dress, that she'd intentionally created the ultimate fantasy for every single guy at the party of undoing each zipper one by one, from her breasts, her hips and up each thigh.

"We all did."

Her eyes widened and she licked her lips as if concerned. "We?"

He adored Vicki, and trusted her in a way he didn't trust any other woman but the ones he was related to, but he had a hard time believing she was surprised by the way she'd looked tonight.

He lowered his mouth to the spot on her neck just below her ear and, after giving it a sharp nip, then licking over the skin, he said, "You had to know what all those zippers would do to a bunch of horny ballplayers."

"No," she swore even as shivers racked her

sweet, soft frame at the next touch of his teeth, then tongue, on the other side of her neck. "My friend Anne is so talented that I had to wear her dress. And I didn't have anything else to wear."

Ryan lifted his head to gaze down at the surprisingly innocent beauty below him. She'd lived for over a decade with artists who, he guessed, partied harder than even the biggest sports stars, that probably slept in kinky groupings even a guy like him had no interest in at all.

How had she kept herself apart from all of it?

"Remind me to thank her next time I see her for the pleasure of unwrapping you like this." He pulled the zipper down again, all the way this time, so that her breasts spilled free.

Ryan froze as he looked down at her.

"Jesus, Vicki." He swallowed hard, tried to grab hold of what was left of his frayed control. "You aren't wearing a bra. And your breasts are—"

There weren't any words for them. Nothing that would even come close to doing them justice.

Against her creamy skin, her nipples were a dark, rosy flush. The tips hardened even more as he stared down at her in wonder.

Vicki was every fantasy he'd ever had come to life beneath him, her body made for sex in its purest, sweetest form, with curves to fit his hands, his mouth, his—

"Ryan?"

He could hear the panic just starting to bubble

up in her voice at the crazy way he was acting, but he didn't have the lucidity anymore to deal with it. All he could do was reach for her with a trembling hand and cup the softest flesh he'd ever touched.

He throbbed so hard in his pants his arousal was almost pure pain rather than pleasure, but trying to keep the reins on his desire for Vicki didn't matter anymore. Nothing mattered but touching her the way she'd touched him, discovering her with his hands on her skin, her sweet moans of need reverberating all the way through him.

When one hand wasn't nearly enough, he covered her with both, splaying his hands over her skin just as she had over him. He could feel the beating of her heart, so fast, so strong through his palms, his fingertips.

Words he hadn't planned on saying, full of emotions he knew he wasn't supposed to feel for just a friend, hung on the edge of his tongue and the only way he could stop himself from saying them was to lower his lips to one beautiful peak and take her into his mouth. Vicki's hands threaded into his hair as she arched closer to him. He began by gently swirling his tongue over her, but then he had to taste her better with his teeth, his lips. She gasped as he nipped at her sensitive skin, then sucked harder, trying desperately to get his fill of her sweetness.

Suddenly, her hips went wild beneath him and he was about to move one hand down to her hips to hold her steady before she unwittingly pushed him over the edge when she whispered, *"Ryan,"* in a raw voice, his name falling from her lips again and again.

My God, he suddenly realized, she was about to shatter beneath him from nothing more than his mouth at her breast.

He cupped her hips hard against him and ground against her the way he'd been wanting to all night. He didn't have time to worry about being gentle, or holding back for fear of shocking her. He never wanted her to forget her first climax in his arms... and didn't intend for a minute to let her escape from the fact that he was the one taking her over the edge of pleasure.

Her skin dampened beneath him as she moved closer and closer to release and it was pure instinct to lift his head from her chest, raise one hand to stroke her cheek as she writhed beneath him.

"Let go, Vicki. Let me see how beautiful you are."

Her eyes fluttered open as her lips parted on a gasp. She arched into him and trembled hard in release just as he took her mouth in a kiss. Again and again he pushed his hips into hers as he held her against him, until finally he felt her go lax and soft again.

Ryan felt wild, like an animal finally released from capture as, with a soft nip at her bottom lip, he pulled back to stare down at the woman he needed more than anyone he'd ever known.

Her eyes were closed and she was still breathing hard as he ran the pad of his thumb over the lips he'd just been devouring. Slowly, her eyes opened and her cheeks flushed even more. Ryan didn't realize he was grinning down at her until she smiled back.

"You're amazing, Vicki."

She blinked once, twice then turned her head a little to the side as if she was suddenly shy. "I didn't know that was going to happen. I'm not usually so—" She shook her head a little, staring at his biceps before saying, "Sensitive."

While he loved hearing that he'd made her feel things she didn't usually feel, he hated the way she seemed almost afraid to look at him. Cupping her jaw gently, he turned her face back to his.

"I may never be able to sit comfortably on this couch again," he teased her with a smile, even though the blood was pumping through his veins so hard he could barely form a sentence.

It was true, of course, that he would be reliving those past fifteen minutes for a very long time. Every time he walked into the living room, he'd see Vicki lying beneath him, her beautiful breasts spilled into his hands and mouth while she arched into him and found her pleasure.

She flushed again, but this time he wouldn't let her turn away from him.

"You're so beautiful when you come," he told her, forcing her to see exactly what she did to him. "Even more beautiful than I thought you'd be."

Again, that little look of confusion furrowed the skin between her eyebrows.

"You have no idea how many nights, how many hours, I thought about you," he admitted to her in a low voice. After all, now that they were finally together for real, there was no reason to hold back his endless fantasies, was there? "I was dying to know how you touched yourself. What you liked. How you liked it. I couldn't stop wondering about the sounds you made when you were close…and when you finally went over."

She didn't say anything, just continued to stare up at him like she couldn't possibly believe what he was saying was true. Wanting her to believe, needing her to know just how much she meant to him—how much she'd always meant—he slid his hand from her hips back to her breasts.

Another gasp sounded from her pretty lips as he cupped her soft curves and ran his thumb over the taut, still-damp peak. "I also," he said in a voice made raw from pure need, "dreamed of seeing you naked one day."

"Ryan…please."

He didn't know if she was begging him to stop divulging his secret desires—or to hurry and make good on them. Not that there was any choice, of course. He couldn't possibly get this close to stripping her clothes from her and not make good on it.

He grinned down at her again, his friend who had just become so much more, thank God.

Benefits had never been this good, that was for sure.

"I always have liked the sound of a woman begging."

Her eyes rolled then, and he was glad to see that her shyness finally seemed to have gone.

"So I've heard," she replied with a sassy lift of one eyebrow.

He had to lower his mouth to one breast and then the other again before asking, "What else did you hear?" When she didn't answer right away, he licked at her again. "Come on, I'm dying to know."

"I can't think when you do that."

His grin grew wider. "Good." Shifting over her on the couch, he sat back so that he could reach the zippers that started just above her knees and ran up the outer length of each thigh. "God, this is hot," he said as he slid the first slowly open, baring inch after inch of her gorgeous thighs.

He could feel her trembling slightly beneath his hand, but it was clearly from arousal, not fear, so he relished it, let the edges of his fingernails scrape softly across the top of her thigh so that she actually shuddered in his hands.

How could he have done anything else but lick his way up the leg he'd just uncovered? Open on one side now, the fabric of her dress was barely covering her sex and he was a beat away from lifting it and pressing his mouth to her heat. Somehow, he managed to pull back to undo the zipper on the other side. He wasn't able to go as slow this time, could barely handle the thought that Vicki was almost naked on his couch.

With a quick yank, he grabbed the dress and slid it completely off her. When Vicki instinctively moved to cover herself, he caught her hands in his and held them over her head.

"You were completely naked under this thing." He was breathing so hard he could barely get the words out.

He was holding her hands up high enough on the couch that she had to arch a little, and in one quick move he reversed the position of their legs so that his were inside of hers and she was open to him, everywhere, all at once.

Ryan had never before seen anyone as beautiful as Vicki.

Not even close.

He knew he was staring at her like he was a teenage boy seeing his first naked girl, but in a way that was what it felt like. All the other women he'd been with fell away—the models, the movie stars, the baseball groupies—all reduced to utter insignificance.

"You should always be naked. You're perfect. Beyond perfect."

Her laughter caught him off guard. "You really do always know what to say to the girls, don't you?"

He loved it when she laughed, but not when it was at her own expense. Or his. "Are you calling me a liar?"

She gave him a look that few people ever had outside of his own family. The one that said she had no problem calling him on his crap.

"We both know I'm not perfect. Not even close." She quickly added, "And I'm okay with it, with who I am. I thought you of all people should know you don't have to say things that aren't tr—"

He closed his mouth over hers before she could say anything else to piss him off, but even lost in the heat of her, he couldn't forget the way she'd doubted what he'd said. What he believed.

What was true, damn it.

He'd show her just how perfect she was…one caress, one kiss at a time.

And he'd keep at it until she believed.

Eighteen

"Leave your hands above your head."

Vicki's eyes widened at Ryan's command, but he didn't stop to soothe her surprise or laugh like he was joking. Instead, he wrapped her fingers around the arm of the couch.

"This will help if you need something to hold on to."

A second later, his mouth was back on hers for one more kiss before he began to run kisses over her face, her eyelids, her earlobes slipping between his teeth for a split second before he drew a small moan of pleasure from her at the flick of his tongue against her neck.

Even as she relished every single second of his attention, every one of his kisses, Vicki couldn't believe it.

Not any of it.

Was she really naked beneath Ryan Sullivan?

Was he really kissing her this passionately? Had she already climaxed, fully clothed, on his couch, with another orgasm hard on the heels of the first if he kept kissing her like this?

And had he figured out the truth about her... that the slightest restraint and the gentle command spoke to all of her hidden desires?

Her ex-husband's crowd had derided her for not joining in their drug-fueled sexual explorations, but the thought of getting down and dirty with any of them had made her sick to her stomach. They'd called her a prude—her husband most of all—and she'd let them. Thank God she'd never dared bare her desires to Anthony after those first few years when he'd seemed blissfully happy just to be with her.

She tensed at the thought that she should be doing a better job of keeping her secrets from Ryan, too.

He lifted his mouth from the underside of her arm, where he was pressing soft kisses, and stared down at her, his eyes so dark with need he stole her breath away all over again.

"You just tensed up."

He was *that* in tune with her body? She'd barely stiffened, but Ryan had noticed.

"Have I done something you don't like? Am I being too rough? Do you need me to try to be gentler?"

She swallowed hard as she shook her head. "You

know just how much I'm liking everything you're doing."

God, she hated the way she kept flushing practically every time she looked at or spoke to him, but she was still trying to make sense of what they were doing. Even more, though, she hated letting her ex into this glorious moment with Ryan for even one single second.

She wouldn't let it happen again.

Turning her full focus back to her gorgeous friend, she said, "I'm guessing I'm going to start liking it even more soon."

His grin came back then, and she swore it had to be the sexiest combination in the world, those dark, intense, sex eyes with the infectious smile.

"Good guess." He stole a kiss, nipping at her lower lip hard enough to sting in the most delicious way. "What about that? Still good?"

She worked to catch her breath. "Yes. Still good."

She loved getting another smile from him, realized she would have done practically anything at that point to get more.

He moved so that his lips were on the underside of her breast. The kiss came first, and then the slight pinch of his teeth on the incredibly sensitive flesh. His tongue licked out over the small hurt before he lifted his head.

"What about that?"

"Mmm," was all she could manage as he moved to give her other breast the same delicious attention. Finally, she managed to get the word, "Good," out of her mouth.

But then, oh, God, he was moving lower, his lips kissing a path of goose bumps that turned into little licks of fire down the center of her stomach.

She wasn't embarrassed at the way she'd come against him earlier when he'd been playing with her breasts and they'd been grinding together. But she already knew that the second that wicked mouth of his made it between her legs, she wasn't going to have a prayer of holding back a second time.

What would he think of her going off again so soon? Would he think she was desperate and hard up? Or, worse, would he finally realize that sleeping with him was her number-one sexual fantasy of all time?

Sure, he'd told her he'd fantasized about her as a teenager. But she could easily discount that—everyone knew teenage boys couldn't control their hormones around any girl with a heartbeat. Plus, as his garage buddy, she'd been the only girl in school who was off-limits to him in that way. No doubt that had done funny things to his head, a classic case of thinking you wanted what you couldn't have.

No question about it, she needed to mentally prepare herself for the press of his lips against her core. Of course she was going to enjoy it. How could she not? But this time, she wouldn't let herself lose all sense.

She'd make sure she kept at least a small piece of herself secret. Private.

Another little bite of Ryan's teeth against her belly brought her out of her dark thoughts and she couldn't help but wonder if he was doing it on purpose to keep her from spinning off too long, too far, while they were together.

"If I had champagne, I'd drink it from you," he said, right before he licked a decadent path down to her belly button. "Right here." He moved lower and slightly to the side to lave her hip bone. "And just below here." With obvious intent, he moved to the other side of her hip. "Here, too."

How, she wondered helplessly as he played with her all-too-willing body, was she possibly going to make good on the silent vow she'd just made?

"Tell me, Vicki, would you like that?"

His voice was low. Raw with desire. And so damn sensual that she was practically coming apart again at nothing more than the way he was stringing words together.

"Would you want me to pour it between your breasts and make you lie still until you're all clean again with nothing but my tongue?"

Seriously, was he trying to kill her?

When she didn't answer quickly enough, he nipped at her again, this time just below her belly button.

"Yes," she gasped, "I'd like it."

She caught the flash of his smile, heard him say,

"Good, because I'd *love* it," before he lowered his head again.

All the while his mouth had been torturing her, his big, strong hands had stroked down the undersides of her arms, and then her back, before moving beneath her hips and cradling her. He turned his head and pressed his cheek against her stomach, holding her like that for several long moments.

Vicki felt beyond precious—and so incredibly safe. And then, in a split second, one small shift of his thumbs against the insides of her thighs replaced safety with a spike of arousal so intense she was almost afraid of the power of it.

A heartbeat later, his mouth was on her, and as he slicked over her with his tongue, slow and sure and so wonderful, all thoughts of fear or safety disappeared as if they'd never been there at all. She heard herself cry out as if from far, far away and her hands slipped from the couch arm as she came apart again, falling down deeper into pleasure with every pass of his tongue, with every wave that racked her, radiating from her core and over her breasts, then down her limbs to the tips of every finger, to her toes.

The pleasure was sweet and heady and she felt better than she'd ever thought possible.

A moment later, Ryan was lifting her off the couch and heading for the stairs. She wrapped her arms around him and buried her face in the crook of his neck. He smelled like sex and sweat and *Ryan*.

If she could have bottled his scent, she thought

with a sleepy satisfaction, she'd surely make mil-
lions.

"Good?"

She could hear the hint of laughter in his voice
as he quizzed her on whether she'd enjoyed herself, and she smiled back even as she licked at his
salty skin.

Oh, but he was yummy. She took another taste
before finally answering him. "Really good."

"It was really good for me, too," he told her as
he kicked open his bedroom door, laid her down on
the big bed in the middle of the room and quickly
stripped the rest of his clothes off.

For the past week, every time she'd gone to sleep
in his guest room, she'd dreamed of being here instead. Only, even in her dreams she hadn't come
close to the reality of just how gorgeous he was
completely naked.

"Great," she said without thinking, "you've just
ruined me for anyone else."

He looked down at his groin—erect in all his
aroused male glory—then back up to her with raised
eyebrows, looking far too pleased with himself.
"Good."

No, she thought, it wasn't good. It was horrible,
because after this ridiculous fantasy came to an end
and she had to rejoin the real world, she really was
screwed. And not in a good way.

She'd already been a goner for his humor. His

kindness. His talent. The way he loved his family and always put them first.

And now *this?*

If she hadn't been so darn relaxed after those two screamingly great orgasms, she would have been mad about it.

Still, he hadn't exactly launched himself at her since they'd come into his bedroom. Pushing away the slight disappointment at that fact, as a wave of exhaustion hit her while she stretched out on the bed, she told herself she was glad that the crazy fog of lust that had been clouding their brains finally seemed to be dissipating.

For one, she could speak to him normally again without all of the blushing and shyness that kept coming over her. He'd join her on the bed soon and they'd finish having sex and then she'd go back to her guest room and they'd both chalk it up to a few hours of momentary madness.

They'd end up laughing about it all in the morning, she thought with an exhausted yawn. Because if she lost him as a friend—

"Sleepy?"

The first hint that she was off base with all her assumptions of fading passion was the easiness of his voice. So dangerously easy, in fact, that the one word sent a shiver through her.

"You wore me out," she teased, trying to keep things light between them.

Didn't he understand that they needed to finish

things up in such a way that they could write it off as water under the bridge in the morning?

Besides, she wasn't the least bit tipsy anymore, so she couldn't possibly blame anything she did—or felt—from this moment forward on the alcohol.

Which meant that everything from here on out would be all her…and she simply couldn't afford to feel too much with Ryan while they were naked and kissing, above and beyond simple physical pleasure.

He took a step toward her. "I'll have to work harder on making sure you stay awake, won't I?"

For all that she wanted to act like what they were doing—and what they had already done—was no big deal, she couldn't manage to lie still and wait for him to come to her. Feeling suddenly vulnerable, she scooted back on the bed.

Ryan's hand on her ankle stopped her from moving any farther away from him.

She swallowed hard as she looked down at where he was holding her, his hand so tan against her pale skin.

He had her other ankle in his other hand a moment later and, before she could remember how to breathe, he was dragging her toward him, the soft bedcover rubbing against her naked back and bottom.

He didn't stop pulling until he had her at the edge of the mattress and had positioned them so that he was standing with his legs between hers. He pulled her legs around him, made her ankles cross behind the small of his back. The bed frame was high enough that his groin was barely higher than hers without his needing to bend his legs.

She didn't know what to reach for or how to respond. She felt lost and completely out of her element. They'd crossed a lot of lines tonight, but none of them had been *that* big, had they? Yes, she came like a rocket from his barest touch, but she was sure he was used to that kind of reaction from women.

But she'd never live down begging...most likely because he'd never let her forget that she had.

Only, the way he was looking down at her, like he owned her body and soul and was beyond pleased with that fact, had her wondering if he knew exactly what she was feeling without her having to say a word.

"This is how I want you, Vicki. Open to me. Ready for me. Always."

His eyes were dark with pleasure as he ran them over her naked body, then back up to her eyes, where she was trying so hard to keep from giving herself away.

Instinctively, she recognized his words as a command. Reminding herself that if she didn't want to follow them she could simply unwind her legs from his body and get off the bed, as he began the slow slide of his hands from her ankles up her calves and then to her thighs, she left her legs right where he'd put them.

And then he was leaning down over her, his sinfully talented mouth a press of heat on the upper swell of her breasts.

She had to touch him, had to put her hands on his chest, then over to the broad muscles of his back. She wanted to memorize every inch of him by touch alone, but her concentration was immediately shot when his erection pressed thick and hard against her belly. He gave her one kiss after another over her collarbone, and then her pulse point, before he found that spot just below her earlobe that made her shiver every time.

"Feeling more awake now?"

He didn't give her time to answer before he was covering her mouth with his. She gave herself fully over to his kiss, loving the way he devoured her and letting herself devour him right back. She tightened her ankles around his hips at the same time that he ground himself against her lower belly.

His hands were in her hair as they continued to ravage each other's mouths, and then he was shifting so that his hips were lower and—*oh, God!*—she could feel the thick, hot length of him slide over her.

She gasped at the extreme pleasure of it and he swallowed her gasp with his own groan as he slid up, then back through the slickness of her arousal.

"I want so badly to love you, Vicki."

His words were a rumble against her lips and she was so lost in desire she could hardly make sense of them. But then he lifted his head to look into her eyes. She'd never seen them so dark, so intense.

There was no trace of the laughing, easy man the rest of the world knew.

It was, she suddenly realized, just the way he'd looked when he'd come to rescue her from James. Like she was the only thing that mattered in the entire world, and he would do whatever he needed to do to protect her and keep her safe from harm.

"Tell me you want that, too."

His voice was raw with desire, but in that moment she could have sworn there was more than just lust behind his request.

"Yes, I want you," she said as she felt the muscles of his back and shoulders flexing beneath her fingers as he worked to hold himself steady over her. "You already know how much I want you."

She needed him closer, needed more than just this tease. But even though she'd just told him what she thought he wanted to hear, he hadn't moved, hadn't taken her the way she so badly needed to be taken.

He simply stroked her face with his hand, his fingertips brushing over her lips, her jawline. She shivered at the gentle, loving touch. She recognized what he was doing, knew it from the way her own hands had to caress a truly beautiful sculpture. She needed to touch it, needed to feel it beneath her hands to let the emotion of it course through her, and let herself become part of it, too.

All night long, she'd been trying to hold back something, anything. But she just couldn't do it anymore. She had to mirror his actions, had to give in to the instinctive urge to memorize him with her hands as well as she was memorizing his kisses with her mouth.

Vicki slid her hands from his shoulders to his face, and when she put her hands on him, he closed his eyes and let out a ragged breath.

Was this what he had been waiting for, for her to give herself over to him fully, completely?

She ran her hands over his face, falling deeper in love with him with every new stroke of her fingertips over stubble and bone and cartilage. All the while, his eyes were closed as he simply let her feel him.

His beauty shook her all over again, just as it had day in and day out from the first day she'd set eyes on him. But to know him like this, for him to not only let her feel him so intimately, but also to practically beg her for it, was beyond anything she'd ever hoped for.

Finally, when her hands rested on his jaw and he opened his eyes again, what she saw in them had those pleas she'd planned on holding back forever spilling from her lips.

"Love me, Ryan. Please don't wait any longer. *Please.*"

She didn't know where he got the condom from and she didn't care. All that mattered was that he had put it on and then he was kissing her again and she could feel him hot and hard and throbbing against her core.

He slid into her with a hiss of pleasure and she couldn't keep her head from falling back, her mouth opening as she gasped for breath. One stroke of Ryan's thick, hard heat inside of her and she was about to come apart again.

Her brain screamed for her to have more control. She couldn't need him so much, shouldn't be so pathetically responsive to every single touch.

Slowly, so damn slowly that she had to clench her teeth together to keep from crying out, he pulled from her before gripping her hips in his big hands and slamming back into her. She couldn't look at him, keeping her eyes tightly closed rather than daring to see the dark fire in his eyes.

She needed to keep them closed until it was over and she could pretend that what they'd shared hadn't been more than just sex between two horny friends.

His hands tightened on her hips. "Don't hide from me, Vicki."

Oh, God, why did he have to talk to her like that? Like he was in charge of every cell in her body?

And, worse, why did it have to turn her insides to goo…and make her immediately respond with even more fire and need?

Angry with herself for having less than no control around him anymore, she closed her eyes tighter. Only, she knew that wouldn't deter him from getting his way, and she was right when he leaned back over her and kissed each eyelid softly.

"Look at me. Please."

His plea undid her. Completely.

Unable to resist him for a moment longer, she looked up at him, her inner muscles clenching even tighter around him as she let his dark gaze all the way inside her heart…and her soul.

"Oh, baby," he said on a whispered groan of pleasure as he pushed in even deeper, "I love the way you come apart when I touch you, when I'm inside of you. You're so beautifully responsive. For *me*." He pulled back, then thrust forward again, causing her to grip him even tighter with her legs, her nails digging into his back in her desperation. "Let go for me while I love you. Let me see you. All of you."

Between the sweet movement of his body inside hers, his coaxing demands and the intense desire on his face, Vicki had no choice but to obey.

His mouth captured her cries as she came harder than she ever had in her life, her orgasm going on and on and on, only to have Ryan catapult her back over again as he called out her name, as he told her again and again how good she felt, how much he wanted her, until he finally let his own control go, too.

Nineteen

Vicki woke up curled into Ryan's arms, the room dark, the covers up over them. His heart beat strong and steady beneath her open palm resting on his chest. Even in sleep, she'd needed to keep her hands on him, to make sure she didn't lose that most elemental of connections.

Panic threatened to crash through the warmth, the remembered pleasures still throbbed between her legs, at the tips of her breasts and on her tingling lips. Dawn would break soon, and then they would have to face reality, cold and hard and awkward.

All she wanted was to luxuriate in her fantasy made real for a few more seconds. Vicki knew it wasn't forever, that their lovemaking had been some crazy blip on the radar screen, but letting herself be held by the man she'd loved forever, breathing him in for just a few more seconds, was something she simply had to do.

Ryan shifted, a low sound rumbling up from his chest as he pulled her closer so that her cheek rested on his chest and her hands slid around his waist.

Vicki's heart fluttered with the pleasure of the sweetest moment she'd experienced yet. Making love with Ryan had been extraordinary, but she felt this closeness way down deep in the farthest reaches of her heart.

A few more minutes. That was all she wanted with Ryan before she slipped from his arms and went back to her own bedroom. But right now it was good, so damned *good* just to be close to him.

Vicki closed her eyes and fell asleep again to the beautiful beat of Ryan's heart.

The next time she woke, she was alone in Ryan's bed, only this time she could smell bacon frying. Her stomach grumbled even as she realized that this morning wasn't like the others they'd shared.

Instead of walking out of her own bedroom fully clothed, she was going to be making the walk of shame out of his.

Hating the way her heart was pounding so hard—*It's just Ryan,* she reminded herself in a firm inner voice—she slid naked from his bed and saw that he'd laid a robe out for her. She loved the way it smelled like him as she slipped her arms into it. The sleeves were so long she had to roll them up several times, then wrap the robe nearly twice around herself before closing it. She was certain she must look ridiculous, but just then she couldn't bring herself to care.

Not when it was almost as good as being wrapped in Ryan's arms.

Besides, the only way to deal with this situation was head-on, she told herself as she opened the bedroom door and headed down the hall. And yet she still couldn't quite bring herself to walk into the kitchen. She needed a few more seconds to try to clear her head of the delicious memories of the way he'd touched and kissed and loved her the night before.

From where she was standing at the top of the stairs, she was able to watch him moving around in the kitchen below. Since he'd left his robe for her, all he had on was a pair of navy blue cotton boxers.

She. Would. Not. Drool.

Okay, so she would. She was only human.

Really, she told herself, it was no different than those shirtless pictures of him working out she'd seen in the press. She'd gotten used to looking at those without having heart palpitations. She could survive this, too.

And clearly, since Ryan was already up making breakfast rather than trying to convince her to go for another round of crazy monkey sex in the morning, he was on board with the get-right-back-to-normal plan.

Ryan looked up and saw her then, his beautiful

mouth moving into a huge smile. "Good morning, gorgeous."

Had he put extra emphasis on the word *good,* or was her mind playing games with her? Lord knew, she'd never say or hear that word quite the same ever again, after last night.

"I made your favorite."

Her heart skipped a beat and she almost missed a step, needing to grip the rail extrahard to steady herself as she realized all over again just how wonderful Ryan was.

If she'd ruined their friendship by sleeping with him she'd never, ever forgive herself.

Whatever she had to do to fix this, she'd do.

Even if it meant giving up the stunning pleasure of any and all future nights in his arms.

"Thank you," she said as she took her plate from the counter and sat at the breakfast table by the window.

"It was my pleasure."

Her entire body tingled at the way he'd just said *pleasure.* For all the warnings she'd given herself since waking up, she was way too close to throwing herself at him and begging him for more of that pleasure. And all the while, he was going about his regular business in the kitchen, turning down the gas burner before he plated more eggs and bacon and toast.

How many times when they were kids, and then

this week, had she watched women throw themselves at Ryan?

He was always kind, even when he was taking advantage of his allure—and especially when he wasn't—but Vicki knew she'd never be able to look herself in the eye if she became one of those women.

Worse, she couldn't stand the idea of Ryan worrying about how to let her down easy.

She waited until he slid into the seat beside hers before planting a smile on her face and saying, "Last night sure was weird, wasn't it?"

Ryan felt everything go still.

Especially his heart.

When he'd looked up to see Vicki standing at the top of the stairs in his robe, swallowed up by the thick blue fabric, he'd been so full of love he'd almost called it out to her right then. But he'd thought there'd be time for that soon, that he could at least let her eat breakfast first before he took her back to bed and opened his heart up to her completely.

"Weird?"

Vicki nodded before taking a large gulp from the coffee cup he'd placed in front of her, then swore. "Ow, that's hot!"

He automatically got up to fill a glass of cold water for her, but his limbs felt strange. Robotic. As if he was only just learning to use them. He handed her the glass and she thanked him as she took it.

He watched the lines of her throat as she closed her eyes and swallowed.

He swallowed hard, too, as he sat back down at the table. He'd been starving when he woke up— great sex always revved up his metabolism—but now it felt like a heavy weight had descended into his hollow gut, pushing out any room for food.

Vicki put the empty glass down. "You're always my knight in shining armor."

She smiled at him, but he'd learned to recognize that smile over the past few days. While it looked real to the naked eye, it was far from it. He didn't know what the hell was going on here, but he was damn well going to find out.

"What's wrong, Vicki?"

She shook her head. "Nothing." Again came the smile that wasn't really a smile. "I just want *you* to know that *I* know last night didn't mean anything."

Again, his heart stopped beating. Right there, with one final thud beneath his breastbone, any doctor worth his salt would have declared Ryan dead.

The night they'd shared had meant *everything*.

He'd begged her to let him love her. And he'd thought she understood that being together was about so much more than just their bodies coming together and finding pleasure.

How the hell had he been so wrong?

In his stunned silence, she continued, "I mean, the sex was really good and everything—" she flushed at the word *good* "—but we both know it was just one of those things that happens when an available man and woman are around each other a lot, you know?" She didn't wait for him to agree or disagree before adding, "And with trying to convince everyone all the time that we're really together, it was inevitable that we'd forget for a little while it was just pretend, and have sex." She reached for the coffee again. "Just to take the edge off, and all."

She put the mug to her lips again, but this time she was careful not to burn herself.

Ryan didn't know what the hell he was supposed to say. He couldn't imagine not touching her naked skin again, not being able to kiss the pulse that throbbed so fast just below her chin, not feeling her buck and cry out beneath him as he filled her.

Everything he'd thought he'd gained in those sweet, dark, perfect hours with Vicki in his arms had just been yanked from him so swiftly and abruptly that he could almost taste the loss of her on his tongue.

But even as he felt that loss, he knew there was only one thing that could be worse than losing the lover who had made him forget any other.

Losing his best friend would be the worst of all.

Which meant that if Vicki thought she'd made a mistake by sleeping with him—and if he didn't want to lose her as a friend, too—he had to agree.

"So," she asked in a voice that trembled so

slightly only someone utterly attuned to her the way he was would have heard it, "are we still okay?"

It was the anguish in her eyes that got him to force the words, "Of course we are," up through his throat and past his lips.

She paled at his totally unconvincing reply and when she said, "Ryan?" in an even shakier voice he didn't think before reaching for her.

Even as he pulled her onto his lap and buried his face in her hair to breathe her in, he knew he needed to be a hell of lot more convincing, instead of sounding like a lovesick fool who had just been dumped by the girl of his dreams.

Reminding himself that he'd already fulfilled so many more fantasies with her than he'd ever dreamed he would—and that he was going to have to be satisfied with that—he stroked her hair and pulled her closer to his chest.

Working like hell to ignore the way her curves fit against him so perfectly, and the fact that the robe was gaping open over her naked breasts while one beautiful thigh was bared at the front opening of the fabric, he said, "We've always been friends, Vicki, and we always will be."

He felt her nod against his chest as he stroked her back and shoulders. He knew he shouldn't keep giving in to the need to touch her like this, but if this was going to be the last time, then how could he help himself?

With his other hand, he tipped up her head so

that they had to look at each other and get past this. And make sure their friendship was safe.

"We had sex and it was great, but we're both adults."

She nodded again, but she still looked too serious. Too worried. It was going to kill him to do this, but for Vicki he'd bury what was in his heart and play it easy for her. Simply because she needed him to do it to make her feel better.

"Just one thing I was hoping you'd promise me. As you probably know, rumor has it I'm pretty impressive." He raised his eyebrows at her and lowered his voice, "Don't tell anyone the truth, okay?"

"The truth?" Her laughter was the sweetest sound she'd ever heard. She shook her head before saying, "Trust me, the truth would make it hard for you to get out of your front door unaccosted ever again."

A moment later she was sliding from his lap and back onto her seat. She picked up a piece of bacon and popped it into her mouth. "What's it like being so good at everything? Cooking. Baseball." She shot him a wicked glance that had his blood pressure spiking. "Sex." She finished the bacon with a lusty sigh of appreciation that was way too close to the sounds she'd made in his bed for him to keep from sweating as he sat next to her. "Truly, it must be exhausting."

"I'm bad at some things."

She raised an eyebrow. "Name one thing."

Making you fall in love with me the way I've al-

*ways been in love with you. You only ever saw the
jock while you let those artist assholes chase you.
And hurt you.*

"Making a clay pot."

She laughed, but shook her head. "You'd get
there with practice."

"Okay, then, I'm a shitty outfielder."

She pointed her fork at him. "Bull. Remember
that game in high school when they played you in
center field? Hate to break it to you, but you were
great."

The word *great* from her lips instantly brought
back the night they'd just spent together, and as
their eyes met and held he was *this close* to chuck-
ing it all in and pulling her back onto his lap so that
he could kiss her and touch her and love her again.

Only, just as he was about to draw her back into
his arms, Vicki gave the barest shake of her head,
so small that he wasn't sure she even knew she'd
done it.

But he heard what she wasn't saying out loud as
if she'd screamed it at him.

No.

"So how'd it go last night?"

Vicki nearly jumped out of her skin at Anne's
question as she finished putting the little sculptures
she'd just made for Summer's birthday party into
the kiln in her studio.

She'd hit a snag on her still-unnamed fellowship

project and had put it away for a few hours to try to sketch herself out of the hole she was in. But when the sketching didn't work, either, she realized she had to face facts.

After what had happened last night with Ryan—what amounted to the most beautiful, stunning, mind-blowing lovemaking of her life—she simply couldn't get her brain to focus on work. On top of that, she was incredibly nervous about going to a family party, even more now that their fake engagement had morphed into an accidental night of sizzling-hot sex.

She could have gone to a toy store to buy Summer a standard gift, but she knew it would make her feel better to get her hands in clay and make one. Evidently the little girl had just gotten a new poodle puppy from Zach's girlfriend, Heather, and was head over heels for it.

After Vicki had made a really fun poodle out of the clay, she decided to make a pretty oak tree for Mary Sullivan, and then when she was done with that, she'd tackled a well-read hardback book in clay for Sophie to put in the library. Vicki had been working with such serious intent for such a long stretch on her fellowship project that she'd been almost giddy from the pleasure of making the cute and funny sculptures.

She barely noticed the sun falling lower in the sky as she moved from one little project to another. What fun it was to have a big family to make things for. She wouldn't have time to make a wine bottle for Marcus or a pair of ballet shoes for Lori, though. Next time.

Her hands had stilled on the book spine she'd been pressing into the clay with her fingertips.

Next time.

What on earth made her think there was going to be a next time?

Pretty soon, she'd be moving out of Ryan's house. She hoped she and Ryan would be able to find time to get together to catch up on life on a regular basis, of course, but once she was no longer living at his house, the two of them would be going their separate ways.

Anne's question had startled her out of her somewhat depressing musings and brought her right back around to the previous night.

And all the amazing sex she'd had with Ryan.

"Everyone loved the dress. Of course you knew they would. It's an awesome dress."

Anne's smile was wicked…and pleased. "Awesome, huh?" She raised her eyebrows. "Dare I hope my awesome dress ended up in shreds in your gorgeous man's bedroom?"

Vicki automatically started to shake her head, but quickly realized there was no point in trying to pretend it hadn't been the most glorious night of her life. Especially with the engagement ring Ryan had given her hanging between her breasts on the gold chain.

It had been a long time since she'd had another woman to confide in. Justifying it by telling herself that Anne's knowing only gave more credence to the false engagement, Vicki pulled the ring out from under her tank top. "He gave me this."

Anne's eyes went wide as she grabbed it, inadvertently pulling Vicki forward while she inspected the ring. "He has great taste. Are you free tonight for a bottle or two of champagne? And could he bring a few of his gorgeous baseball-playing friends?"

"I'd really love to," Vicki said, "but I've promised Ryan I'll go to a family birthday party with him tonight."

Anne clapped her hands together. "Even better— you can wear another one of my dresses. Who needs this fellowship when I have you to wear all my clothes?"

She had pulled Vicki halfway down the hall by the time Vicki could get out the words, "I don't know if that's such a good idea."

Anne put her hands on her hips. "Why? You were stunning last night. And clearly, the dress made an impression on your man."

But that was just the problem. Ryan had *loved* the dress…and he'd loved stripping it off her even more. Vicki's body started heating up all over just thinking about it.

If she wore another one of Anne's brilliantly sexy designs, he might think she was trying to say that she wanted a repeat of last night. Which, of course, she did, because how could anyone *not* want that?

But God, this morning had been awkward enough.

Last night had been an accident. A sexual slip-up. Two bodies in motion colliding without premeditated intent.

She couldn't imagine how awkward it would be if he thought she was actually trying to seduce him this time. Instead of letting her down easy, he'd be forced to take much more drastic—and obvious—steps.

But since she couldn't say any of that to her out-of-the-big-lie-loop friend, Vicki grabbed on to the only excuse she could think of. "The party is for an eight-year-old. I'm sure everyone will be wearing jeans."

"Or pretty little sundresses," Anne shot back. "A couple days ago I didn't know why I was so compelled to make this dress, since I can't use it for the fellowship. Now I know. It's my engagement gift to you."

With that, Vicki knew she had no choice. She let Anne drag her into her own studio and hand her a pretty summer dress made of dozens of light and colorful layers.

And, despite knowing better, she couldn't help wanting to knock Ryan's socks off one more time.

Twenty

Ryan stood in his brother Gabe's living room surrounded by his family, a big group of strangers and a dozen rambunctious eight-year-olds. And yet all he could see was Vicki.

Summer had just barreled into Vicki's waist to give her a huge hug. Clearly, the eight-year-old girl loved the poodle sculpture Vicki had made her. She'd surprised Sophie and his mother with fun little sculptures as well, and he knew they wouldn't stop gushing over the unexpected gifts for a very long time.

As she chatted animatedly with Summer, there was nothing fake, nothing affected, about Vicki, not from her soft hair to her unpainted fingernails to the sweet curves that had transfixed him since he was a teenager. To make matters worse for the hard-on he was working like hell to hold at bay, she was wearing another pretty dress that simultaneously hid and showcased her incredible figure as the breeze played through the fabric.

Ryan's chest squeezed tight at her beauty.

Smith handed him a beer. "Some pretty big bets were going down today in the production offices for the play-off games. You ready to make us all some money?"

Ryan took a slug from the bottle, his eyes never leaving Vicki. "I'll do my best."

Instead of taking the hint that he wasn't up for shooting the breeze tonight, Smith kept right on talking. "I enjoyed the shaking down we did today for your school sports fund. Kind of nice to be on the other side of the demanding, for once. Ever feel like everyone just wants something from you?"

Depending on his mood, Smith could be disturbingly blunt…or as opaque as it got. Clearly, he was in one of his deep—and talkative—moods.

"Well," Ryan drawled, "considering my brother just told me to pitch a no-hitter so he wins his money back on a bet, yeah, I guess I do know how that feels."

"You're lucky to have her, you know."

Ryan finally shot Smith a look to see what he was playing at. "Vicki?"

"You've been friends since you were kids, so you know she's not hanging around because of what you could do for her, or for the fame that comes with being your fiancée."

"She's not my—"

"Right." The one word was loaded. "Funny how the way the two of you look at and touch each other makes it hard for any of us to remember that it's all just a lie."

Ryan's teeth clenched at the way his brother had just pointed out the obvious. He couldn't keep from wanting Vicki. Loving her. Not even when she'd all but asked him to do just that this morning when she'd called their night together "weird" and then said her silent no to ever being intimate like that again.

Frustration had him lashing out at a brother who didn't deserve it. "Not everyone is as good an actor as you are."

Smith gave him a hard look. "Then maybe you should quit trying so hard to pretend."

Finally, his brother left him alone again and Ryan's gaze immediately went back to Vicki.

All day he'd been turning their situation over and over in his head. Yes, he knew she thought making love had been a mistake. A *weird* mistake. But he hadn't forgotten the way she'd responded to his touch...and that there hadn't been one single weird thing about the way she'd arched and cried out against him and begged for more.

The thing was, even before he'd known just how amazing it was to make love to her, Ryan had wanted more.

Everything.

He wanted everything.

Not just to give Vicki his heart, but to know that she wanted to give hers to him, too.

Ryan hadn't had to fight for much in his life. School, sports, friends, women—they'd all come easily. Even his friendship with Vicki had always been natural, comfortable—easy—right from the start.

But he wasn't satisfied with friendship anymore.

Not when he wanted what his parents had shared.

Not when he wanted what his brothers and sisters were finding for themselves, one after the other.

And not when he held Chase's baby daughter, Emma, in his arms and wondered what his and Vicki's children would look like.

All her life, Vicki had kept reaching, kept believing, kept trying to turn her most passionate dreams into reality.

Now it was finally his turn to reach. To believe. And to try.

Ryan Sullivan had finally found something that mattered enough to fight for.

Love.

"I'm so glad you could come to Summer's party," Mary Sullivan said when Vicki joined her on the patio.

"You know how much I love spending time with your family. And Emma is positively gorgeous." Zach and Heather's dogs had clearly adopted the baby as they flanked her pink-and-purple vibrating baby seat. A moment later, Jake helped Sophie up from the nearby couch, her belly looking even bigger than it had just a day ago. "And I'm so glad things worked out so well for Sophie and Jake."

Summer's grandmother, who had flown out from Minneapolis for Summer's birthday party, smiled and said, "Congratulations on your engagement."

Vicki worked to smile back and say, "Thank you," without faltering. Thank God Mary already knew the truth, or she would have felt even worse about the situation than she already did.

The other woman turned to Mary. "You must be so thrilled to know that another one of your children has found *the one*."

Mary put her arm around Vicki and didn't miss a beat in the game of pretend they were playing. "I couldn't be happier for Vicki and Ryan. He had such a crush on her when they were in school together. It was amazing for me to see him be so serious about a girl when he'd always been so relaxed about them all before."

Wow, Vicki thought, now she knew where Smith got his acting chops.

Mary turned to her and added, "The night he went over to ask you to the prom and found out you had already agreed to go with someone else... Well, it just about broke my heart to see him like that."

Forgetting they were supposed to be pretending, Vicki blurted, "He was going to ask me to the sophomore prom?"

Summer's grandmother cut in to ask, "He never told you?"

Vicki shook her head, wondering if Mary could have made that up. "No. He never told me."

At her unspoken question, Ryan's mother patted her arm and nodded. "It's true, Vicki. He really did go to ask you to the prom. I know how worried he was about doing something that might ruin your friendship. Asking you to that dance was going to be his big risk. Unfortunately, he never got to take it." Mary's eyes held hers. "Until now."

Summer's grandmother was saying something about romantic love stories and long-lost high school sweethearts, but Vicki could barely keep track of it. Fortunately, Mary seemed to understand that she needed to be left alone with her thoughts.

Vicki had been so careful to keep herself from getting hurt every step of the way with Ryan this past week. But as she watched Ryan pick up Emma and give her kisses all over her face that had the baby nuzzling even closer to him, Vicki suddenly wondered if what she'd thought had been so smart had actually been blindingly stupid instead.

As they drove through the city back to Ryan's house, Vicki was as nervous as she'd ever been. Ryan was strangely silent, which was okay, since she couldn't have made small talk if her life had depended on it.

Oh, God, she couldn't believe what she was

thinking of doing—that she was actually toying with the idea of confessing her feelings to him after all these years. Because, last evening, after her body had given away far more than she'd ever planned while in his arms, it was still possible to write that off as "just sex."

But once she'd crossed the "I like you as more than a friend" line with actual words, there was no taking them back...or trying to attribute them to one crazy night.

At the beginning of this week, for her own good, she'd made a vow to be calm and rational rather than too passionate. Okay, so she'd blown it last night. But clearly, if she wanted it, there could be tons more passion and way less calm and rational in her future.

But was the greatest sex in the world worth risking her heart and her friendship with Ryan?

When they finally arrived home, they walked inside and she put her things down on his kitchen counter, the same way she had so many nights before that week. Only, tonight everything felt different.

Different enough that she suddenly blurted, "You were going to ask me to the prom?"

"I had it bad for you even then."

Slowly, she turned to face him. He stared at her and she stared back. Time stood still as she tried to read what was in his eyes.

"Ryan?" His name on her lips made them tingle. Made her want. Desperately.

"It won't be weird this time."

Vicki's heart was pounding so hard she could barely hear her own voice over it.

"Promise?"

"I promise."

Just that quickly, the fire that had been sparking and kindling between them all night long finally burst into flames as he cupped her hips and pulled her tightly against him, her palms grazing his jaw as she moved to thread her fingers into his hair.

Their mouths licked, sucked and even bit at each other as they made it over to the couch. Vicki clenched Ryan's shirt in her fist and pulled him down, her core clenching with heat as he moved his heavy weight over her.

They'd gone so slow their first time, needing that pace to feed their discovery of each other. But she wouldn't survive that tonight, not when she was already this desperate for him to take her, to make her his again.

The buttons of his dress shirt flew in every direction as she ripped open his shirt and pressed hungry kisses on his chest. She flicked her tongue over him and he groaned her name into her hair even as he yanked her dress off her shoulders.

She loved how rough his hands were as he shoved the fabric down off her chest, her hips and then her legs.

He pulled back to take in her nakedness. "I don't think I'll ever get over how good you look lying naked here on my couch." A moment later, his arms were lifting her and he was saying, "I can't wait to see how you look in my shower."

He kissed her all the way up the stairs and down the hall past the guest bedroom to his own bedroom. Her heart pounded as much from the arousal he so effortlessly built in her as it did from knowing she was going to be in the shower with him soon.

Quick and dirty sex on his couch would have been so much easier to write off as another crazy impulse.

But he didn't even bother to do more than kick off his shoes and then slide hers off, too, before walking into the huge, glass-enclosed shower with her still in his arms. He turned on the water. She knew in that moment that he was doing exactly what she'd been trying to avoid—simply following his impulses.

Thank God.

He moved them so that he could watch the warm water pulse and flow over her chest, and then lowered his head to her breasts. As his mouth covered one taut tip, she held on to his neck even as the sweet pleasure coursed through every cell in her body.

His skin was getting wet and so were her hands, but before she could slip, he put her back down on her feet and pressed her up against one tiled wall.

He pressed her legs wide open with his, and took her hands in his to hold them up against the tiles on either side of her head.

She felt owned.

Possessed.

Utterly, completely claimed by the heat in his eyes as his gaze ran down her body, then back up to her face.

"Every fantasy, Vicki." His words were raw. And so low she could barely hear them over the spray. "You're every single fantasy I've ever had."

Her breath came fast as she let herself look at him, too. His chest was tanned and beautifully muscled. His wet button-down shirt clung to his shoulders and arm muscles in a shockingly sexy way. Not to mention the way his jeans cupped his enormous erection and clung to his taut thigh muscles.

"You are, too," she whispered, barely getting the words out before he captured her mouth in a kiss so searing the water could have been cold and she would still have been warm.

"You have no idea how many dirty things I want to do with you right now."

The warmth coiled down low in her belly let go at his heated words. She was already risking so much with Ryan tonight.

Why not one more thing?

"Good thing we're already in a shower, then."

His eyes lit at the realization that she'd just given him permission to do whatever he wanted with her, and then his mouth covered hers again for a brief, intense kiss.

He let go of her hands to cup her breasts and she threaded her hands into his wet hair to hold him there against her as he laved and sucked and nipped at her sensitive flesh.

"God, I love your breasts," he murmured against her chest as he moved to taste the other one.

They'd always been big, ever since puberty, and more than once she'd wished she didn't have to deal with them. But right in that moment, she'd never been so happy for her abundant flesh, if only because it meant more kisses from Ryan across every inch of them.

"You have no idea how many nights I dreamed of doing this when we were in high school."

She could barely catch her breath enough to ask, "How many?"

"All of them."

His thumbs and forefingers moved to replace his mouth as he kissed his way down her stomach. He dropped to his knees in front of her. Vicki's legs trembled as he moved lower and lower to where she was so wet, so ready for him, that the barest touch was going to send her over.

But instead of pressing his mouth to her, he pulled back and just stared at the wet curls between her legs. His hands moved from her breasts to grip her inner thighs and open her more to him.

He'd gone down on her the night before, but

being in the shower like this as he stared at her really did feel dirty...in the best possible sense of the word.

She could still hardly believe that it was Ryan between her naked legs, the best-looking man in the world kneeling in front of her, ready to worship her with his mouth and hands.

"Gorgeous." He pressed a soft kiss to her curls. "Absolutely gorgeous." He slid two fingers into her and groaned the words, "So wet. And hot."

As Vicki's inner muscles automatically clenched around him, he dragged his fingers from her, then pushed them back in.

"You're going to come for me, aren't you?"

Oh, yes, that was exactly what she was going to do for him.

She bucked into his hand and then his mouth as his tongue found her. Her cries of pleasure bounced around the shower walls as he pushed her harder, higher, until she was a trembling, postclimactic mess.

Ryan grasped her hands in his again and, before she could get her synapses to fire, he had her turned around and shifted so that her hands were flat on a tiled ledge that held his soap and shampoo.

He held his hands over hers and braced her hips with his. "Are you steady enough to stay like that on your own while I get my clothes off?"

Oh, God.

"Yes." Barely.

He ran his hands all the way up her arms and then down her back to the flare of her hips before he stopped. "Your ass is a goddamned miracle."

She wished she had the kind of experience with men and sex to answer him in a flirtatious way, but her earlier quip about being in the shower seemed to be the full extent of her sexy repartee. Especially when he palmed her cheeks and squeezed them.

A gasp of pleasure fell from her lips as he sparked her desire anew with shocking ease, the fingers of one hand slipping into her again as he undid his pants with the other.

And then his hand was gone and he was pressing up and into her on a groan, his hands coming around to cup and squeeze her breasts as she gripped the tiled shelf.

"Hold on tight," he growled.

His command barely pierced the fog of lust and pleasure in her head before he was pounding into her hard, fast and so deep. His hands moved from her breasts to her hips, gripping her so possessively, so perfectly, that she had no choice but to succumb to feeling him everywhere…and loving every single second of being completely under his power.

Somewhere way down deep it felt as if she'd been made with these curves just so Ryan could hold on to them when he was taking her, sending her to the edge again with his fierce lovemaking.

"Again, Vicki. I need to feel you come around me."

His deliciously dirty words were the final push

she needed to catapult up, up, up, and then as her forehead dropped onto the tile between her hands, she was pushing back against him at least as hard as he was into her, giving him exactly what he'd just demanded.

With every clench of her inner muscles around him, he grew harder, thicker, until he suddenly pulled out, one hand moving between her legs to squeeze out the final tremors of her climax even as he worked himself in his other hand.

Utterly lost in their dirty-sex shower world, Vicki didn't think before turning and moving to her knees in front of him to take him into her hands and mouth.

She barely heard his groan through the pounding of blood in her ears. For the first time in her life she understood the thrill of tasting a man like this, the arousal that pumped onto her tongue with every stroke of her hand around him, the sweet rapture of knowing she was giving him as much pleasure as he'd just given her. Twice, already.

She wanted to see his face when he came, but when she looked up through her lashes at him, she was surprised to see him staring back down at her in wonder.

And then he was down on his knees with her on the shower floor and his mouth was on hers, the taste of both of them merging until she couldn't tell one from the other. She was just about to climb over him when he abruptly pulled back and cursed.

"I need a condom."

He gripped both of her hands and pulled her dripping wet from the shower, and across the bathroom floor to his bed. He was so strong—and so worked up—that he all but threw her down on the covers to wait for him as he yanked open his bedside drawer, found a condom and ripped it open.

She couldn't wait for him to get it on, and their hands tangled together on his hard heat as they slid the latex down. And then his hands were on her breasts again and his mouth was on hers as he was pushing her back onto the bed and shoving her legs open to push inside of her.

The sweet force of his desire for her—and hers for him—had her losing her breath again. She arched away from his mouth to throw her head back and gasp for air as she circled his hips with her legs and gripped his neck and shoulders. And, oh, was she glad for her strong sculptor's hands as they rode each other hard, Ryan finally cresting the edge he'd been coming to again and again, while Vicki erupted one more beautiful time beneath her best friend.

Twenty-One

The lights were still on in Ryan's bedroom, the sky dark outside his window, when Vicki woke in his arms a while later. As soon as she shifted, he spoke.

"I wore you out."

He effortlessly maneuvered her so that she was lying flat on her back and he was leveraged on his right arm looking down at her. Looking so pleased with himself.... She couldn't resist smiling at him.

"You did. Three times, actually."

He grinned back at her and for a moment it was as if nothing had changed and they were just two friends who enjoyed each other's company.

Only, that wasn't even the slightest bit true.

Because everything had changed.

Everything.

As the smile fell from her lips, Ryan's expression grew serious, too.

"Don't tell me it was weird again, Vicki. Not when we both know it was anything but."

She hated knowing she'd hurt him this morning by stupidly blurting out that dumb word. "No, it wasn't *weird.* It was great. Last night was great, too. But—"

He stopped her with a kiss. One that was just as sweet as it was sinful.

"I'm going to let you finish saying what you have to say so that you can get every single one of those *buts* out of your system." He stared down at her, his eyes dark with intense emotion. "And then you're going to listen to what *I* have to say. So go ahead. Get it all out."

In the wake of his kiss—and the press of his hard muscles over her—she had to work really, *really* hard to ignore the fact that she and Ryan were completely naked in his bed. The problem was, she knew he was right, that if she didn't give voice to all of her worries now, the next time they ended up in bed together, things would only become more confusing between them.

"I know you would never hurt me, Ryan. Not on purpose, anyway. And I would never want to hurt you, either. But—" she paused, hating what came next "—I just don't see how this can end any way but badly when I'm made for the long term and you're not."

A tic jumped in his jaw as he stared down at her. "How can you say I'm not made for the long term?"

"How long has your longest relationship been?"

"A few months." His gaze softened as he added, "But none of them were you, Vicki."

His sweet words warmed her. Of course they did. But she still had to ask, "And how many women have you been with?"

Something flashed in his eyes and it looked a heck of a lot like remorse. "I've already told you that none of them mattered to me. You're the only one who has ever meant anything to me."

The twisting of her stomach at the thought of all those women had her nodding. "You're right, I don't want—or need—to know the number." Besides, if she extrapolated from their one year together in high school, she could make a pretty good guess.

"I don't see what my past has to do with our future."

"Here's what—you've been with lots of women whom you freely admit didn't matter. I've never done that." Vicki lifted her chin and met his gaze squarely. "In my entire life, I've been with two men."

She could read the shock on his face, loud and clear. "Hold on a second. You were a virgin when you met your husband?"

She didn't want to be embarrassed about her choices. Not when they'd felt like the right ones at the time.

"I wasn't a total prude during college. I'd fooled around with a handful of guys, but I couldn't justify sleeping with them when I knew I wouldn't be with them past the next semester."

Besides, none of them had made her insides turn to goo or made her heart flutter in her chest the way she'd hoped they would.

Precisely the way Ryan did.

"I can't believe your bastard ex-husband got to be your first."

She could see how jealous he was about it. It shouldn't have made her feel good, but it did.

She gave him a wry smile. "He loved it, of course. I think it made him feel like the conquering hero. You know, going where no man had gone before and all that. And, stupidly, I thought we were going to be together forever. Maybe if I had stayed twenty-two, it would have worked out, but I had to grow up at some point. Everything changed once I wasn't that impressionable, starstruck girl anymore." And still she'd hung on, hoping that they could work things out, hoping that she didn't have to end up a failure at love, too.

"I'm not like that, Vicki. I'm not like him."

"I know." She had to smile at Ryan as she brushed her hand lightly over his stubbly chin. "That's one of the reasons I allowed myself to sleep with you. Not just because my hormones were taking over, but because I trust you."

"Then keep trusting me when I say that I've wanted to be with you since we were fifteen. Even before you saved me from that car, I wanted you,

Vicki. All those stories I've told these past few days about trying to get you to notice me and losing you to another man were true."

"I love hearing you say all that, so much so you wouldn't believe it. But even though I've only been with two men, I've seen enough to understand that wanting rarely becomes more than that."

"What about the fact that since you've been back, everything's been better?"

"I guess that's something," she admitted in a cautious voice.

"It's a hell of a lot more than *something*. Vicki, I want you to give me a chance. I want to be your boyfriend. I want you to be my girlfriend. I want you to stop assuming that I'll be wanting out in a few weeks. Vicki, our relationship is *real*. I want you to believe that."

"It all sounds so good," she said slowly.

"It will be good. I promise."

His confidence was one of the things she'd always loved about him. But life had never come as easily to her as it had to him. Not even close.

She needed to be realistic…and make sure that what they were doing didn't end up ripping away one of the most important people in her life.

"What if it doesn't work out? What if all we're feeling is the rush of new excitement at finally getting to be more than friends?"

"I've had it bad for you for fifteen years. My feelings have never gone away. They've only grown bigger, stronger with every year we were apart. And every time I look at you, every time I touch you, you're even more beautiful than you were just seconds ago. Now that we've gotten horizontal—and vertical—a couple times, I'm pretty sure you've wanted it, too. We've waited half our lives for this chance to be together. Do you really think we're going to blow it now?"

She wanted so badly to believe that they wouldn't. But she'd been down that road before; she had followed her passions, and she'd been wrong.

She had to be pragmatic for once. Practical. Especially now when so much was at stake.

"Of course I don't think either of us would go into a relationship planning to screw it up. I just need to know— If dating doesn't work out, will we still be friends? Or will it be too strange, too hard, too awkward, to see each other all the time?"

Especially if it turned out that she wasn't enough for Ryan Sullivan after all.

He blew out a hard breath. "You keep saying that I'm not a forever kind of guy, but you're the one who keeps talking about things ending."

She was surprised to recognize the truth in what he said. He was right.

"I'm just scared that we'll make a mistake we can't recover from. Where we are right now, I think we can probably still step back and be okay. But if we go further and if it all goes wrong?"

"What if I told you that I see us together forty

years from now, with kids and grandkids and you with clay under your fingernails and me coaching the Little League team down the street? And what if I told you that I'm in l—"

She jumped to press her fingers against his mouth. She tried to catch her breath at the fairy tale he was painting for her. It was the very same one she wanted more and more with every passing year. A future full of kids and grandkids wrapped up in a close-knit family who loved and laughed and fought as a unit.

Of course she wanted him to love her back, but she couldn't bear to hear him say it after they'd just had such great sex. Not if she'd always be afraid that was the only reason he'd said it.

"I think this is a good time to remind you that after spending more than a decade on different continents, we've only spent a week together and had sex twice."

He pressed a kiss to her fingertips before sliding his fingers through hers and lowering their hands. "True, but it's been really awesome sex."

His sudden grin reminded her so much of the boy she'd first fallen for so many years ago. She laughed despite the serious tone of their conversation.

And then he put her hand palm down on his chest and her laughter and his grin both fell completely away.

It was testament to just how well he knew her that he understood that when words were failing, the only surefire path to get to her emotions was through her hands.

"Be with me, Vicki. For real this time. And let me convince you that you'll never need to know the answers to those questions."

Vicki's vows to herself to be cautious were slipping away. His dark eyes and the strong, steady beat of his heart beneath her hands told her that she was mere clay in *his* hands.

"I want to be with you, too," she said softly. "But even though we started out things in reverse, I think we need to take it slow. Just to be sure that we don't mess everything up."

"Slow, huh?" Her heart dropped when he frowned. "I don't know if I can promise to go slow with you in bed."

Relief flooded her. "Don't be stupid." She grabbed another condom out of the side table, then pushed him down on the bed and straddled him. "Hot, fast and *dirty* sex is grandfathered into this discussion."

He grinned at her even as he pulled her mouth down to his. "Then what do you say we have a quickie before I ask you out on our first official date?"

Moments later she was answering him by sinking down onto his hard heat. For the next few minutes she let the sweet press of his mouth against hers, the rough caress of his needy hands over her skin push

away her doubts, her fears…and the sure knowledge that nothing had ever come easy to her before.

Especially not love.

Twenty-Two

Ryan paced around his house all day, unsettled, expectant…and nervous. He had waited fifteen years for his first real date with Vicki and now it was going to happen as soon as she arrived home from the studio.

The past year had been a master's course in love as he'd watched his brothers and sisters fall one after the other. Regardless of how much he'd razzed each one of them along the way, he'd paid close attention to their soul-deep emotional connections, to the humor they shared…and to the sparks that lit and crackled like firecrackers between them.

Maybe it was too much to want a first date to do all those things. After all, until now he'd been happy with dinner and a movie and uncomplicated sex. But there was no point comparing Vicki to any of the other women he'd dated.

And yet Ryan knew that even if he pulled off the

best first date in history, it didn't mean his work was done as far as Vicki's heart was concerned.

Because she hadn't let him say he loved her.

He understood that she'd been hurt badly by the only other man she'd ever allowed herself to trust. He knew she was wary of taking the leap again with him. But the difference was that he would never hurt her.

Never.

By the time Vicki walked through his front door and smiled with obvious pleasure at seeing him, he was *way* past the first date they hadn't even had yet.

Fortunately, he had the presence of mind to know that doing her up against the front door couldn't possibly be construed as perfect first-date plans.

Just like blurting out "I love you" wasn't going to fly, either.

"How was your day?"

She looked radiant as she walked into the kitchen and dropped her bag on the counter. "Amazing. My project really started to come together today, in a really big way. Thank God."

How was he supposed to control himself when she was glowing like that?

He put his arms on either side of her shoulders, effectively trapping her against the kitchen island. "I can't wait to see it." He lowered his mouth to hers and said, "I couldn't wait to see you, either," before kissing her softly, forcing himself to remain gentle rather than giving in to the nearly overpowering urge to lift her up on the counter and take her right then and there.

"What about you?" she asked when he let her up for air. "How was your day?"

"Life is good." She was so soft and sweet against him that he could hardly remember what he'd done all day. "Smith helped me convince a bunch more filthy-rich people to part with some of their fortunes by giving schools the money for sports programs. I don't know why I didn't think to pull him in before now."

She grinned. "I can only imagine the two of you together. Those poor billionaires didn't stand a chance, did they?"

Did she have any idea how pretty her mouth was when she was smiling at him?

"Are you ready for our date?"

She moved her hands around his back and pulled him closer. "Almost."

"Is there—" He had to clear his throat to push past his lust. "Is there something you need to do first?"

"Yes." She went up on her tiptoes. "More of this."

Her mouth had barely touched his when he had her up on the marble counter, a fistful of cotton fabric in his hands. "You said you wanted to go slow. We can do this date without sex, Vicki."

Ryan couldn't believe he was saying this. The thought of walking away from all her heat, her sweetness, was almost unbearable. But he didn't want her to have a single reason not to go out on the date with him. He couldn't let her think all he wanted her for was sex.

"If you need me to control myself," he promised, "I'll find a way to do it."

"I guess that means you're a stronger person than I am," she said as she took his shirt in her hands and yanked it over his head. "Because there's no way I can wait for the date to be over to have you."

She took his face in her hands to kiss him again, but even though there was nothing in the world he wanted more, Ryan had to make absolutely sure she wouldn't use their predate sex as a reason to back away from him later.

"You and me, we're about more than great sex."

She licked at his lips. "Of course we are. But the sex is a really fantastic bonus, don't you think?"

He had to kiss her again once, then twice, before saying, "The best bonus in the world."

An hour later, they were walking hand in hand onto the same wetland path they'd walked so many times before as teenagers.

"I can't believe you brought me back here." She squeezed his hand tighter as she pulled him toward the water, murky green as it slowly flowed along the peninsula south of the city. "Ready for the plunge?"

Side by side, they squatted down on the muddy

edge to stick their hands underwater. Vicki looked down at their hands just under the surface, then back at him.

"This is a really lovely first date. Thank you."

"Even the part where I tore off your clothes the second you walked in the front door?"

She shot him a wicked—and well satisfied—grin. "Especially that."

"Do you know what I always wanted to do out here?" he asked her.

"Probably the same thing I wanted."

In perfect sync, they leaned in to kiss each other. But just as their lips were about to touch, Vicki's heels started skidding on the muddy bank.

Her wide, laughing eyes were the last thing he saw before she toppled into the water...taking him with her.

Ducks scattered into the sky as they splashed their way to the surface. Laughing too hard to bother climbing out of the sludgy water, they held on to each other, and the ducks that had flown away settled back down to swim around them.

A clump of something green and gooey clung to Vicki's hair, mud streaked her cheek...and still she was the most beautiful woman in the world.

"What are you looking at?"

"You," was all he could say. "Just you, Vicki."

And then he gave up on talking altogether to make good on the wet-and-dirty wetlands kiss he'd wanted to give her fifteen years ago.

* * *

Twenty-four hours later, Vicki hummed along with the pop song she'd had on repeat for the past two days as she worked on her new project. Cheesy love songs performed by sixteen-year-old kids were her weakness. Serious artists, she knew, were supposed to be above all that. But she'd never been any good at looking, sounding or acting the part of the serious artist.

Then again, she hadn't thought she'd be able to pull off the role of Ryan Sullivan's fiancée very convincingly, either.

Of course, that had nothing whatsoever to do with her acting skills…and everything to do with the fact that she'd lost her heart to him so long ago.

It wasn't hard to act besotted when you actually felt that way—when every night you spent together was so special. Especially last night, when he'd taken her back to the wetlands.

She knew how busy his life was now as they headed toward the play-offs, yet he'd squeezed her into every free moment. As much as she loved it, she couldn't live with herself if she'd unwittingly stolen him away from his friends and family. Hopefully, she thought as she looked out at how low the sun was in the sky, he'd had a great practice and was headed out to have a beer with the guys.

Yes, that was what he needed. Some guy time.

She would darn well ignore her feelings of missing him over the eight or so hours that had passed since he'd kissed her awake this morning. She blushed at the delicious—and decadent—memory of the good-morning Ryan had given her before heading out to the stadium.

Realizing her hands had stopped working at least fifteen minutes ago and that her focus was slightly shot for the time being, she carefully moved her fellowship project over to her worktable against the wall.

Somehow, she realized, she'd let herself start to plan for the future. One that Ryan—and his family—were a big part of.

Her stomach clenched as she mentally looked down the road she'd been walking these past couple days with Ryan. When they'd agreed to start dating—postshower-wall-banging sex—she'd told him they should take it slow.

And now here she was having a hard time doing that herself.

There was no guarantee things would work out between them, despite how incredibly compatible they were. She didn't doubt her feelings for him, knew they wouldn't ever lessen. But Ryan had the whole world at his feet. And even though he was already one of the top athletes in the world, she knew he hadn't yet reached his peak. He would go from pitching to something even bigger, she was sure of it. She wouldn't stand in his way. And she would never—*never*—allow herself be an albatross tied to him as he climbed higher and higher.

Her studio light flicked on and she was momentarily blinded. A few seconds later, she realized Ryan was walking toward her. Before she could even register what was happening, he pulled her to her feet and gave her a hard, hungry, possessive kiss. She could taste his need. And, strangely, his relief, as well.

"Jesus, Vicki, you need to answer your phone."

Her pupils were still trying to adjust to the bright lights as she worked to keep her balance after Ryan's brain-sizzling kiss.

"My phone?" was the best she could do by way of a response. It was hard to come up with something better when she was at the perfect height to stare straight at his gorgeous mouth. She couldn't resist taking her own tiny little taste of him.

"You weren't at home, and I've been calling you for an hour." Ryan pulled back, his dark eyes flashing dangerously. "No one was answering out front."

She wished her hands weren't covered in wet clay. Otherwise, she could have stroked the worry from his face. "I lost track of the time. You shouldn't have worried."

He abruptly let go of her and walked back to her door to kick it shut. Maybe it would have scared her if some other man had acted like this, but she didn't feel even the slightest twinge of fear with Ryan.

Only the fast sizzle of arousal…and anticipation of just how he would take her this time.

Plus, she couldn't help but think she knew why

he was acting this way. Until she gave him the commitment she knew he wanted, how could he do anything but doubt her? One way or another.

He locked her door before moving to yank down the blinds on one of the big windows. "All goddamned day long I thought about you." He yanked down another blind, so hard it rattled against the glass. "Every second at the stadium, every second of my meetings. I was waiting for it all to end so that I could get home and spend my last night before leaving for the play-offs with you." Frustration fairly rolled off him. "But you weren't there."

She stood in the middle of her workroom, paralyzed by the desire—and possessiveness—in her normally calm and easygoing friend's eyes as he quickly covered the distance between them.

"We agreed to go slow," she reminded him, and herself, even though slow was the exact opposite of what she wanted right now. Fast and hard and breathless was all she could think about even as she told him, "We've spent the past six nights together. I wanted to give you space to go out with the guys."

"I've had a lifetime of space," he growled. "I don't need space. I need you, Vicki. *You.*"

She was shell-shocked by his intensity.

And honesty.

"Then take me, Ryan, because I need you, too."

He yanked off his shirt and then hers, stopping only long enough to run his fingers over the engagement ring hanging on the chain between her breasts.

Her leggings were gone a second later and then he snapped open the clasp at the back of her bra and it fell, too. All that remained was for him to push his thumbs into the sides of her panties and shove them down over her hips and thighs.

Her hands were wet and covered with clay, but Ryan clearly didn't care as he threaded his fingers into hers and backed them up against the nearest wall. He lifted her hands up over her head and lowered his mouth to her breasts, roughly rubbing the stubble on his chin over her, making her flesh even more sensitive as he laved first one breast and then the other with his tongue.

Even lost in the sweet shock of arousal, Vicki realized she was surrounded by all of her favorite things.

Clay. Sculptures. Ryan.

Full to bursting with a joy she hadn't ever let herself believe could be real, the next thing she knew Ryan was kissing her again and letting her hands guide his now-clay-covered palms over her breasts.

Every inch of skin he touched came alive beneath his fingers, marking her with clay, claiming her as his with every caress.

Wanting to mark him, too, desperate to feel his heat and strength beneath her fingertips, she laid her hands over his shoulders and slowly slid a path of clay down over his chest and then his abdomen.

He pushed himself between her naked thighs so that the zipper of his jeans—and the huge bulge behind it—was a deliciously hard press of heat into the vee between her legs, making her gasp as he hit just the right spot. Always incredibly attuned to her body, he reached for one thigh and slid his hand down to grasp her beneath her knee, pulling her leg up and around his waist.

Vicki was entirely sensation now, a bundle of nerves ready to spring apart at any moment. But she didn't want to go there alone.

Suddenly clumsy with desire, her hands shook, fumbling at the button and zipper on his jeans. He moved his hands from her breasts just long enough to pull a condom out before his pants and boxers fell to the ground.

So strong, he lifted her up and she wrapped her legs around his waist just as he lowered her down onto his pulsing shaft. Both of them breathed out hard at the sweet moment of connection, her body a perfect fit around his, and then he was cupping her hips hard in his hands and riding her against the wall while she kissed him with more than just her mouth. Her entire heart and soul were there in every slick of her tongue against his, in every gasp of ecstasy…and especially in the explosion of pleasure that soon overtook them both. They clung to each other for several long moments, working to catch their breath. She loved the way Ryan kept holding on to her as if it didn't even occur to him to ever let her go.

"I like dating you," he said into the curve of her shoulder.

She laughed before losing her breath all over again at the aftershocks that her body made jostling over his in laughter. Thirty minutes later, when they'd pulled their clothes back on over their clay-covered bodies and were sitting on the floor devouring the slices of pizza that were left over from lunch, and with Ryan's fake-engagement ring lying between her breasts, Vicki realized it was the craziest second date she'd ever had.

Crazy...yet so right.

Twenty-Three

Vicki snuggled in closer to Ryan. He had a habit of kicking off the covers while they were sleeping, but as long as he was there to keep her warm, she didn't mind.

A few minutes later, alarms started to sound from around the room. "Time to wake up, sleepyhead. You have a plane to catch." She softened her words with a soft flick of her tongue across his earlobe.

He groaned and tried to pull her closer, but as much as she wanted to let him drag her beneath him to make their morning even more perfect, first she needed to wiggle out from beneath his arm to find his various alarms and turn each of them off.

By the time she clicked off the last one, he was sitting up in bed giving her a very appreciative—and smoldering—look.

"You look so good naked, you've just given me a new idea."

She raised an eyebrow even as she moved toward his outstretched arm. "Are you sure it's a *new* idea?"

He pulled her over him so that she was straddling him over the covers. "I think we should make this a clothes-free room."

She laughed and kissed him. "Okay."

His large, extremely talented hands cupped her breasts and, as he lowered his mouth to them, he said, "If I'd known it was going to be that easy to convince you, I would have said the whole house should be a naked zone."

Her laughter stopped the second his tongue slicked over her. She threaded her fingers through his hair and held him against her as he feasted on her.

She was panting as she said, "Maybe."

He lifted her head. "Say that again?"

She gave him a wicked smile. He needed to get on the road soon, but if they worked fast, they could squeeze in a little fun, couldn't they? "Make me say it."

Just that fast, her wrists were in his hand, her gentle morning lover turning deliciously dominant in a split-second changeup.

Ryan's free hand moved between her legs and his mouth covered hers as his fingers played over her aroused flesh.

"You ready to talk yet?"

Talk? She could barely breathe.

"Okay, then. You've left me no choice but to get

serious with you." He moved his hand down to the top of her abdomen and stopped right there—such a good tease.

Already overflowing with want, Vicki gasped out the word, "One."

"One what?" His fingers went a little lower, just brushing against her curls, but no matter how she tried to move against his hand, he held firm.

"You can have me naked for one day."

"Where? Just in the bedroom?" He nipped at her earlobe with a possessive growl. "Or the whole house?"

He moved his hand even lower, but still not low enough.

She all but moaned the words, "The whole house."

He grinned down at her, but his eyes were dark with desire. "Only once?"

She couldn't believe what she was about to promise him. But no one had ever made her feel so desired—or safe—that she could even consider agreeing to stay naked for one full day with him.

"At least once."

"Every month." His words were a seductive flicker of warm breath and stubble over her breasts and stomach as he kissed his way down her body until his mouth was hovering right over his teasing hand. "Promise me a naked day every month and I'll give you what you want."

If she'd been able to, she would have promised

him anything, everything, but all she could manage was, "Please, Ryan."

She'd stopped trying to quiet her pleas when they were in bed together. Not only because it didn't feel like she was giving up any of her power to him when she begged…but also because she knew how much he liked knowing he was making her crazy.

His mouth came down on her at the exact moment his fingers slid inside, and Vicki instantly came apart in a flash of brilliant, beautiful color.

Moments later, he moved over her, inside her, and she was wrapped all around him and he was wrapped around her, too, and it was all so beautiful and perfect that she knew it couldn't possibly get any better.

"I love you."

They were the three words she'd waited half her life for Ryan to say. Not only to hear him say it… but also to believe it could be true.

She'd been so young when she'd learned not to get too attached to anything since her father would be stationed somewhere new at least every year. But that one year with Ryan had been different. So special that she hadn't been able to keep herself from losing her heart to him. Just like this week, when she'd given him her heart all over again.

And still, even when he'd told her how he felt about her, and that he wanted their fake relationship to be real, she'd held herself back out of fear that their friends-to-lovers story was too good to be anything but fiction.

Only, as they lay together, with his heartbeat thudding in time with hers, Vicki felt closer to Ryan than she'd ever felt to anyone else. Close enough that she finally allowed herself to give voice to the feelings she'd once believed would forever remain silent.

"I love you, too."

The joy on his face at her confession had her heart clenching hard in her chest and tears coming so fast they were already slipping down her cheeks one after the other.

"God, it's good to hear you say that. So damn good, Vicki. Say it again."

"I love you," she whispered again and again between kisses, and even though they were already so close, she needed more.

And as their words of love for each other tangled on their tongues and mouths, their morning quickie turned into something even hotter and sweeter with Ryan's fingers threading through hers. He took her body—and heart—up to the highest peak she'd ever crested. One more beautiful time.

Vicki was towel drying her hair as Ryan gathered up the last of his things to head out for the airport. They'd used up every single second of their final morning before the play-offs—and then some, she thought with a smile.

She put on her usual studio uniform of a tank top and pair of leggings and headed out to the kitchen. Her smile grew even bigger as she thought about how she could make Ryan's day just a little bit better before he got on the plane for Saint Louis to play the Cardinals in the first game of the play-offs.

He was staring at his cell phone, and she couldn't see his face as he said, "Thanks for calling about this, Smith."

When he kept scrolling down the screen, she took the chance to stare at him for a few seconds... and to reflect on the shocking fact that he was all hers.

Oh, how she was going to miss him while he was in Missouri for five days. How had she ever managed to go so many years without seeing him when now she was barely going to make it a week?

Thanking God he'd be back from his games just before the fellowship board made their decision, she wrapped her arms around his waist and laid her face against his back. "Okay, you can have it." He turned to face her and she was grinning as she said, "One completely, totally naked d—" Vicki's words fell away as she saw his face. "What's wrong?"

"Smith just called to let me know about some new press."

She tried to shrug off the quick hit of panic by joking, "If it's just more awful pictures of me—"

"It's a video interview with your ex."

At that point, even Ryan's warm hands on her

arms couldn't keep the chill from moving over her. "What did he say?"

"Stupid stuff. He's obviously upset that you've moved on."

She could see how angry Ryan was, the muscle jumping in his jaw, the murder in his eyes. She looked at his phone on the counter. "Is this what you were watching?"

Reluctantly, he handed it to her and held her even closer as she started to watch the interview, his arms around her obviously meant to keep her steady.

Vicki's heart pounded hard as she scanned through the first minute or so where Anthony talked about his latest successes and achievements. Without appearing to be bragging, he'd always been a master of letting people know just how well he was doing. He'd been equally as good at tearing her to shreds. Something she didn't fully appreciate until she was already married to him—every word from his tongue was a sharpened knife.

Finally, she came to the part of the interview that had her heart almost coming to a complete stop in her chest.

"Thirty years have come and gone since your first important sculpture appeared on the art scene," the interviewer said. "Tell us about the many changes we've all witnessed in your work over the past three decades, especially in the past twelve months."

"I know what you're really asking," Anthony replied as his self-deprecating laughter faded away, leaving behind a deep, strong ache. "True love, broken hearts—how can they not impact a person? It doesn't matter if you're an artist or an accountant, when love comes into your life and turns it upside down, there's love in everything you do." He paused and weighed his next words carefully before softly adding, "And if love leaves—when love leaves—everything you touch is replaced with brutal pain."

"He always thought he was such a poet," Vicki snarled.

"He's an ass," Ryan agreed, but she was already watching more of the interview…enough for her anger to turn to nausea.

"Your ex-wife is newly engaged. Not to an artist this time, but to professional baseball player Ryan Sullivan."

"I wish them nothing but the best," Anthony said. He lit a cigarette and took a few strong pulls on it. "Perhaps because of what I do, I've always been attracted to beauty. Victoria is, undoubtedly, a beautiful woman, one I knew I had to have the moment I saw her. I have no doubt her new fiancé feels the same way." His brow furrowed as he jammed his cigarette into the ashtray before saying, "I just hope he knows to be careful…to make sure he comes first."

"Do you believe your ex-wife used you to further her career?"

Anthony stared into the distance for a long time

before finally shaking his head. "I'd like to believe that's not the case."

"Oh, my God, I can't believe he all but said that I used our marriage to try to advance my career!" The phone fell from her hands, but Ryan just let it fall and pulled her closer.

"I'm sorry, Vicki." Ryan kissed the top of her head and his hands stroked down her back. She realized she was shaking against him as he said, "I'm sorry you were ever married to him. I'm sorry I wasn't there with you all these years. My lawyer is going to make that reporter wish she was—"

"It's not the reporter's fault." Funny, her voice sounded so steady when her insides felt like they'd shattered into tiny little shards swimming around inside her chest, a thousand little cuts nicking her as she rewound and replayed Anthony's words in her head. "She didn't put the words into his mouth. He's the one who thought I was using him, even though the truth is that marrying him was the worst thing I could have done for my career."

Anthony had always made sure to shove her into a shadowed background whenever she made the mistake of trying to catch even the smallest piece of the limelight that he'd already claimed for himself.

"He's an idiot. We all know it."

"You know it. I know it. But he just gave voice to what people have always, and will always, think. They think I used him." She made herself meet

Ryan's concerned—and angry—gaze. "They'll think I'm using you, too."

"You can't let him win. Not when he's nothing but a bitter, self-absorbed prick."

She didn't want to let Anthony have any more of her soul than she'd already lost to him during their marriage. The only problem was, she couldn't completely discount the fact that her ex might be just a little bit right, as well.

"What about the fact that I didn't tell you I was here until I needed you to step in with James to keep the fellowship from slipping away? Or what about the fact that I wanted to be with you for so long but was so afraid to actually tell you how I felt that I created this lie and pulled you and your family into my messed-up life? What if some part of what Anthony is saying about me, about the way he thinks I use people, is actually true?"

"Stop it."

Ryan put his hands on her shoulders, but even though he was holding her firmly in front of him, his fingers on her skin were gentle. Loving.

"You reached out for me because I'm your friend and you were in an ugly situation. I came because I love you and would do absolutely anything for you. If you think I give a rat's ass what anyone else thinks about you and me and our relationship, then you're going to make me question everything you just told me in bed this morning."

His eyes held hers, dark, intense and full of unconditional love.

"Don't do that, Vicki. Don't even think about taking it back, not after I've waited so goddamned long to know that you feel the same way I do."

Tears spilled down her cheeks. "I would never take it back."

Finally, he smiled at her as he brushed his thumbs across her cheeks. "And I would never let you." His phone rang again and he cursed when he looked down at the screen lying on the floor. "I've got to get on the team plane." He cupped her face in his hands. "Promise me you won't let any of the stupid things some asshole said in an interview get in the way of finishing your brilliant sculpture. Especially not when you know he probably made sure that interview ran to coincide with his joining the fellowship board this week. You gave him ten years. He doesn't deserve even one more second."

Vicki had been on the move her whole life. She could feel that desperation to leave—to bury the past, to start over again in a place where her past didn't matter and no one knew her—beginning to take her over. If she left, she could still hold these memories of being so close to Ryan this past week inside herself forever. And no matter how far she went, she knew she would never forget what it felt like to be in his arms, to feel safe and cherished.

But…leaving Ryan once when she was just a teenager had nearly destroyed her.

How could she even think about running from him now?

Especially when his open arms were the only place she ever wanted to run to again—and he was oh-so-right about Anthony not deserving even one more second of her energy.

A heartbeat later, his hands were in her hair and her mouth was under his as he kissed her so thoroughly, so passionately, that everything fell away but how much she loved him.

When he finally let her go, she didn't open her eyes right away. She just let herself feel the hard, fast beat of his heart beneath her outstretched palms as she worked to catch her breath.

"All those years that he and I were together, I ignored that little voice that told me something wasn't quite right with our marriage. It was so much easier to listen to his voice and to everyone around me who said I'd be crazy not to want him. And he was so smooth, always had the perfect excuse for everything. I thought I could make him into the husband I needed. Over and over that last year we were together, I dreamed I was trying to carve marble with my fingers. I longed for tools to chip, to carve, to sand. But all I had were my hands, and they weren't enough. I could give my entire life over to it and I still wouldn't have made the slightest dent in the stone. The dreams stopped the night I left."

She opened her eyes and held Ryan's gaze as

she admitted, "I'm still learning to listen to that little voice."

"What is it telling you?"

She went up on her tiptoes to press a kiss to his mouth before whispering against his lips, "To give you that promise."

And to love him with her entire heart...and soul.

Ryan had barely closed the front door behind him when her phone rang. The past few days she'd gotten used to ignoring the calls from reporters and bloggers, but when she recognized the Italian country code, she knew she had to pick up.

Of course Anthony wouldn't be happy with merely giving the horrible interview. He'd want to make sure she saw it so that he could rub it in her face.

Damn it, she wasn't going to let him run her in circles. "Your tricks don't work on me anymore, Anthony, so you might as well quit trying."

There was a pause on the other end of the line. "Signorina Bennett?"

Oh! It wasn't her ex-husband calling. It was an Italian woman. One who was clearly confused by Vicki's outburst.

"*Sì,* I'm sorry, this is Vicki Bennett."

"I apologize for calling you with no warning," the woman said in perfect English with a pretty Italian accent. "I am with the Museum of Contemporary Sculpture in Matera. We have been reviewing your work for the past few months and I am calling with some very good news. We have selected a dozen of your works to be put on display, and would be very pleased to offer you an artist-in-residence position."

While she'd been in Prague, Vicki had sent packages to a dozen museums around the world with artist-in-residence programs, deciding she would let fate be her guide.

She'd thought fate had chosen San Francisco. And Ryan.

What the heck was fate up to now?

Knowing the woman likely expected her to accept on the spot, Vicki finally managed to at least say, "I'm thrilled that you've chosen my sculptures for your museum, of course, but—"

The women cut her off by informing her of a much larger yearly artist-in-residence grant amount than she would make in San Francisco.

If she even won the fellowship.

"We would like to give you some time to consider the position, of course. But we absolutely must know by the end of the week so that we can prepare the exposition and accompanying literature in time for your arrival. I'm sure you understand our position. We have emailed you all the details."

The woman did not have to spell it out any further. If she didn't accept within a week, the opportunity would go to another sculptor.

And she would have lost the biggest chance she'd ever had.

Taking the residency in Italy was about more than that. It also meant it didn't matter if she got the San Francisco fellowship or not. Which meant that she didn't have to worry about James or Anthony… and she and Ryan wouldn't have to pretend to be engaged anymore.

But it would also mean leaving Ryan.

Yes, she knew they could probably figure out a way to make a long-distance relationship work, at least for the first few months once the season ended and his schedule was more flexible. But as soon as the next baseball season began, nine months would go by before he would be able to get on a plane to Europe.

She pulled the ring out from under her shirt and instinctively curled her hand around it. It wasn't real.

But could it become real with more time? With more honesty? With more risk?

And more faith?

Vicki thanked the woman again and promised her she would read through everything carefully, and that she would have an answer for her very soon.

Twenty-Four

As soon as Ryan boarded the Hawks' team plane, he was pulled into a strategy session with the pitching coach and catcher. They planned to study the lineup of the opposing team and go over the strong and weak points of every hitter. He already had a good sense of who was hot, who chased the fastballs and which batters he could fool with his changeup. But his brain kept spinning back to Smith's concerned phone call and the way Vicki's face had fallen when he'd told her about the interview with her ex.

On his way to the airport Smith had asked him if there was anything Ryan wanted his PR team to do. His brother was perfectly happy to use his connections to take down Vicki's ex, especially within a community of ultrarich movie people, many of whom had thrown plenty of money the sculptor's way over the years.

It had been really tempting to let Smith do that, just as he'd been all for his brother taking James apart. But Ryan couldn't forget what Vicki had said that first night at the cocktail lounge. *If I win the fellowship, I want to know that it was because of the quality of my work.*

Smith and Marcus and the rest of the well-connected Sullivan clan could easily pull every trick and favor in the book for Vicki. But doing that would strip away her victories just as badly as her ex-husband had stripped them from her during their marriage.

Of course, Ryan still wanted to fly to Italy to rip the dickhead's heart from his chest for hurting her.

The second the plane touched down, he called her. "I hope you have clay all over your hands," he told her voice mail. "I miss you already. And I love you. Call me when you get this."

By the time the Hawks arrived at Busch Stadium for a light workout, Ryan was more than ready to blow off some steam. He worked out so hard, in fact, that Bobby, the pitching coach, had to pull him aside.

"Looking good out there, Ryan. We're getting ready to head out for dinner. You ready to go?"

Ryan put down the weights he'd been lifting, knowing it was time to quit ripping his body apart today. As the Hawks' ace on the team, he was pitching the first play-off game. He knew better than to blow out his muscles the day before a game, especially a huge one like this. But he'd never experienced such frustration before. Not since the day he'd watched Vicki ride her bike away from his house as a teenager after telling him she was moving again. He'd ended up running after her, running long after she was out of sight, running until his legs had finally given out.

He hadn't made it to the game at the high school that night. It was the only one he'd ever bailed on.

Just thinking about what he'd seen in Vicki's eyes that morning—knowing she'd been thinking of leaving him again after what her ex had said—had all of those emotions rounding back on him. Only they were bigger, stronger now than they'd been when he was just a kid with a massive crush on his best friend.

"I've got a few things to take care of," Ryan said as he and the coach headed toward the locker room. "I'll get something to eat later tonight."

The gray-haired man he'd worked with for the past decade leveled a stare at him. "You need to talk anything over, give me a call. Doesn't matter how late, I'll be around."

Ryan appreciated the gesture, but there was only one person he needed to talk to right now. He grabbed his bag without hitting the showers and headed for the hotel. His phone rang just as he was closing the hotel room door behind him.

"Hi, gorgeous."

"Ryan." Vicki sounded a little flustered and shy. "Hi."

Damn, he loved the sound of her voice.

Even just the sound of her breathing.

"Hi," he said again, grinning into the phone as he heard her putting her keys down on the kitchen counter.

"Are you in the middle of something?" she asked.

"Nope. The night's all mine." And he planned to spend it with her. "What about you?"

"I just got home."

He'd never had anyone waiting for him before, and the thought of coming home to her kisses in a few days sent warmth moving through him. He loved picturing her in his house.

At long last, the frustration that had been riding him all day started to dissipate.

Of course he wanted to hear about the progress she'd made on her sculpture, and he needed to make sure she hadn't let her idiot of an ex-husband derail her. But first he needed to make sure she understood that all the miles currently between them didn't mean a damn thing…and wouldn't stop him from loving her just as thoroughly as he would have if they were standing in the same room.

"Remember what you were about to offer me right before I left today?" He couldn't wait for her reply before saying, "Your first naked night is tonight." He grinned even wider at her stunned silence. "I sure hope you aren't saying anything because you're too busy taking off your clothes."

Finally, she gave a little laugh into the phone. "Actually, I'm standing here wondering if you've been watching the X-rated channels in your hotel room."

"I don't need porn when I've got plenty of triple-X pictures in my head of you in the shower, in your studio and in my bed." He let the images of what the two of them had done in all those places run through her mind for a few seconds. "Put the phone on speaker, place it on the kitchen counter and take off your tank top."

"You're serious?"

"You have ten seconds to take it off, Vicki."

"Or what?" Her voice was breathy now, and obviously aroused. "You're all the way in Saint Louis."

God, he loved her. How playful, how strong, how loving she was. All the years they'd spent apart, he'd been searching for a woman like Vicki. If only he'd realized long before this week that he'd never find a replacement for her—that she was the only woman he'd ever love—then maybe they wouldn't have wasted so many years apart.

They couldn't get those years back.

But they could make the most of every single one they had left.

And they damn well would.

"You're right," he agreed in a deceptively easy voice that he intended for her to see right through.

"But I'll be back home in five days." He let her register the sensual threat—and promise—in his words. "Your time is up. Where's your tank top?"

He heard her swallow before answering. "In my hands."

"Drop it on the floor."

The sound of the fabric dropping to his kitchen floor got him so hard he had to adjust himself again in his shorts as he sank down on the hotel room couch.

"I want you to take your leggings off next. Tell me when they're gone."

He let himself picture Vicki balancing first on one leg and then the other to slide the fabric off.

"They're gone."

"What else do you have on?"

She paused just long enough for him to know it was going to be good. "Pink lace."

"Your breasts look incredible in that bra." He could barely get his brain to function well enough to ask, "Are you wearing the matching thong?"

"I pulled that off along with my leggings. Wait a second and I'll get the bra off, too." He heard the click of the front clasp of her bra opening. "Okay, that's everything."

"Jesus, Vicki." He slid his shorts off and reached for himself. "You're killing me here."

She laughed softly into the phone before saying, "Now that you've got me naked for the rest of the night, what are you going to do with me?"

"I'm going to love you, sweetheart." He couldn't have hidden the emotion in his voice from her even if he wanted to.

He didn't want to hide his feelings for her ever again.

"Ryan." His name was a whisper on her lips, one that reverberated way down into his soul.

"Cup your breasts for me. Do it the way I would if I were there."

He loved the little moan that escaped her right before she said, "I wish you were here. Tell me what to do, Ryan. Tell me how you want me."

Oh, hell, he almost lost it right then and there. "Lick your thumbs, then brush them over yourself like they're my tongue." He could imagine the taste of her so well it was almost as if he was in California with her sensitive flesh taut and so damn sweet against his tongue. "God, you taste good."

"I love your mouth on me. The scratch of your stubble against me, the way you start to suck and bite at my skin when you lose control."

"I'm losing control now." He couldn't see her smile, but he knew her well enough to be absolutely certain that her gorgeous lips were curving up at the edges. "I need to touch more of you."

"Where, Ryan? Tell me where."

"Leave your left hand on your perfect breasts and start moving the right one down over your stomach and keep going. I'll tell you when to stop."

A few moments later, her swift intake of breath

told him that her hand had reached the sweet, slick flesh between her legs.

"You've stopped already, haven't you?"

"I—" She panted. "I need—"

"I know what you need, sweetheart." Because he needed it, too. Not just tonight. Not just for a few months.

Forever.

"First I want you to tell me how you taste." He'd planned to make her beg, but he was the one saying, "Please."

He swore he could hear the slow slick of her tongue over her damp fingers. "A little salty." She paused. "And a little sweet."

"You're so beautiful. So perfect." His breath was coming as fast as it did when he ran sprints. "Walk over to the couch and lie down on it. Pretend I'm there with you. Over you. Sliding into you."

"Oh, *God,* Ryan. *Yes.*"

"Are you touching yourself?"

"Yes, and I'm so close."

"I am, too." He'd never been so turned on in all his life, but instead of telling her that, the words that came were, "I love you. So damn much."

She gave a low cry of pleasure before her breath whooshed into his ear. "I love you, too."

With the crystal clear picture in his head of her gorgeous naked curves bucking up into her hands, he gave up his own control and let his release follow hers.

* * *

Vicki couldn't believe she'd just had phone sex with Ryan.

And it had been *amazing.*

She wanted to clasp the knowledge to her chest and hold it there, along with all their other firsts. Wanting him as close as she could get him, she shifted on the couch to pick up the cell phone from the counter.

"You're not putting your clothes back on, are you?"

Even though he wasn't there to see her, she still flushed at her nakedness…and the shockingly sweet fact that he'd asked her to strip down less than a minute after picking up her call.

She put the phone to her ear and said, "I promised you a full day, didn't I?"

His laughing response was layered with un-quenched desire. She knew exactly how he felt. Her orgasm had been fantastic. But it wasn't nearly enough to quench her need for him.

"I hope you made good on your other promise to me."

She wrapped the blanket from his couch around her and sat down. The message he'd left for her had been full of love. And worry. She didn't want to add to it. But she also wanted—and needed—to be completely honest with him from here on out. She was tired of the lies.

And she refused ever to tell another one to the man she loved.

"I had a great day at the studio, even though everyone had already seen the interview by the time I got there."

Ryan cursed. "I take it James came by?"

"Everyone but him, actually. I know we're all supposed to be competing for the fellowship, but everyone was really great about it, especially when they learned that Anthony has been added to the board." She'd been more than a little surprised by the support from her fellow artists, and not just the ones she thought of as friends.

"No one wants to be sold out like that."

Vicki wasn't surprised that Ryan had cut right to the heart of it. Whoever said jocks were dumb or clueless had never met her ballplayer.

"And they know you, how hard you work, how passionate you are about everything you do."

"Thank you for always believing in me. And for loving me."

And yet even as she felt his support all the way down in her core, she had to pull the blanket tighter around her shoulders to try to combat the chill that was trying to take her over as she worked out how to tell him about Italy.

"Something else happened today, didn't it?" he asked.

When would she stop being surprised that he knew her better than anyone? And that he could read her silences better than anyone had ever understood her actual words?

"I got a phone call. From Italy. It wasn't Anthony," she said quickly, before Ryan got the wrong idea. "A major museum of contemporary sculpture wants to put together an exhibition of my work."

"That's amazing, Vicki. Why didn't you tell me the good news as soon as we got on the phone?"

"Because—" she could feel every single mile between them and knew how much farther away she'd be if she went to Italy "—they don't just want my sculptures. They want me, too. As an artist-in-residence. For at least a year."

"Italy is a big deal, isn't it? Bigger than San Francisco."

She couldn't lie to him. "Yes, it's a big deal."

Ryan was silent for several brutally long moments. "You know my mother was born in Italy, don't you?"

"I do." When Vicki had complimented Mary on her spaghetti sauce, his mother had told her about learning it from her Italian grandmother.

"And did you also know there's an Italian national baseball team that isn't half-bad?"

Quickly putting it all together, she said, "You're not going to play baseball in Italy, Ryan."

"It would be fun."

"Don't be crazy," she said when she realized he was serious. "You can't give up your career for me and a year in Italy that might not mean anything at all in the long run."

"I know you've never come first before, not with your family or your ex-husband, but I meant it when I said I would do anything for you. *Anything.*"

"But your career—"

"Has been great. And you know what? I would trade every single win to have spent those years with you."

"No, you wouldn't." Her eyes felt wet with the tears she was trying to hold back. "But I love you for even thinking it."

"Yes, I would," he countered. "And I love you, too, *amore mio.*"

When he called her "my love" in Italian, more tears fell.

"The museum gave me a little while to decide, so don't quit the team just yet," she told him in as light a voice as she could, as though the whole idea of him quitting the Hawks was utterly preposterous.

Which it was. Vicki would never in a million years force him to choose between her and baseball. Yes, she'd heard what he said. And she believed he meant it.

But how could she ever forgive herself if she took him up on it?

When she had married Anthony, she hadn't realized all the things she'd be giving up. If she turned down a year in Italy, at least she'd be doing it with her eyes wide-open.

Knowing they weren't going to make any more headway tonight, she said, "Now that we've covered my day, it's your turn to tell me all about yours. Especially the part where you got sweaty and your muscles bulged."

"Well," he teased her back, "I got this phone call tonight...."

For the next hour they shared the little details of their day that no one else would have cared about, but that meant the world to each of them. Then, later, Ryan convinced her to take the phone into the master bathroom and get into the bathtub. Calling out his name after having followed his wickedly sensual instructions to the letter, she momentarily forgot that she'd ever had a worry in her life.

Twenty-Five

Ryan would gladly have stayed on the phone with Vicki all night, but she'd insisted he get some sleep before his big game. She'd whispered how much she loved him one more time before she disconnected.

But even with her soft, sweet words of love playing on repeat in his head, he couldn't sleep.

They hadn't talked about Italy again before disconnecting, but it was clear that they both knew a long-distance relationship between San Francisco and Matera was next to impossible given his career. Sure, there were weeks here or there where he could leave town and work out from the road, but as soon as spring training started, he would be locked into a home-and-travel schedule that was set in stone.

After waiting so long for Vicki to finally be his, he wanted—needed—more time laughing with her, loving her. Not less, damn it!

If he asked her to give up Italy for him, he knew

what would happen. Just as she'd thrown herself in front of a car for a stranger in high school, she'd let him wrap his love around her like a chain.

The question wasn't whether she'd stay. Not when he already knew she was planning to turn down the residency in Italy and the triumph that she deserved after so many years of playing second fiddle to her ex-husband's ego.

The only question that remained was how much she'd end up hating Ryan after she'd given up the chance of a lifetime for him.

Somehow, some way, he needed to stop her from making a choice she'd regret forever.

The moon was still high in the sky by the time Vicki gave up on sleep. She knew Ryan wouldn't like her driving through some of the sketchier districts at 3:00 a.m., but she couldn't spend one more second in his big bed without his arms around her. She'd even tried curling up on the couch, but thinking about their lovemaking on the soft cushions only made her miss him more.

What, she wondered as she let herself into the dark, empty fellowship building, was he doing right now? Was he missing her the way she was missing him? Or was he worrying about her news of a possible residency in Italy?

She hoped he was sleeping. He needed to be fresh for the first play-off game. And she would never forgive herself if his performance on the mound took a hit because he was worrying about her.

The smell of clay settled her down some, along with the promise she'd made Ryan to hold her focus on her sculpture. Before they finally put down their phones earlier tonight, he'd made her promise again. And she knew he was right, that working with clay was the one thing guaranteed to make her feel better.

Especially when her only other guaranteed cure was in Missouri right now.

Amazingly, once she sat down to work, the hours flew by until the sun rose and filled her studio with light. It was only when her stomach started cramping from hunger that she realized it had to be close to noon.

She had to find a TV—and fast—so that she could catch Ryan's game.

Vicki grabbed her bag and was skidding down the hallway when Anne caught her. "I'm starved. Want to go grab something?"

"I can't." She ignored her stomach growling loudly in protest. "Ryan's first play-off game is about to start. I've got to find a TV."

"I know just the place. It's a sports bar with the cutest bartender on the planet. Going there for lunch with you will give me a good chance to flirt with him some more. Not to mention the street cred I'm going to have by hanging out with the star pitcher's girl." Anne grinned unabashedly. "Follow me."

Vicki would never have found the sports bar on her own and was beyond glad to see the game was only just starting. All of the big-screen TVs in the bar were tuned in to the game, and the patrons were completely focused on the satellite images. She and Anne slid onto the only two bar stools available just as Ryan took his place on the pitcher's mound.

"Seriously," Anne said as she slid a menu in front of Vicki, "that man of yours is too gorgeous to be real. We can still be friends even if I can't help fantasizing about him, right?"

But Vicki barely heard her friend's joke as the cameras pulled in for a close-up on Ryan.

She frowned at the expression on his face…and how tired he looked. She knew the first play-off game was a big deal but, even under major pressure, he always looked relaxed enough for one to think that for him it was nothing more than a pickup game between friends on a local field.

When the bartender asked her what she wanted to order, she pointed to the first thing she saw on the menu. She knew she wouldn't be able to eat a bite while she was watching the game.

Ryan looked down at the catcher, got the sign, went into his windup and threw a blazing fastball over the plate for strike one. She felt some of the tension leave her body, but when his next two pitches missed the plate, she tensed right up again.

She had nothing riding on whether the Hawks won the game or not, but she knew how seriously

Ryan took his job. He felt responsible, not only to the team that signed his paychecks, but also to the Hawks' enthusiastic fans.

A few moments later the count evened out at two balls, two strikes and then Ryan threw a high outside fastball. But the batter didn't chase it. With one more ball to throw, she watched the catcher give Ryan a sign and then he threw a fastball that hit the low outside corner of the strike zone.

Only, instead of calling it strike three, the home plate umpire sent the hitter to first base with a walk.

Vicki could see how shaken Ryan was by the call. In an uncharacteristic move, he glowered at the umpire before turning to face center field as he visibly worked to compose himself to face the next batter.

But after four more pitches, the count was three to one. Ryan missed badly on the next pitch, putting runners on first and second base with nobody out and the Cardinals' two power hitters waiting their turn. The Saint Louis fans were on their feet, screaming at the tops of their lungs, trying to rattle Ryan as best they could. Clearly, they were beside themselves with joy watching the league's best pitcher tumble into a world-class meltdown.

The TV in front of the bar was turned up loud enough for Vicki to easily hear the announcers discuss Ryan's uncharacteristically bad pitching.

"Ryan Sullivan has always made his job look so

easy. In all the years I've seen him pitch, I can't re-call ever seeing him choke like this."

Another announcer agreed. "There's no question that he's in his prime in terms of age and strength. Even so, the first game of the play-offs is a bad time for any ballplayer to be dealing with personal issues, no matter how talented."

"Looks like the pitching coach has just called a time-out. He's heading out to the mound to have a word with him," the first announcer told the audience.

"If they're thinking of pulling him, it's a good time to do it, before his arm wears out. This way they can use him three days out instead of having to wait four full days before his next start."

Vicki's heart stilled in her chest as she watched the pitching coach say something to Ryan. She wished she could read lips to know what Ryan's reply was as he shook his head and held firm on the mound.

"Sullivan just got engaged, didn't he?" the first announcer asked.

"Sure did. The story I've heard is that they've known each other since high school, but only started to date again recently. Sounds like something right out of a fairy tale, doesn't it?"

"Unfortunately," the other man replied, "it doesn't look like he's living a fairy tale right now."

It wasn't just the announcers who were trying to make sense of what was happening on the field.

The fans who had gathered in the bar to cheer on the Hawks were grumbling about Ryan loading the bases within five minutes of hitting the mound. Fortunately, Anne was too busy flirting with the young bartender down at the other end to have heard anything the announcers said.

If Vicki had never come back into Ryan's life, he wouldn't be suffering now. And yet she still couldn't make herself wish away the past week they'd had together…or the unexpected love they'd found with each other.

The pitching coach was still conferring with Ryan, but when she looked more closely at the screen, she realized something was different.

Her body recognized Ryan's determined look, and the dominance in it. Probably because it was the same look he'd given her in bed—a look that always turned her insides to goo.

Even though the announcers were surprised when the coach returned to the dugout, Vicki wasn't. Ryan stayed right where he was.

"Looks like he's staying on the mound for at least a few more pitches. I don't know about that decision, given the fact that the Cardinals just sent in their cleanup hitter. He slammed forty-nine homers during the regular season."

"This is a do-or-die moment for Ryan Sullivan and the Hawks," the announcer said in a hushed voice. "Another walk will force in a run. A home run and this thing is practically over in the first inning."

Ryan waved off the first two signs from the catcher until, finally, he got the sign he wanted. His face was a picture of perfect concentration—and beautiful determination—as he took several deep breaths, went into his windup and uncorked a fastball that caught the inside corner of the plate level with the batter's knees. Two great pitches later and the umpire barked, "Strike three!" giving the out sign with his hand and arms. The crowd in the bar let out an audible sigh of relief while the TV announcers analyzed what had just happened.

After Ryan struck out the fifth-place hitter on five pitches—a mix of fastballs and changeups—the stadium became eerily quiet. And then, one more time, three straight blazing fastballs hit the corners with precision. Ryan was taking no prisoners and didn't give the batter even a hint of a chance.

The inning was over. Ryan had climbed out of a deep hole. And the Hawks were back in the game.

Big-time.

Vicki cheered along with the rest of the crowd in the bar as one of the announcers said, "Looks like the Ryan Sullivan we all know and love is back."

Throughout the rest of the game Ryan's determination and strength of will never wavered, to the point where the announcers agreed that it might have been his best pitching ever. Though she knew he wouldn't get her message until the game was over and he'd finished dealing with the press, Vicki pulled out her phone to text him.

That was when she finally saw his message to her.

I love you. Remember, you promised to kick butt in the studio today.

She smiled at his sweet yet tough message. She texted him back.

I love you, too. Looks like we're both kicking butt today. I'm so proud of you.

Anne left the bar before the game ended, happily returning to the studio with the bartender's phone number programmed into her cell. Even though Vicki hadn't had so much as a bite of her burger, she was too amped up now to eat. She put a twenty down on the bar and practically ran back to her workroom.

Most artists claimed that the end of a project was the easiest for them, but it had always been just the opposite for Vicki. The final days on a sculpture usually felt like they dragged on forever while she second-guessed and endlessly refined and then triple-guessed the whole damn thing from top to bottom.

But, amazingly, instead of flailing in these final

important moments, she suddenly felt like she was mining a whole new bottomless well of inspiration.

Love.

Much as she hated to admit that her ex had been right about anything he'd said in that horrible interview, the truth was that Ryan's love had completely changed her.

To actually *know* such a big love when she was in his arms and they were laughing or kissing or talking was so monumental that she could truly feel the energy of that love pouring from her fingers.

Vicki couldn't believe she was actually smiling at her ex getting something right. Had she finally managed to move beyond her past…and into a beautiful future with Ryan?

She looked down at her sculpture of the hands. One hand was utterly masculine, the other feminine yet strong. She'd worked hard to make sure that neither hand grasped at the other and that there was no desperation in their hold. Only love, pure and sweet and *real*.

It hit her, suddenly, for the very first time, that she didn't need to fiddle or worry over or doubt this sculpture anymore.

It was done. And it was good.

Really good.

She had Ryan to thank for all the beautiful inspiration he'd given her this week…and hopefully would for a long, long time to come. He was her anchor, there to keep her safe and grounded when she needed him, but always ready to rise up to explore new journeys and adventures with her.

Yes. That was what she'd call her fellowship sculpture: *Anchor*.

One after the other, new ideas for future sculptures came to her. A baby's hand held so gently in her father's. A mother and son holding hands as they walked through a field of wildflowers. Another of a girl and boy, older still, siblings as bonded to each other as Ryan and his siblings were.

Needing to share her joy and excitement with the person who meant everything to her, Vicki reached for a rag to clean her hands so that she could call Ryan. Hopefully he would be done with his postgame interviews by now. When she realized all of her rags were too filthy to make a dent in the clay on her hands, she got up and went into her supply closet to grab a clean pile.

She was on her tiptoes reaching for the top shelf when she heard footsteps come down the corridor.

Figuring it must be Anne, back to dish over the bartender, and still giddy with the knowledge that she'd made something truly beautiful, Vicki turned around to greet her friend with a smile.

Too late, she realized it wasn't her friend who had come to see her.

James Sedgwick closed the studio door behind him.

Twenty-Six

"I heard you hadn't showed up at the reception for the fellowship contenders." James looked extremely pleased about this information. "Everyone else is there, so it's just you and me in this big building."

Vicki had been so swept up in Ryan and his game and finishing her sculpture that she had forgotten all about the reception. "Shouldn't you be there at the museum?"

"I'll get there when I get there," he said with an arrogant shrug of his shoulders. "They'll wait for me."

He moved into her studio to stand beside her sculpture. He ran his hand over it suggestively and possessively. Her stomach roiled watching him touch it.

"Judging by today's play-off game, your fiancé obviously wishes you were with him in Saint Louis tonight instead of here working on your project."

Of course James would know that Ryan was out of town. And of course he'd waited to corner her again, knowing full well that there was no one to protect her.

"Ryan pitched a brilliant game," she countered. "Just like always."

"Yes, I suppose he did. Once he regained control of his emotions." He shook his head as he regarded her finished sculpture. "I see you didn't take any of my advice on how to improve your work. Emotion is fairly dripping from this thing." He shook his head in disgust.

Despite the size of her studio, James was too close, just as he'd been so many times before. Only, today, something was different.

She wasn't afraid of him anymore.

Even as anger simmered, she remained outwardly calm as she asked, "Why are you here, James?"

"Last year's winner sold her fellowship project for one million dollars. She has turned down more commissions this past year than most artists will be offered in a lifetime. She was talented, but not nearly talented enough to manage everything on her own. *I'm* the person who helped her, both through the fellowship program and with contacts for her future. You could have that, too, Victoria."

Vicki remembered seeing the news of the sale and the pictures of the beautiful artist whose smile didn't quite reach her eyes. Probably because she'd sold herself to this horrible man for seven figures. No wonder Anthony and James had always been friends. They were two peas in a pod, the only difference being that her ex-husband had gone one step further and rather than making her his mistress he had actually married her.

She'd been accused by Anthony of not getting to where she was on her own merits, and maybe there had been some truth to that. Especially after she'd asked Ryan to rescue her rather than rescuing herself that first night.

The thing was, all this time she'd been beating herself up for asking Ryan to rescue her, but instead she should see it as the gift it had turned out to be. Because if this nasty man in her studio hadn't creeped her out so much, who knew how long it would have been before she'd got up the nerve to call Ryan in the first place?

To have missed out on even one of the sweet, funny, comforting and sinfully sensual moments she'd experienced with Ryan would have been a far bigger crime than asking for help from her friend.

Was she still afraid that things could go wrong? Of course she was, because she was human. She'd made mistakes. She hadn't trusted her instincts nearly often enough. And she'd broken her own heart in the process.

But even as true as all those things were, she loved Ryan enough to push those fears aside and put her entire heart—and soul—on the line for him.

And for herself.

No longer able, or willing, to hide her disgust of James, she said, "I'm glad you're finally being clear. So now I'll be just as clear with you. Whatever I achieve, whatever commissions come my way, I'm going to get them on my own merit, not because you've directed me like a puppet. I know you're going to vote against me, along with Anthony. And I know you will both do whatever you can to turn the rest of the board against me, too. But neither of those things changes the fact that I wouldn't work with you for all the money in the world."

Just that fast, his distinguished face contorted into a nasty scowl. "In that case, don't do it for the money or the fame. Do it for your precious baseball player. I'm sure his team and fans would just love to know all about your fake engagement. It will make them all look like such fools." He leered at her figure and she felt as if spiders were crawling all over her. "If Ryan is willing to lie for you, you must really be worth it. I'm offering you the world, Victoria. My silence—and support—can both be yours. All you have to do is take them."

"Get out."

He smiled at her, a baring of teeth with absolutely no joy behind it. Talk about *fake*.

"You really are sweet, aren't you? Too sweet to even know how to play off your own lie convincingly. What a pleasure it will be to show you just how enjoyable the darkness can be. You hard-to-get types are always the most fun. I'm going to give you so much, Victoria. So much more than Anthony ever did." Rage, and something that looked like jealousy, flicked on in his eyes. "I saw you first, you know. All those years ago, I was the one who spotted you in the group of students, but I never even had a chance to introduce myself. Anthony stole you from me. Now I'm stealing you back."

He punctuated his words by moving to the door and locking it. The click was horribly loud in her quiet studio.

So much of Vicki's life had been about not following her instincts, but that was about to change. She wouldn't beat herself up anymore for all the times she hadn't listened. But she would celebrate the fact that she'd finally started to pay attention to that little voice in the back of her head that had always been so much smarter than she'd given it credit for.

Right now the little voice was telling her that James was suave and cultured and charming and rich enough to always get what he wanted. But he would never claim her. He was not just going to roll over and play dead just because she said no. Even screaming no at him wouldn't make a difference—not in this empty building.

So she would *throw* the word at him instead.

"You're right," she said finally as he stalked her, surely, confidently. She moved toward her laden table of sculptures, so many of them false starts on the way to creating the sculpture that finally expressed everything her hands—and heart—had in them. "Ryan and I aren't engaged."

His eyes filled with triumph. "That first night during cocktails, I knew he'd never kissed you before." Fury rose again. "Did you really think you had pulled one over on me? No one pulls the wool over my eyes, Victoria."

She'd counted on her admission to buy her a little time, and it had. Just enough time to get within reach of her sculptures.

He moved closer. "Now it's my turn to see just how sweet you taste."

Even as revulsion swept through her, she felt surprisingly calm. Steady.

She reached for *Anchor* to throw it at him, but stopped just before her fingers could grasp it.

It was good, damn it.

Too good to waste on a creep like James.

She wrapped her fingers around one of her heaviest sculptures. "One thing about having a pro pitcher as a best friend—you learn how to always hit your mark. The size of your head will only make it easier."

She was just lifting the clay up to throw it at him when he covered his head with both hands and skittered back so fast he could have been wearing roller skates.

"This is your last warning to stay the hell away from me." She lifted her heavy sculpture higher and wound up to let it rip, but a beat before it left her fingers, he fumbled for the door lock and popped it open.

"I'm going to ruin you," he snarled. Then he fled like the coward he was.

Vicki was still holding the sculpture over her head when she realized he really was gone…and that she'd been the scary one this time.

She waited for shock to take her over, just as it had after she and Ryan had narrowly missed being hit by the car. But instead of dealing with shaking hands and a pounding heart, she felt clean. As if finally giving voice—and hands—to her rage had wiped years of frustration right out of her.

Just as she'd told Ryan a week ago, there was no guarantee that anyone would believe her claims about James's behavior. Especially if he was already on his way to begin spreading rumors about her, likely claiming that *she* had come on to *him*. But if there was a chance that she could stop anyone else from ever being on the receiving end of one of James's oh-so-generous offers, she had to at least try.

Vicki put her sculpture back on the shelf, wiped her hands on her shirt and picked up her cell phone to make a few very important calls. "This is Vicki Bennett. There are a few things you should know about your fellow board member, James Sedgwick."

Twenty-Seven

The Hawks were still celebrating their first play-off game win, but even though Ryan's pitching was one of the major reasons everyone was on such a high, the main person he wanted to celebrate with wasn't there. He'd seen guys duck out of parties like this dozens of times over the years to go call their girlfriends and wives.

Now it was his turn.

He dialed Vicki's cell as soon as he walked out of the bar, but she didn't pick up. She'd promised to keep her phone somewhere she could feel it buzzing, even if she was working with her headphones on. Ryan began to run possible scenarios through his mind—maybe she just needed to clean up before answering her phone. But he couldn't stop worrying that James would try something with her while he was gone. Even though the guy had definitely kept a low profile around Vicki over the past few days, Ryan didn't trust him for a moment.

When her voice mail beeped, Ryan left a message. "I have been thinking about you every single second since we hung up last night."

Mostly, he'd been thinking about how easy it would be to let her turn down the Italian residency just so he could keep the status quo in his life. Doing that would be just as easy as everything else had been for him.

But easy was overrated.

He wanted to earn Vicki's love. He wanted her to know, unequivocally, that he'd fight hard for her heart— and for her happiness—every single day of his life.

"I'll be waiting in my room for you," he continued, teasing, "It will probably save time if you have your clothes off already when you call me back."

The bar was only a couple blocks from the team's hotel, and he was just about to walk in the front door when a cab skidded to a stop in front of the building. The door was flung open and every wish he'd ever had came true as Vicki jumped out and into his arms.

She rained kisses over Ryan's cheeks, his chin, his eyelids, until he finally managed to capture her mouth with his. He never wanted to stop kissing her, never wanted to put her down, but the sooner he got her up to his room, the sooner she'd be naked and he'd be making love to her.

"I can't believe you're here." Of course he'd given her his hotel information, but he hadn't dreamed she'd be able to show up here to make all his dreams come true.

"I had to come. I had to be here with you so I left the studio this morning and hopped the next plane to Saint Louis."

Hand in hand they walked inside, but instead of being able to head straight toward the elevators, a group of teenagers circled him asking for autographs.

When he hesitated, Vicki assured him, "We have all the time in the world."

Without once letting go of her hand, he signed autographs and had pictures taken with the kids and answered their endless questions until he was finally able to say good-night. When he realized that waiting for the elevator would only bring on a fresh rush of fans, he dragged her off to the empty stairwell beside the elevators.

As soon as the heavy metal door clicked shut, he told her, "I want to go to Italy with you."

She wrapped her arms around his neck and whispered against his lips, "Who needs Italy when we've got a stairwell in Saint Louis?"

Of course he had to kiss her. And of course their kiss quickly morphed into his pressing her against the gray-painted wall so that he could get closer to her.

When she smiled up at him, he realized the shadows that been in her eyes since she'd returned to San Francisco were finally gone.

"You don't know what it means to me that you'd be willing to give up so much for me," she said. "But you don't have to. Not this time, anyway."

"A residency in Italy at a major museum is what you've always wanted. I've had the big prize, many times over. It's been fun, but now it's your turn. Why would you turn down the opportunity of a lifetime?"

"Because I've finally figured out what I want, Ryan. What I've wanted all along." She pressed another kiss to his lips. "You're hard everywhere I'm soft. You love a crowd when all those people make me want to run in the opposite direction. You're easy and effortless, I'm always twisting myself up trying for something just out of reach. I thought those were all the reasons we could never work as a couple. But I was wrong, so very wrong." She moved her fingertips over his jaw. "Our differences are exactly why we're so good together."

"Two halves of a whole."

"Exactly." She smiled up at him. "Which is why I want *you,* Ryan."

"You have me. Forever. And you deserve Italy, too."

"I know I do."

He was transfixed by the look in her eyes that told him she finally understood—and owned—the depths of her own talent.

"All my adult life I've been striving for the big career, for the recognition. My ex fed right into this, both during our marriage, when success always seemed just out of reach, and then after our divorce, when I wanted to win just for the pleasure of spiting him and showing him how wrong he was about me. The call from Italy should have been the greatest moment of my life. But while it felt great to be wanted and respected, I'm finally listening to that little voice inside of me."

She paused and pressed her hand flat to his chest, right over his breastbone. "Every other word that voice says is your name, Ryan. The truth—*my* truth—is that Italy isn't a step up if it's also a step away from you and the future we're building together."

"But will you be happy taking the San Francisco fellowship when you could have had Italy?"

"Actually," she informed him with a lift of one eyebrow, "I can pretty much guarantee that I won't be getting that fellowship."

"Screw James and Anthony. Your project is brilliant. The other board members will make sure you get it."

She made a face. "James came to my studio today. He had another charming offer for me."

"That's it!" Ryan exploded. "I'm going to k—"

"You don't need to do anything to him. I already did."

She told him everything, every word, every nuance, of her showdown with James. And then she told him about the phone calls she'd made to the other members of the fellowship board to tell them about what James had done, not only to her but likely to more women, as well.

"Today when I was putting the finishing touches on my project I remembered something I'd known a long, long time ago, but I'd forgotten somewhere along the way. From the first moment I picked up that ball of clay in Mr. Barnsworth's art class, I loved the way it took shape beneath my fingers. As long as I have that, I'll always be happy, whether I'm making sculptures of poodles out in the garage or trying to sculpt water in some fancy art studio with my name out front in big, bold letters." Her smile was radiant. "Everything I've ever wanted, everything I've ever looked for, was there the whole time. It was inside of me." He could feel his heart beating through to her palm as she said, "And you."

"I know you wanted to go slow," Ryan began, but even as he was saying the words, he reached around the back of her neck to undo her necklace, getting down on one knee.

Not both.

One.

Vicki opened her mouth, but no sound came out, even though his name was right there on her lips.

"I know it's only been a week since you came back to California. I know we've only had two official dates. Well, one, actually, since I mostly just ripped your clothes off and took you in your studio the other night, so it might not count as an actual date. And I also know we're in the middle of a dirty stairwell in a Saint Louis hotel right now."

Finally, laughter bubbled from Vicki's lips.

Because even when Ryan was down on one knee, he was still her friend.

Her best friend.

And he still made her laugh…all while making her burn hotter than she'd known her inner thermostat could go.

"I've already lost fifteen years without you. I'm not going to waste another second. You're everything I've been looking for. You're everything I've ever wanted." Ryan looked at their linked hands, her sculpture come to life. "That night we held hands in the water outside my house, I felt the same thing you did, Vicki. That nothing, not even water strong enough to carve cliffs, is as strong as our connection. Nothing is ever going to break us apart. Not jobs or miles or creepy bastards. Make me the happiest man alive. Say you'll marry me and wear this ring." His mouth curved up into another beautiful grin that took what was left of her breath away. "Let me be the one for real this time."

One more time, her whole world came down to her hands, to the deliberate way she held out her left ring finger for Ryan, to the cool slide of platinum across the heated surface of skin, and then to the scruff of his jaw against her palms as she held his face and kissed him.

"You've always been the one, Ryan. You always will be."

A heartbeat later, he scooped her up into his arms and was practically jogging up the steps.

She was laughing even as she asked, "What floor is your room on?"

"The tenth."

She only laughed harder at the thought of him trying to run ten floors with her in his arms, but she knew better than to try to stop him when he was hands down the most determined man she'd ever known.

Of course, she wasn't surprised when he made carrying her up ten flights of stairs look so easy. He was barely even winded as he pushed open the door to his room.

What did surprise her, however, was when he put her down on the bed, telling her to stay put in that deliciously dominant voice of his, before moving back into the front room to make a phone call. Wondering what he was up to, her heart pounding in anticipation, a few minutes later she heard a knock on the door and Ryan saying thank you to someone in his low voice.

His gaze was full of wicked intent when he came into the bedroom, his hands held behind his back. "Remember what I wanted to do to you our first night together?"

Even though it had barely been a week since they'd first made love, that night had been such a blur of pleasure and sensation that all she could think to answer was, "Everything?"

She loved the purely carnal sound of his laughter.

"You always have been able to read my mind," he teased her. "Now take your clothes off and I'll show you."

He sat back on the couch against the opposite wall, still hiding whatever was in his hands.

Even after making love several times that week, she was amazed to realize there were still so many firsts for them, like stripping down for Ryan. She'd done it over the phone the night before, but never in person. He'd always ripped the clothes off her before she could do a thing to help.

Inherently shy, it was tempting to just quickly shove off the tank top and leggings she'd worn from the studio to the plane and beg him to join her on the bed. But that wouldn't be fair to either of them.

Slowly, she got up off the bed and walked across the room to stand in front of him. With every step, Ryan's gaze heated up more and more. Her nerves gave way to a rush of joy.

He was hers.

And she was his.

Keeping her gaze locked with his, she reached for the hem of her tank top and slid it up over her waist, then her breasts, one slow inch at a time. By the time she pulled her shirt up over her head and uncovered the black lace, air was whooshing out of Ryan's lungs.

"Gorgeous, Vicki. You're so damn gorgeous."

She was smiling by the time she threw her top to the side. "Wait," she teased, "there's more."

Her thumbs went into the waistband of her leggings a moment later so that she could slide them down over her hips to reveal the matching lace thong. Just as her leggings fell to the floor and she stepped out of them, he wrapped two big hands around her bared bottom cheeks and pulled her into him so that he could press kisses against her stomach, her hip bones and then the sheer fabric covering her sex.

Her breath was coming fast now, faster still when he slid two fingers beneath her panties and into her. A heartbeat later, she was lying on the couch and he was lowering his deliciously heavy weight on her so that they could kiss and grind against each other.

Maybe it was because they had first fallen for each other as teenagers, but she loved the way they always got down and dirty on the couch like two horny kids who couldn't get enough of each other even when a bed was just feet away.

He levered himself up from her just enough to remove her bra and panties, but once she was naked, instead of coming back into her arms, he simply stared.

"I can hardly believe you're mine." His whispered words were filled with awe. Pure, never-ending desire.

And so much love it filled her to overflowing.

"Always," she whispered back. "Forever."

She was reaching to pull him in for more kisses when her elbow smacked into something hard. And cold. And wet.

"Sorry about that," he said as he lifted her elbow up to press a kiss to it. "I'll make it up to you, I promise." He pulled a champagne bottle out of its hiding place. "Surprise."

She tried to smile back at him, but it was hard to pull it off when all she could think about was what he was planning on doing with the champagne. She watched with heady anticipation as his deft fingers worked the cork. It popped open and champagne sprayed all over her breasts, making her laugh in surprise as the cold, fizzing droplets covered her.

"You did that on purpose, didn't you?"

A flash of his wicked grin was the only answer she got before he lowered his mouth to her sensitive flesh and licked off every last drop. When he found a particularly sensitive spot, and then another, she threaded her hands into his hair to hold him against her.

Finally, he lifted his head to stare down at her with his dark, intense eyes.

"I think we're ready to start now."

He hadn't even started yet?

Oh, God… She was never going to make it out of this hotel room in one piece.

And that was just fine by her.

* * *

Ryan wanted to savor every single second with Vicki. It meant everything to him that she trusted him to love her the way she deserved to be loved.

Gently, he ran one finger down between her breasts to her belly button. "Do you know what they call this part of a woman?"

She shook her head, her eyes wide and filled with heat.

"The champagne line."

A soft whimper left her pretty lips and he had to press a kiss to them. She licked the bubbly from his tongue and he was tempted just to take her right then and there and forget about the full bottle of champagne. But he'd have a lifetime to take her hard and fast.

Tonight, he wanted to cherish. To treasure.

To love.

He lifted her arms above her head one at a time and curled her fingers around the arm of the couch. Her back arched just enough to make the slight indentation on her torso slightly more pronounced.

He stared down at her, the woman he'd waited half a lifetime to finally make his own.

"Perfect."

With a quick lick over the tip of each breast, he finally tilted the bottle over her. Champagne pooled between her breasts for a split second before beginning the slow, sweet slide down toward her belly button.

His groan sounded in the room a beat before he leaned down to lick his way up over the fizzy liquid from her waist to her breastbone. One by one, Vicki's fingers slipped from the couch until her hands were in his hair again and she was arching into his mouth.

A moment later, Ryan lifted her up off the couch. He'd given slow his best shot.

But he *was* known for speed after all.

He carried her over to the bed and left her arms just long enough to put on protection. And then he was sliding in deep and she was gasping out his name. He stilled and stared into her eyes.

"That first day we met, when I was lying over you on the grass, I knew you were the one."

Vicki smiled up at him, even more beautiful now than she'd been all those years ago when they'd lain together on the high school lawn.

"I did, too."

Twenty-Eight

Four nights later, Vicki and Ryan walked into the San Francisco Museum of Modern Art hand in hand for the fellowship awards ceremony.

"He's here." Ryan's low voice vibrated with anger.

He wasn't just her best friend and fiancé; he was a Sullivan. He would always want to protect—and avenge—her, especially when it came to her first husband.

She squeezed his hand as Anthony made his way across the room straight toward them. "I'm glad he's here." And it was true. She actually appreciated this opportunity to see her ex again. It was her chance to finally put him where he belonged.

In the past.

But before her ex-husband could get to her, a beautiful woman approached her. "Are you Vicki Bennett?"

Vicki had never met the woman before, but she recognized her nonetheless. It was the woman in the picture with James. The one who had sold her soul to a sadistic devil for a million-dollar prize.

"Yes, I'm Vicki."

"I'm Kris. I worked with—" the woman faltered, paused, regrouped "—with James. I was last year's sculpture winner. I just heard the fantastic news that he's been kicked off the fellowship board. Off all of them, actually, including the board of this museum." Before Vicki could respond, the woman said, "I don't normally do things like this," and then strong sculptor arms were coming around her in an unexpected hug. "Thank you for doing what I didn't have the strength to do."

Vicki had spent plenty of time on the phone with several of the board members during the past few days. Again and again she'd gone over what had happened with James, but it wasn't until the board called her with the good news about James's dismissal that she'd known for sure they believed her.

The woman's eyes shone with unshed tears as she took a step back. "I never should have said yes to his offer to 'help' me. Everything I have now feels like it's been tainted with ugliness. I'm going to leave, go somewhere new, start over where people don't know about the mistakes I've made."

Vicki had been mulling over the Italian residency for the past few days, but any way she looked at it— and despite Ryan's obvious willingness to chuck it all in for her—she couldn't quite picture herself in Europe again. Suddenly, she knew exactly what she was going to tell the museum curator.

"I've recently heard that there is a yearlong residency opportunity in Italy for a sculptor. Does that sound like something you might be interested in?"

The woman's eyes grew big. "Are you kidding? I'd jump on a plane to Italy in a heartbeat. There isn't one single thing tying me to San Francisco."

Whereas everything in the world that mattered to Vicki was right here.

As they exchanged contact information and Vicki promised to make the call to the museum as soon as the awards ceremony was over, she finally realized she hadn't introduced the woman to Ryan.

"Kris, this is my fiancé, Ryan Sullivan."

She was the first woman Vicki had ever met that didn't look like she wanted to eat him up as she said hello. It made Vicki like her even more.

After she walked away, Vicki said, "I really hope I can help make the residency work out for her."

Ryan pulled her closer. "You're amazing."

"She needs Italy. I don't."

He was bending down to kiss her when they realized Anthony was standing right in front of them.

"Looks like I finally get to meet my replacement."

There was a wide smile on her ex-husband's face as he held out his hand for Ryan to shake, one Vicki recognized as false. Anthony's sculptor's hands had drawn her in from the start, but now, as she watched the two men's hands come together, she was struck by how small and pale Anthony's were.

He leaned in to give her a kiss on each cheek, as if to indicate that there were no hard feelings. It was surprisingly easy to let him play the benevolent ex-husband when he meant so little to her now.

Especially when she knew he'd never have the power to hurt her again.

"No," she told her ex in a perfectly pleasant voice, "Ryan isn't your replacement. You were right when you said I'd never find anyone like you, Anthony."

With that, she turned her full attention to the man she loved, who loved her back every bit as much. "You're so much more to me, Ryan."

And if she couldn't help but feel a tiny little rush of pleasure at Anthony having to watch his ex-wife's big, strong, gorgeous pro-baseball-playing fiancé claim her mouth in the middle of the museum floor, well, she was only human after all....

When they finally came up for air, Anthony had taken his position on the stage with the rest of the board. The stage lights were bright and nerves fairly vibrated off the walls from the dozens of artists hoping to win a fellowship position. Fellowships would be awarded tonight to one painter, one photographer, one digital artist, one clothing designer, one mixed-media artist and one sculptor.

As they began to announce the winners one by

one, Vicki's hands grew sore from clapping so hard, especially when Anne's name was called. Not only were her clothing designs brilliant, but she'd also created all of the textiles from scratch.

Anne winked at her from the stage and Vicki hugged Ryan even tighter. "I'm so glad we came tonight. I wouldn't have wanted to miss seeing her win."

Finally, they were down to Vicki's category. Anthony came forward holding a thick white envelope.

"It was a great honor to be asked to join the fellowship board this year. Some magical essence in San Francisco's salty air not only makes the sourdough bread unparalleled, but it seems to have worked the same magic on all of you. In the thirty years that I have been invited to judge similar competitions, I can honestly say that I have never seen such an impressive group of projects."

Events like this, Vicki had to admit, were where Anthony excelled. Up on stage, he was both confident in his position and generous with his compliments. And the truth was, she wouldn't have married him if he hadn't had any redeeming qualities. She didn't doubt that he'd loved her. He simply hadn't had the capacity to love her right.

"Every board member agreed that the winner's sculpture was not only risky and engaging to the senses, but also beautifully and skillfully executed. I'm extremely pleased to present this year's sculpting fellowship to Victoria Bennett!"

As *Anchor* was brought to sit on a table beside the lectern and lit with another spotlight, Ryan leaned over and whispered, "Just like I've always known. You're brilliant."

She hadn't prepared for this moment, hadn't thought there was any chance of her winning the fellowship with James and Anthony voting. She probably would have stood there with her mouth hanging open in surprise if Ryan hadn't put his hands on her waist and said, "Go be a superstar. It's your turn this time," before giving her a gentle nudge toward the stage.

The applause became deafening as she made her way up to the stage. She'd searched for validation for so long that even though she no longer needed it because she'd finally learned to believe in herself, she let it feel good, anyway.

Really good.

Vicki took the envelope and the pretty little statue from Anthony. She'd never been particularly comfortable speaking in front of groups of people but, tonight, with Ryan and her new artist friends cheering her on, she felt steadier and stronger than she ever had before.

"I thought I had known exactly why I had boarded that plane in Prague to come to San Francisco. I wanted to win the fellowship, of course, but it was more than that. I believed I needed it."

She looked down at the trophy and envelope in her hands for a long moment before gazing back into the crowd of important curators and collectors and fellow artists, all the people she'd been so hoping to impress tonight.

"But I was wrong."

She turned to look back at Anne, who was standing behind her on the stage. "Coming to San Francisco was about making good friends." She looked out into the audience at Ryan. "It was about going back into the past to find new love." He blew her a kiss she swore she could feel land on her cheek. "And it was about finding out what I'm capable of." She ran her hand over *Anchor*. "I'm proud of the work that I've done here. Really proud."

She smiled at each of the board members, wanting to acknowledge their recent support. "Thank you very much for choosing me this year, but I'm afraid I won't be able to accept the fellowship."

As she turned and handed her trophy and envelope to Anthony, then picked up her sculpture, it occurred to her that the last time she'd seen him look that surprised was when she was leaving him.

She knew accepting the fellowship would be good for her career, but from here on out she wanted her sculpting career to reflect passion and joy, and not be a reminder of the darkness into which James had tried to pull her.

Vicki had faith that other opportunities would come her way. And until then…

She walked into Ryan's open arms, her winning

sculpture cradled between them. He grinned down at her. "Can I drive you home?"

The years immediately disappeared until it was just the two of them again, a girl and a boy who had become friends in an instant...and who would end up sharing the rest of their lives together.

"Sure," she said, "if you don't have anywhere else you have to be."

He put his arm around her shoulders and walked beside her. "Nothing more important than hanging out with my best friend."

They were halfway across the room when she felt her phone buzz in her purse. She handed her sculpture to Ryan so that she could pull it out of her bag. She was surprised by the name on the screen.

"Your brother Smith is calling me. Do you have any idea why?"

Ryan shook his head. "Nope. He hasn't said anything to me."

She picked up. "Hi, Smith. If you need Ryan, he's right here."

"You're the one I'm looking for, Vicki, and I'm really glad I got you. Any chance you could drop by the set first thing tomorrow morning? I've got the set designer coming in and we both need to sit down with you to discuss the pieces we'll need for the movie."

She'd felt perfectly calm while dealing with Anthony and turning down the fellowship. Only now did she feel like her head was spinning and her fingertips were buzzing.

She recognized that feeling.

Inspiration.

"I'd love to meet with both of you, Smith. Thanks for the opportunity."

"I'm the one that should be thanking you for agreeing to jump into the deep end so fast. I'll text you the details for the meeting. Bring a piece that represents your style, okay?"

She looked at her sculpture in Ryan's arms. "I've got just the one in mind. See you tomorrow morning."

Turning to Ryan, she said, "I'm going to work with Smith and his set designer on his new film. You didn't have anything to do with that, did you?"

"Trust me," Ryan said as she slid her phone back into her purse and he handed *Anchor* back to her. "Smith takes his movies way too seriously to do anyone a favor. He wants you on his movie because you're the best."

She was about to press a kiss to his lips when a gray-haired man stepped in front of her. "Ms. Bennett, I'd like to introduce myself. I'm the curator for the Marina Gallery in Sausalito. We're very interested in your work."

And with that, Ryan stood proudly beside Vicki while she finally had her day in the sun.

Epilogue

Three weeks later

The whole Sullivan crew was congregated at Smith's house and there was nothing he liked more than sitting back and watching the mayhem created by his brothers and sisters and their significant others and kids and stepkids and dogs. Only Ryan, who was pitching in Detroit, and Vicki weren't there.

"Everyone, this is it!" Lori called out. "If he nails this pitch, we win the World Series!"

Even the animals quieted down as Ryan looked in for the sign from the catcher, shook off the first two then nodded yes to the third. He went into his windup and broke off a slow curve that split the plate in half. The batter was completely fooled, the bat frozen on his shoulder.

"Strike three!"

On the screen, as the Hawks' players charged

out of the dugout, then jumped on one another like little boys in a sandbox, Ryan's entire focus was on Vicki as he blew a kiss up to her in the stands.

Lori hugged Megan and Summer. Chase and Chloe danced with baby Emma between them. Marcus and Nicola used the win as yet another excuse to kiss each other. Zach and Heather tried to calm down their overexcited dogs while Summer's poodle puppy peed in the middle of one of Smith's priceless Aubusson rugs. A very pregnant-with-twins Sophie and Jake stayed right where they were on the couch and everyone came over to hug and high-five them.

Smith danced his mother, Mary, into the kitchen. Together, they pulled several bottles of Marcus's finest champagne out of his wine cooler, along with a couple bottles of sparkling apple juice for Sophie and Summer.

More cheers rang out as they popped open the corks. Once every glass was filled high enough for bubbles to skid across Smith's kitchen counter and everyone had a glass, Lori said, "To Ryan, for winning the World Series!"

"And for winning Vicki's heart, too," Sophie pointedly added.

Everyone clinked to that, then relaxed back into their seats.

"So," Chase asked as he put down his glass and

bounced his adorable little girl on his knee, "how's casting going?"

"Good," Smith said. "We've just signed Tatiana Landon."

"She was amazing in *Midnight Lake,*" Chloe said.

"And she seems so sweet in her interviews," Heather added.

"I think she's pretty," Summer said. "Can I meet her?"

Smith ruffled her hair. "Of course you can."

His family was right. Tatiana was a talented, sweet and beautiful twenty-one-year-old actress. Funny, then, that he hadn't given her a second thought since they'd signed the contracts.

No, it was Tatiana's older sister he couldn't stop thinking about.

Smith had never let a woman distract him from his work. And given the fact that he was finally directing, producing and starring in a movie in his hometown, his focus was tighter than ever.

Valentina Landon was a watchdog for her younger sister…and she clearly didn't trust him—or like him—one bit.

Still, none of that stopped him from wondering about what lay beneath Valentina Landon's armor. Smith grabbed a roll of paper towel from the kitchen and then got down on his knees beside Summer to help her clean up the mess the puppy had made of his rug. "So, Summer, have you got any hints for how I can get a girl to like me?"

* * * * *

Turn the page for a sneak peek
of the next book in THE SULLIVANS *series,*
COME A LITTLE BIT CLOSER
Available soon in print from Harlequin MIRA

One

Smith Sullivan loved his fans. They'd supported him from the start of his career and had helped his movies gross nearly two billion dollars worldwide. Without them, he wouldn't be in San Francisco today, about to begin filming the most important movie of his career.

So even though he had at least a dozen other important things to take care of before filming could begin, Smith headed straight toward the large group of beautiful women gathered outside the barriers his crew had erected around Union Square where they'd be filming today. Some of the women had brought their young children with them, but most of them were alone, and quite clearly available.

As he approached, he said, "Good morning," with a smile that held even as the crowd pushed in closer to him.

One smile and two simple words was all it took

for a woman to reach out to shake his hand. She pressed a piece of paper with her name and phone number into his palm. She was dressed in a tight V-neck top and short skirt despite the cool fog hanging over the square.

"I'm so excited about your new movie, Smith," she purred. She ran her hand up his arm as if they'd met before and knew each other well enough that he'd want her to touch him.

"Thank you…" He paused, waiting for her to say her name, since he'd never set eyes on her before this morning.

"Brittany."

He smiled down at her. "I'm looking forward to you watching it, Brittany."

"Oh, I can't wait," she said in a husky voice. "And I want you to know that I'm free anytime while you're filming, if you want to talk about it. Or—" she licked her lips "—for anything else you want to do while you're in San Francisco."

Following her lead, one after the other, the women shook his hand and passed him their phone numbers while telling him that he was their favorite actor and that they'd seen all of his movies. This same scene had played out hundreds of times over the past fifteen years, and the truth was that if he'd still been in his twenties, Smith would have been more than happy to take his pick of the beauties back to his place for a night, a week, or even longer if the woman was easy enough to be with.

But thirty-six was a long way from those early, wild years…and he was tired of waking up next to naked women whose names he didn't remember, who had never made him laugh, whose families he'd never meet. What a contrast that was to the way so many of his siblings had recently found love. They all seemed to be getting married and having children. Every week he updated the screensaver on his phone with a new picture of his little niece, Emma. Soon his sister Sophie would have her twins, and he couldn't wait to upload a picture of all three Sullivan babies.

Still, even after witnessing just how powerful real love could be and just what amazing things could come from that love, it was hard to break the cycle. Because without those strangers in his bed, he was alone.

Alone in another hotel. Alone in another city. Alone in another country. Away from his family and friends. Surrounded by people who either wanted something from him or treated him like a god rather than a man.

Yes, he could have his pick of these women, but he knew what they wanted: to date *Smith Sullivan*. And as the past couple years had ticked by, part of him had begun to wonder if he would ever find a woman who not only meant something beyond a few hot hours between the sheets, but who also wanted him for more than his fame.

Of course, Smith was still a man. A very sensual

man who adored women of all shapes and sizes. He knew that a few nights of hot sex didn't add up to much in the long run, but he would never be immune to beautiful women.

More specifically, he thought as Valentina Landon walked past in a thick, long wool coat to fight the early-morning chill, her eyebrows raised as she took in the women gathered and giggling around him, he was drawn to one woman in particular.

"Valentina," he said with the intention of making her stop in her tracks.

She turned to look at him without the slightest bit of the flirtatiousness that the two dozen women he'd just been speaking to had been pouring all over him. "Yes?"

"Do you and Tatiana have everything you need this morning?"

"Everything's perfectly in order, thank you," she said in a crisp voice. "Do you need anything from us before filming begins in—" she looked at the slim watch on her wrist "—an hour?"

"Just let me know if you or Tatiana have any problems or need anything from me at all."

She nodded, her pretty mouth softening slightly as she said, "Thanks. We will." Unfortunately, just then her gaze caught the pile of telephone numbers that had been pressed into his hands and her eyes narrowed in disgust.

And yet as she walked away with her lips pressed together in clear disapproval, she was beautiful.

Smith turned back to his fans and thanked them all for their support one more time before heading back to the trailer that was doubling as his office during filming. Dumping the women's numbers on his desk without giving them a second thought, he grabbed his script and laptop and walked back out. He was just sitting down in the makeup trailer when his phone buzzed; the key electric was alerting him to a lighting issue that needed to be worked out before filming could begin.

It was just the beginning of what would be an incredibly busy day on a set that was all his this time. And as Smith dealt with the first problem of what would surely be many before the day was through, he knew he wouldn't want to trade his career for any other. Not for the beauty of his brother Marcus's winery in Napa Valley, not for the thrill of Ryan's World Series wins pitching for the Hawks, not for the speed of Zach's race cars.

Smith couldn't wait to begin filming *Gravity*.

The young woman in the middle of the sidewalk was utterly beautiful, and yet the way she moved, dressed, wore her hair with pink streaks, her makeup artfully smudged and dark around her eyes, gave her away in an instant as an overwhelmed early-twentysomething on her own in a big city for the first time. With wide eyes she took in San Francisco—the buildings, the traffic, the people rushing all around, the fog rolling in from the bay. For a moment, her mouth almost curved into a smile, but a flash of something that looked too much like fear held that smile back from her full lips.

A stray dog skittered over her cheap, red-plastic boots and the longing on the girl's face was almost painful as she knelt down to reach out to the mangy animal. Instead of coming toward her open hand, the dirty little dog turned and ran as fast as it could in the other direction.

Her big green eyes suddenly filled with the slightest sheen of tears, which were blinked away just as quickly. It was impossible not to wish that she'd find happiness and love and everything else she'd come to San Francisco for.

Down the street, a businessman dressed in a dark suit, impeccably tailored and very, very expensive, was talking on a phone and moving fast, faster than anyone else on the sidewalk. His conversation held his complete attention, his expression forbidding as he issued directives one after another in a hard voice. Everything about him spoke of his power...and to just how closed off his heart was.

Fury crossed the man's face a beat before he spoke loudly into his phone, his entire attention turned to the conversation so that he didn't take notice of anyone on the street around him. There wasn't even the slightest pause in his gait as he kicked the girl who was still kneeling on the pave-

ment staring after the dog who hadn't dared to trust her.

Thousand-dollar Italian shoes jabbed hard into her stomach, and as she cried out in pain, he finally stopped cursing into his phone, looked down at the dirty sidewalk and noticed her.

It was the ultimate picture of how far the girl had fallen. And yet in that moment when she should have been cringing, her fear and sadness finally receded.

This time she was the angry one, and even though the man had kicked her hard enough to shove the air from her lungs, she was young and agile enough to be back up on her feet and in the man's face less than thirty seconds later.

It didn't matter that she was so much smaller than he. It didn't matter that his clothes were worth more than what she'd managed to save over the past year working double shifts in the ice cream shop in her hometown.

It didn't even matter to her that people had stopped on the sidewalk to watch the scene.

"Do you think you're the only person who matters?" she yelled at him. "Talking on your phone, ignoring everyone, kicking anyone who gets in your way?"

Before he could answer, she got closer and poked him in the chest.

"I matter, too!" Her mouth trembled now, just

barely, but somehow she managed to get it under control as she repeated, "I matter, too."

Throughout her tirade, the man stared down at her, the phone still held to his ear, his dark eyes utterly unreadable. He was clearly surprised by what had happened. Not just that he'd stumbled over her, but by the way she had sprung up to scream at him. And yet there was more than surprise in his eyes.

There was awareness that had nothing to do with anger...and everything to do with her incredible beauty, made even more potent by the flush on her cheeks and the fire in her eyes.

Everything that surrounded the two of them fell away as she searched the businessman's face for a reaction, but he was impossible to read—and on a sound of disgust, she pushed away from him and started to move back down the sidewalk.

But before she could get lost in the crowd, a large, strong hand wrapped around her upper arm and stopped her from getting away. She whipped around to shake him off. "Get the he—"

"I'm sorry."

His voice resonated with genuine regret— deeper, truer than anyone who worked with him might have thought he was capable of feeling. Even, perhaps, the man himself.

Bravado had been all that held the young woman together. She did not know that this was a man who had never apologized to anyone for anything in his life. Hearing his words, she lost hold of the strength she'd been clinging to by her fingernails.

Her first tear had barely begun to fall when she finally pulled herself free and started running through the crowds, intent on getting away from the man whose apology had touched her despite her anger.

The man's deep voice called out to the girl as she pushed through the crowd. She was small and fast and he lost her at the busy Union Square intersection. The pink streaks in her hair were the last thing he glimpsed.

As the rest of the world rushed around him, most people either talking or texting on their phones, their attention on anything but the people around them, the man stood perfectly still.

And utterly alone.

Valentina Landon held her breath until "Cut!" rang out. Moments later, applause and cheering came from the crew, who had been held spellbound by the scene.

Somehow she got her hands to move, to come together in a basic approximation of clapping, but she was too moved by what she'd seen to put anything behind it. That had been the first scene on the first day of photography for *Gravity*. The story had immediately grabbed for her gut and twisted it hard. Smith Sullivan had not only written the screenplay, but he was also directing, producing and starring in the film.

Tatiana Landon, Valentina's younger sister, was an incredibly talented actress with ten years of experience behind her. She'd been hired for dozens of TV episodes, had shot a couple of sitcom pilots over the years and, most recently, had played important supporting roles in two feature films. But *Gravity* was her first lead in a major motion picture.

Valentina had always been proud of her sister, but what they'd all just witnessed from Tatiana had been so stunningly good that Valentina was still having trouble catching her breath. And she knew why.

Smith Sullivan had brought out every last ounce of magic her sister possessed.

Just then, Tatiana moved back down the sidewalk toward Smith. Valentina could read her sister like an open book, and though she was smiling at the applause from the rest of the cast and crew, it was clear that the person she really wanted a comment from was Smith.

So much like the character he was playing, for a moment it was hard to read his face until he reached out to put his hands on either side of Tatiana's shoulders and said loudly enough for everyone to hear, "You. Are. Perfect." He was grinning widely as he planted a kiss on her forehead.

Tatiana blinked up at Smith, pleasure and pride

mixing with the stars in her eyes a moment before her lovely face broke into a blinding smile.

In the span of one terrible heartbeat, the ground fell away from Valentina's feet as she watched the interaction between her sister and the movie star… and every one of her fears for her sister's welfare pushed to the forefront.

She couldn't forget the way he'd flirted and charmed the legion of female fans who had waited to catch a glimpse of him just outside the set earlier that morning. He was the cliché of a movie star. The women had fawned all over him and she had no doubt that he'd loved every second of the attention, not to mention the dozen phone numbers he'd held in his hand. Valentina had no trouble imagining just how giddy with anticipation the women were over whom he would pick to warm his bed tonight.

Like hell if it was going to be her own sister.

So when Smith went to watch playback, Valentina didn't think, didn't stop to assess whether her actions were wise as she pushed through the crew to get to him.

"We need to talk. In private. Now."

She kept her voice pitched low and even, though she knew everyone would likely be gossiping about her nervy move within seconds of their leaving the set. They would all be wondering what possible beef she could have with the great Smith Sullivan.

Valentina headed toward Smith's trailer, which had been moved to the Union Square site for the first day of filming, and even though she hadn't waited for his reply, she could feel his larger-than-life presence behind her every step of the way.

New York Times bestselling author

BELLA ANDRE

introduces the fifth novel in her eight-book series The Sullivans!

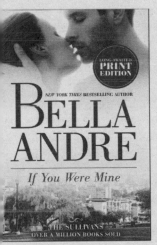

The last thing Zach Sullivan wants is to take care of his brother's new puppy for two weeks. That is, until he meets the dog trainer. Heather is bright, beautiful…and she just might be the only woman on earth who wants nothing to do with him.

Heather Linsey can't believe she agreed to train Zach's new pup, especially since his focus seems to be more on winning her heart than training his dog. But Heather's determination to push Zach away only fuels his determination to get closer—and the connection between them grows more undeniable. Will the biggest Sullivan bad boy of all tempt Heather into believing in forever again?

If You Were Mine

Available now, wherever books are sold!

Be sure to connect with us at:
Harlequin.com/Newsletters
Facebook.com/HarlequinBooks
Twitter.com/HarlequinBooks

HARLEQUIN® MIRA®
www.Harlequin.com

MBA1560R

#1 New York Times Bestselling Author

DEBBIE MACOMBER

First comes friendship...

Back in high school, Maggie Kingsbury and Glenn Lambert were close friends. But life took them in different directions. Now they meet again—as maid of honor and best man—at a wedding in San Francisco full of *White Lace and Promises*....

And *then* comes marriage!

Lily Morrissey decides it's time to find a husband, preferably a wealthy one. It's a strictly practical decision, and she enlists the help of her best friend, Jake Carson, in the Great Husband Search. That's when Lily's feelings for Jake start to change. Because they're *Friends...And Then Some.*

Available wherever books are sold.

Be sure to connect with us at:
Harlequin.com/Newsletters
Facebook.com/HarlequinBooks
Twitter.com/HarlequinBooks

www.Harlequin.com

MDM1580

#1 *New York Times* Bestselling Author

ROBYN CARR

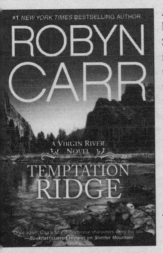

At twenty-five, after five years as her mother's caregiver, it's time for Shelby McIntyre to experience freedom and adventure. Time for travel, college and romance. But when she visits Virgin River she runs into Luke Riordan, decidedly not the Mr. Right she has in mind.

A handsome Black Hawk pilot, Luke exited the army after twenty years, four wars and having been shot out of the sky three times. At thirty-eight he's tough and jaded, with a major in one-night stands and a minor in commitment avoidance.

Technically, these two are all wrong for one another. But sometimes what you want and what you need are two different things...two very good things.

Available wherever books are sold.

Be sure to connect with us at:
Harlequin.com/Newsletters
Facebook.com/HarlequinBooks
Twitter.com/HarlequinBooks

MRC1582

#1 *New York Times* **Bestselling Author**

SHERRYL WOODS

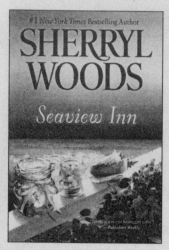

Hannah Matthews is undeniably tough—a single mom, a top-tier PR exec, a breast cancer survivor. She prides herself on being able to handle any crisis. But with her grandmother balking at going into a retirement home, her daughter unexpectedly pregnant and an old flame suddenly underfoot, Hannah is facing a few crises of her own. And being back home on Seaview Key is definitely adding to the stress.

Luke Stevens understands crisis. While serving in Iraq, his wife dumped him for his best friend— with whom Luke shares his medical practice. Seaview Key seems like the perfect place to hide out for a while. The last thing he expects is to fall in love…with his old hometown and with Hannah.

Available wherever books are sold.

Be sure to connect with us at:

Harlequin.com/Newsletters

Facebook.com/HarlequinBooks

Twitter.com/HarlequinBooks

HARLEQUIN® MIRA
www.Harlequin.com

MSHW158

REQUEST YOUR FREE BOOKS!

2 FREE NOVELS
FROM THE ROMANCE COLLECTION
PLUS 2 FREE GIFTS!

YES! Please send me 2 FREE novels from the Romance Collection and my 2 FREE gifts (gifts are worth about $10). After receiving them, if I don't wish to receive any more books, I can return the shipping statement marked "cancel." If I don't cancel, I will receive 4 brand-new novels every month and be billed just $6.24 per book in the U.S. or $6.74 per book in Canada. That's a savings of at least 22% off the cover price. It's quite a bargain! Shipping and handling is just 50¢ per book in the U.S. and 75¢ per book in Canada.* I understand that accepting the 2 free books and gifts places me under no obligation to buy anything. I can always return a shipment and cancel at any time. Even if I never buy another book, the two free books and gifts are mine to keep forever.

194/394 MDN F4XY

Name   (PLEASE PRINT)

Address   Apt. #

City   State/Prov.   Zip/Postal Code

Signature (if under 18, a parent or guardian must sign)

Mail to the Harlequin® Reader Service:
IN U.S.A.: P.O. Box 1867, Buffalo, NY 14240-1867
IN CANADA: P.O. Box 609, Fort Erie, Ontario L2A 5X3

Want to try two free books from another line?
Call 1-800-873-8635 or visit www.ReaderService.com.

* Terms and prices subject to change without notice. Prices do not include applicable taxes. Sales tax applicable in N.Y. Canadian residents will be charged applicable taxes. Offer not valid in Quebec. This offer is limited to one order per household. Not valid for current subscribers to the Romance Collection or the Romance/Suspense Collection. All orders subject to credit approval. Credit or debit balances in a customer's account(s) may be offset by any other outstanding balance owed by or to the customer. Please allow 4 to 6 weeks for delivery. Offer available while quantities last.

Your Privacy—The Harlequin® Reader Service is committed to protecting your privacy. Our Privacy Policy is available online at www.ReaderService.com or upon request from the Harlequin Reader Service.

We make a portion of our mailing list available to reputable third parties that offer products we believe may interest you. If you prefer that we not exchange your name with third parties, or if you wish to clarify or modify your communication preferences, please visit us at www.ReaderService.com/consumerschoice or write to us at Harlequin Reader Service Preference Service, P.O. Box 9062, Buffalo, NY 14269. Include your complete name and address.

ROM13R

BELLA ANDRE

31560	IF YOU WERE MINE	___ $7.99 U.S.	___ $8.99 CAN
31559	I ONLY HAVE EYES FOR YOU	___ $7.99 U.S.	___ $8.99 CAN
31558	CAN'T HELP FALLING IN LOVE	___ $7.99 U.S.	___ $8.99 CAN
31557	FROM THIS MOMENT ON	___ $7.99 U.S.	___ $9.99 CAN
31556	THE LOOK OF LOVE	___ $5.99 U.S.	___ $5.99 CAN

(limited quantities available)

TOTAL AMOUNT	$ _____
POSTAGE & HANDLING	$ _____
($1.00 for 1 book, 50¢ for each additional)	
APPLICABLE TAXES*	$ _____
TOTAL PAYABLE	$ _____

(check or money order—please do not send cash)

To order, complete this form and send it, along with a check or money order for the total amount, payable to Harlequin MIRA, to: **In the U.S.** 3010 Walden Avenue, P.O. Box 9077, Buffalo, NY 1426-9077 **In Canada:** P.O. Box 636, Fort Erie, Ontario, L2A 5X3.

Name: _____
Address: _____ City: _____
State/Prov.: _____ Zip/Postal Code: _____
Account Number (if applicable): _____
075 CSAS

*New York residents remit applicable sales taxes.
*Canadian residents remit applicable GST and provincial taxes.

HARLEQUIN® MIRA®
™ www.Harlequin.com

MBA0114BL